I0684306

Praise for *Across the Savarmati*

"Sriram Ananth's *Across the Sabarmati* is part coming of age story, part sociology of the aftermath of the 2002 political violence in Gujarat, and part investigation into the process of coming to terms with class (and caste) privilege.

Sabarmati is the fictionalized story of Jayram, a young middle class man from the south, who, on a whim, volunteers to help out with relief efforts in Gujarat after the brutal anti-Muslim riots. The experience changes his life and his sense of self. He finds himself coming to terms with denial, simmering hatred, and the possibility of human solidarity and love, in a word filled with political manipulation, tragedy and destitution. Most importantly he must deal with his own complicity with the system that has made the tragedy possible.

Sabarmati captures the feel, smells and tastes of urban India in the crucible that fuses history, tradition and neo-liberal globalization."

- **Tim McCaskell, author of** *Race To Equity: Disrupting Educational Inequality*

****

"A chronicle of crimes perpetrated against the Muslims of Gujarat by fascist Hindu groups in the 2002 Gujarat riots, this novel documents the horror and pain of the victims, trauma of the survivors, as well as vicarious trauma of those delivering help and aid. This book is a riveting account of how human souls can reach lowly depths of inhumanity and take pride in subjugating, shaming, dishonouring and destroying the essence of what makes us human. While classified as fiction, this book is more a memoir, a tale of growing up, an accidental rite of passage for a young man in search of life's meaning who in questioning his own privilege, both inherited, as an upper class Hindu Brahmin, and acquired, as a member of an educated upper middle class society, searches for answers in a dark world of death and destruction. Jayram, the

i

protagonist, encounters pain, suffering and slow death of the people on one side of the Sabarmati river and love, friendship and self-discovery on the other. The river is a symbol of the division of the community as much as a divide that speaks to personal inner struggles of Jayram.

This story raises a number of critical questions and urges all humans to reflect on them at a global level; questions that probe the depths of hatred that breed in our modern day societies in the name of nationalism, tribalism and communalism. In the depths of darkness, it also shines a light on the compassion and resilience of many-- Hindus, Muslims, Dalits and others who worked to rebuild, restore peace and bring comfort to the suffering and the scarred. This account highlights the short lived interest of yellow journalism in a horror story while giving us a glimpse of storytellers, such as Maria, invested in documenting such horrors with real hope of history not repeating itself. It gives us a sense that while murder and killing ends the suffering of the victim at once, the long term trauma of witnesses to the horrors, as well as victims of the powerful weapon of rape, will die a slow death and alter the individuals and society forever.

Across the Sabarmati is a very difficult book to read, certainly not a book that you will finish in a sitting. If the plot was merely a figment of the author's imagination, it may just be another sad tale. However, the events in this book are palpable and the characters real people in a real part of the world who lived through and survived these horrific acts. The most shocking aspects of the Gujarat tragedy are the real life events in Indian politics, the impunity given to the perpetrators of the crimes at the highest political levels to the police forces, all of whom became bystanders condoning the crimes they were duty bound to prevent. It is a commentary on the nature of deep rooted communal tensions in the world's largest democracy; tensions that raise their ugly head, too often leaving millions of Indian citizens form the minority communities, vulnerable and fearful.

Sriram Ananth succeeds in drawing his readers in by relating a personal and a moving record as a witness to genocide. He leaves his readers to ponder the transformation of Gujarat, the birthplace of Gandhi, the father of Indian nonviolent movement, to a place with a very violent and gory recent history."

- Idrisa Pandit, Religious Studies scholar, University of Waterloo

****

"The Importance Of Self-Reflection In Achieving Revolutionary Change:

How do people change? What are the steps that it takes for someone from a privileged class, gender and ideological position to become a revolutionary? What failures might we suffer along the way? What lines do our movements still need to overcome? What does this mean in real life? In my life? To me, these are the questions asked and unpacked in the insightful "Across the Sabarmati"—a new and first novel by one-time Fellow Worker Sriram Ananth. And despite the author's insistence that the "quality of writing hovers between mediocre and average," the book unfolds with compelling and daring self-reflection, unpacking his experiences in the aftermath of a recent grisly history that is both important and largely unknown outside the author's native India – the Hindu fascist riots in Gujarat that killed thousands of innocent working class Muslims and others in the winter of 2002. It is also a stunning portrayal of a particular period of time of street-level fascism in India, one that is perhaps gone, but perhaps not. Fascist upsurges are an inevitable consequence of the racist capitalism that defines our lives, and can only be stopped by eliminating its roots in the system itself, an important insight well beyond India. This warning and lesson transformed the author into adulthood, birthed him a new life, and burdened him too with the question of revolution and solidarity across class lines and now, across oceans as well. As part of an internationalist workers' movement and as an organization of new, experienced, and growing organizers who are increasingly facing the need to diversify who we organize with, honest books like this are an invaluable contribution to our collective coming of age. I can only hope that more workers take the time to write the important realities of their lives, stresses, mistakes, repetitions and all. After all it is in our lives – not in a fantasy – that we have a world to win."

- David Boehnke in *The Industrial Worker*

****

"A powerful and compelling personal narrative, *Across the Sabarmati* offers an unflinching glimpse into a world that is rarely seen and exposed- communities and lives after the storm has hit, forgotten people who must continue to live every day with the impact of horrific violence and trauma long after the world has turned away.

The author carries the reader with him on his complex, turbulent personal journey of trying to do direct support work for people in crisis, while grappling with difficult personal issues around his own identity and privilege. The story is told with remarkable candour, honesty and humour, and asks important questions that are salient for anyone who has considered the nature of aid work, community violence and of humanity itself."

- Swathi Sekhar, Member, Immigration Legal Committee and Prisoner Correspondence Project, Toronto

****

"Drawing on his own experience, Ananth provides a humane telling of the humanitarian relief response to an inhuman horror. The 2002 gruesome state sponsored pogrom by Hindu fascists in Ahmedabad, Gujarat, India where thousands of Muslims were murdered, maimed and made refugees when their bodies and homes were burned on the altar of political expediency. The protagonist, a young idealistic and upper-caste Bangalore university student named Jayram Krishnan, is compelled to travel north to assist with the relief effort in spite of his parents' concerns. For Jayram, and the reader, it's the trip of a life time. Along his journey of self - discovery he learns many valuable lessons about power, class, faith, friendship, gender, love and betrayal. For Jayram, and the reader, they're lessons we'll not soon forget."

- T. Turner, Member, Toronto District Labour Council

****

"More than anything else, I found the writing courageous... such as the word play on the chant 'Jai Sri Ram' where author Sri Ram calls his protagonist Jay Ram. In a passage in the book, Jayram wants to carry on even after hearing about the brutal slaying of the cripple. Once you realise that a mindless act was carried out over a period by a substantial number of people, the actual details of individual act do not surprise any longer. Jayram is courageous and does not flinch from expressing his anger against all and sundry that he finds less than acceptable. It's prose that comes straight from the heart. And we need plenty more of these that question the absurdity where an Indian Muslim must prove their patriotism or leave."

- Milind P., Blogger, *Random Keystrokes*

****

"Sriram Ananth's debut novel *Across the Sabarmati* transports us to the streets of Ahmedabad shortly after the city has been marred by bloody riots that have seen thousands of muslims killed, and many more forced into refugee camps. Drawing from his personal experiences doing relief work under these circumstances, the author takes us on a gripping journey that exposes India's communal violence, and enables us to understand the roots of the hatred that breeds such grotesque episodes of carnage. Courageously honest and daringly self-reflective, perhaps the greatest contribution of *Across the Sabarmati* is the unforgiving mirror it holds up to its readers, encouraging us to come to terms with our own privilege and compelling us to act."

- Yogi Acharya, Community Organizer, No One Is Illegal - Toronto

Across the Sabarmati

An Autobiographical Novel

Sriram Ananth

Broken Shackles Press
35 Saranac Boulevard, Suite 103
Toronto, ON, Canada M6A 2G5

Email: brokenshacklespress@gmail.com

Published by Broken Shackles Press

Copyright © Sriram Ananth 2014
All rights reserved

ISBN: 978-0-9881122-0-9

Cover image by Sriram Ananth

Dedicated to Varun Shankar
1986-2004

for your compassion,
for your love,
for putting a face on that ethereal beauty in
humanity worth fighting for

thanks Vaddu

Across the Sabarmati

Acknowledgements

Writing a fictionalized account of a real-life encounter that involves political violence and trauma is always a little tricky. The best part about it however is that you get to take a stab at creative writing while still narrating a cathartic story of pain and justice. I decided to pursue the project as an autobiographical novel, as opposed to a non-fiction memoir, for a couple of reasons. One, because of the pain ingrained in the experiences and the impact it had on me; it helped to write it in the voice of a nominally different protagonist in order to reproduce as honest an account as possible. Two, in order to attempt a tighter narration, I threaded the story around four fictional characters, who are directly modelled after four amazing real-life people but with other, equally inspiring, people collapsed into those characters. The experiences narrated are all true to the best of my memory.

The quality of the writing hovers somewhere between mediocre and average, but hopefully valiantly so. It's not an award-winning piece of literature, but I hope it does what it seeks to do, and that's give an honest reflection of a struggle to find humanity.

As far as thanking people goes, I'll keep the platitudes and spread to a minimum, and stick to thanking those elements of humanity who were special to me during the evolution of this project:

Monica, Amit, Vipul, Farooq, Shahnawaz, Tina, Kanika, Maha, and Kallu for Gujarat 2002;

Vipul, Ayesha, Piyush, Shireen, Farooq, Rupal, and Nitya for Gujarat 2008/2009;

Amma, Appa, Pooja Didi, Shyam, and Abhay for giving me the fall-back safety of Bangalore;

Fizz, Vaddu, Shankar Mama, and Pratima Aunty for my childhood;

And finally, Sus, for being there in love and struggle.

~ Prologue ~

When it first began, the media started calling it another
religious riot, one of many in India's history. Everyone in
India knew how it started. Most believed it was in retaliation
for the burning down of those ill-fated train compartments on
the Sabarmati Express. Fifty-eight Hindus were killed that day
when the S-6 coach went up in flames in the wee hours of the
morning on February 27, 2002 as it trundled into Godhra
Junction. No one had heard about Godhra before that
infamous day; the town was now on the headlines of every
national daily. The rioting started the very next day in the
bigger cities of Ahmedabad and Baroda. The "Godhra Riots"
as they were being called mostly occurred in the rest of
Gujarat, and were the first riots in India to be telecast live on a
slew of 24 hour news channels. It looked like your typical
back-and-forth religious rioting - "they killed some of our
people, we're going to kill some of theirs" kind of thing. The
kind that occurred in some Indian town or the other every few
years. They usually lasted a few days at the most before order
was brought in. Some poor folk would get killed or injured in
those few days, a few reports would come in the newspapers,
and life would soon limp back to normal. In any case, nothing
much really affected well-off folk like us, barring the odd
curfew or Section 144 of the Indian Penal Code.

We lived a fair distance from what was happening in
Gujarat, over a thousand miles away in fact, down south in the
city of Bangalore. But the news channels brought the riots
into our living room like it was happening right in front of us;
a gory blow-by-blow account of the mayhem presented by
attractive reporters in sleek studios, ad breaks and all.

Mind you, religious rioting wasn't something we were
unaccustomed to hearing about.

When I was much younger and not old enough to
internalise religious violence, I remember the adults speaking
about some stray incidents of rioting in Bangalore when the
Babri Masjid was demolished in 1992 in Ayodhya. I was
twelve years old at the time. My friends and I were happy that
schools closed down that day because of a curfew. Pictures
were flashed in all the major newspapers of Hindu mobs

1

breaking down the dome of that historic mosque, one of the oldest in India. But even then, the real bloodshed happened in Mumbai. Three years later, I remember watching Mani Rathnam's film, *Bombay*. It was made before the spree of jingoistic name-changing for large Indian cities. The film showed the violence as equal on both sides, with the same number of Hindus and Muslims killed. In the synthetic quasi-secular tradition of Bollywood, the film depicted the rioting instigated rather equitably by leaders of both religions. The caricature of the rabidly fascist Bal Thakeray, was played by a buck-toothed, normally-comedic, Bollywood actor, clad in a saffron shirt. The generic Muslim leader was a stereotypical angry mullah with a long beard and green robe. As far as I could tell, it was a film about poor Hindus and Muslims killing each other in the slums of Mumbai. It registered as information, but didn't really hit me as something that I needed to be concerned about.

I did remember an argument at home, after coming back from the theatre, between my father and his brother.

"We have to realize that even if equal numbers of Hindus and Muslims died, Muslims are barely 15% of the population, so they're definitely much more marginalized in many ways." Appa said, trying to reason with his brother.

My uncle retorted, "That may be true...but we all know that the violence is always started by the Muslims. What goes around comes around."

My father, in characteristically commanding fashion, admonished his younger brother, "You know that's not true. Leaders on both sides are the problem. I think you ought to understand that we're a secular country...we cannot afford to have religious fundamentalism of any kind, or anything that causes these divisions."

My uncle refrained from saying anything, sullenly ceding ground to his elder sibling.

It wasn't just religion that instigated rioting in India. In Bangalore the closest I had come to witnessing a riot was actually due to water. The Kaveri water dispute between Karnataka and Tamil Nadu flared up with protesters in both states demanding the bulk of the water from that beautiful river. I remember my parents getting a little worried about the potential for the protests to get more violent, especially since we were a Tamil family living in the biggest city in Karnataka. So we decided to play it safe and remain indoors for the weekend.

There was another time when a riot was almost instigated by the irrationally loyal fan-base of a local cinematic idol. I remember riding my motorbike with my friend back from college that day and seeing a bunch of guys walking around with sign boards and flaming torches. They were demanding the release of Kannada film star Rajkumar, who had been kidnapped by the legendary Tamil nationalist brigand, Veerappan. One of the protestors hit the bike as he ran away from the baton-waving policemen dispersing the mob. We nearly crashed, but I managed to control the vehicle and ride safely home, following which I had to calm my friend down from his manic hysteria.

Those were the two times I came closest to experiencing political violence during my youth. But they were stray incidents and, all things considered, fairly harmless ones at that. They could barely be classified as experiences really.

Truth be told, most of what I knew about political violence came vicariously from books. Our house in Bangalore was a veritable library. We had two floor-to-ceiling wooden shelves in our spacious living room just for books. I loved the ones on world history. They told me things I felt like I needed to know. I devoured these books growing up. I loved reading about how things came to be, voyeuristically studying specific moments in history, especially the many times when society boiled over. Some of these books detailed violent events which couldn't be classified as mere violence. They told me what to watch out for. As a teenager I had read about the Holocaust perpetrated by the Nazis, the Stalinist gulags in the Soviet Union, the Armenian genocide carried out by the Turkish state, the bloodbath orchestrated by the United States upon the Vietnamese, the India-Pakistan Partition in 1947, the massacre of Bangladeshis by the Pakistani government in 1971, the Khmer Rouge purges in Cambodia, the madness that was Rwanda, and scores of other episodes of insanity in our recent past. Episodes where people were brutalized, women raped before being killed, infants butchered before being burnt; episodes where carnage became human nature.

I also read about the efforts of brave humanitarians, people who struggled against tremendous odds to end the violence, to deliver hope, to bring justice; regular folk who fought the good fight. The everyday Albert Schweitzers and Mahatma Gandhis of the world. They were inspiring portrayals of inspiring people. Those stories were the primary reason I studied the various brutal moments in humanity's short history. Those stories provided the all-important silver lining when coming to terms with our violent past. Those stories, of great heroism and courage, were stories I wanted to be a part of. It was moving to read about them, particularly because I always imagined myself as one of those people.

I wanted that experience and realized that there was a chance I could get it in Gujarat.

~ Chapter 1 ~

The decision to go didn't settle down well with my predictably cautious family. My parents, never having ventured too far out of their world, started immediately fearing the worst. This was precipitated of course by the daily, almost ghoulish, reports in the newspapers of the bloodshed. When I told them I was going to Gujarat, they initially thought I was going to work with survivors of the 2001 earthquake, which was safe to do and could be celebrated as humanitarian work. Apolitical humanitarian work.

And it wasn't just them who resisted the idea. As was the wont of my extended family, they chimed in with unsolicited advice. With a melodramatic gasp, my grandmother pleaded with me not to go and suggested volunteering at the Ramakrishna Ashram for a few months.

"Why don't you just spend a few months there *kanna*? They do some wonderful charity work in the nearby villages and they are a good, pious organization." she said, her voice tinged with exaggerated angst.

Later, during a family get-together, my uncle gave his engaged and condescending take on the situation.

"What if you're working in one of the Muslim slums and then a riot breaks out?" he asked in a patronizing rhetoric. "They'll obviously target you. It's a very communal place Jayram, and you have no experience of such a situation. And with your name, the Muslims won't spare you during a riot. It's a violent situation, and you should know that."

I rolled my eyes but didn't say anything.

My stubbornness took over. Indeed whatever doubts or fears I might have had evaporated into thin air when my folks protested my decision. Being the maverick was no more an irritant I had to put up with. I embraced it fondly. It was my identity within the family, and it made me arrogant. I was the gutsy one, the one willing to risk it all – as long as there was an audience to showcase it to – while they were desperate for security in their little Brahmin cocoons. My man-child ego simply would not allow me to stay back now.

My parents finally relented. But I was to wait until after Akka's marriage as well as ensure that all my applications for higher studies were completed and sent out. She was in America working in a software firm, and had been dating a co-worker, also from India, for about a year. They soon decided to move back to India together and get married. The wedding was slated for some time in the end of March. My brother-in-law was from an army family, but far too independent to continue the family tradition so ended up as a computer-scientist who soon cashed in on India's tech boom. He comforted my parents by talking about the times when his father was posted in Ladakh or Kashmir, and how his family managed to deal with the stress during those postings.

I wasn't in the military though, nor did I have to go because it was part of my job. I merely decided that Gujarat was going to be the place for me to have that humanitarian adventure I had been craving for so long, the kind I had read about in books and seen in movies. This probably made my family think I was being rather cavalier about it. I'm not sure what I was thinking really. There was something about the violence in Gujarat that seemed macabre enough to warrant this off-the-cuff trip. Or maybe I was just paying more attention this time. Either way, something in me felt like I needed to find out more by actually going there.

I think what really pushed me to go was a report on a major English news channel. It was about a Muslim woman. She had miraculously survived the violence, but lost her 5 year old son to the fury of the mobs and was badly injured herself. The reporter said that she had been assaulted by some members of the Hindu mob that attacked her neighbourhood, but was in too much shock to talk about it on national television. She survived because she had gone unconscious, and the mob thought she was already dead.

Something snapped in me when I saw that news item. I had been reading about the bloodshed in the national dailies for a week until then. But this story of a wailing Muslim woman, face blurred to protect her identity, on an English news channel that was about to go for a commercial break advertising *Fair And Lovely* facial cream made me nearly double over. It's not too uncommon to see poor wailing people on Indian news channels, and often just before commercial breaks advertising facial cream. I don't know why this left me feeling like I just had the wind punched out of me, sitting in my comfortable living room in Bangalore, sufficiently far away from the madness. I must have indeed been paying a little more attention this time.

It was mid-April by the time I actually got moving. I finished sending in my applications for higher studies in America and Europe. Felt safe in knowing that with my high GRE scores and engineering degree, I would get into a good university for my Masters with a scholarship. By the time the admissions were confirmed it would be another six months. Following that I would have to get my student visa and make travel arrangements to start my studies early next year. It gave me a good amount of time to have a really comprehensive stint of volunteer work. An experience I could carry with me for the rest of my life. Something that would hold me in good stead as I moved along in my career. I felt a certain sense of security knowing that my future was on a good wicket, while still having the time to gain another completely different experience. In addition it was bound to look good on my CV. After all, many companies looked to hire people with solid extra-curricular activities. I had it all planned out.

I travelled by plane – Air India. It was more expensive than the train, but the convenience made it worthwhile. My family and friends came to see me off. It felt like I was going to fight a war. An unnecessarily teary goodbye took place at the airport. To my surprise it was Appa rather than Amma who started sobbing. She was emotionally tougher than him, even though he saw himself as the patriarch of the household. Amma merely hugged me tight as I got ready to leave and then asked me to go comfort him as he broke into tears. It felt nice knowing that I had this social support base in Bangalore.

I was quite nervous boarding the plane. For all my bravado, I had never really ventured to do anything like this. Had never really stepped outside my sequestered life in Bangalore. All the rebelling I had done until then was quite safe and within my middle-class environs – excessive sports, bar-hopping with friends, faux-Western culture, non-controversial student-activism, skipping classes, playing mediocre rhythm-guitar in a pretend rock band, general rabble-rousing with friends, or smoking the occasional joint with my cousins.

Rebelling isn't supposed to be that safe.

~ Chapter 2 ~

I stepped out of the airport in Ahmedabad, Gujarat's biggest city, not knowing what to expect. For starters, I had never travelled north of the Vindhyas in India. Had generally remained in my own little cosy, comfortable corner in the South. I really didn't know what to expect in a world so far away from Bangalore, especially one that had experienced such crazy violence. I wondered if I would witness movie-like scenes of mayhem. Would there still be fires burning all around the city as I had seen in the news? Would there be blood on the street? Would I have to duck and cover from police gunfire or angry mobs?

To my surprise, there was nothing out of the ordinary. Nothing I wouldn't have found in most other Indian cities. I stepped out of the airport and found exactly what one would expect to find outside any airport in the country. A line of taxies with uniformed drivers, a clutter of auto rickshaws with less-uniformed drivers, and a few shops scattered around selling ridiculously over-priced snacks and insipid beverages. The place even smelled cleaner than the airport in Bangalore.

This is the airport, I thought. They must have good security here.

I hailed an auto rickshaw after moving sufficiently away from the rush of taxi drivers aggressively affirming that they could get me to my next port-of-call in air-conditioned comfort at barely-higher rates than a rickshaw. The trick I learnt to dealing with their vigorous self-promotion was a single-minded determination in sticking to one's plan of hailing the cheapest mode of individualized public transportation available at airports. Even the slightest hesitation, a momentary turn of the head or a fleeting glance, would have resulted in my bags being unceremoniously yanked by one of the drivers who had clearly misunderstood the meaning of commercial hospitality. Said bags would have then been stuffed into the trunk of a taxi that cost twice as much as a rickshaw, but that I was now obligated to take simply because I displayed a moment of weakness and didn't feel like making a fuss. Past experiences had made me wiser.

I got into one of the rickshaws after confirming with

the driver that he would charge according to the meter. I didn't fancy getting cheated as soon as I landed in the city. He agreed, and we soon sped off.

As we trundled to the Behavioural Science Centre in St. Xavier's College, I was sure I would find signs of rioting and violence. But there was nothing along the way either. The usual bustle of cars, scooters, bikes, carts, a stray beggar or two, surprisingly clean roads with vendors and pedestrians on sidewalks lined with shops. Exchange the Gujarati signs for Kannada ones, throw in a few potholes, and I might as well have been in Bangalore. It was mildly unnerving.

I ventured a question to the driver in my modest Hindi, "*Bhai saab*, is everything ok after the riots?"

He replied with a *paan*-filled gurgle, jutting his lower jaw out to prevent the juices of the betel leaves from spilling out.

"Riots will keep happening in this city *saab*."

"So is everything ok then, have the police controlled everything?"

"Nothing happens here, this is the New City. Problems are there, but nothing much."

He spat out some red *paan* juice as he said this.

He didn't seem like he wanted to chat much, so I dropped it. I did, however, get a chance to examine the inside of his auto rickshaw in detail.

In Bangalore, auto rickshaws often had various faith-based stickers on the inside of them, alongside popular Bollywood actors and actresses. Christians liked to put large stickers of the cross with a picture of Mary or Jesus or verses from the bible. Muslims generally had a small sticker with the name of Allah in Arabic or maybe a picture of the *Ka'ba*. Hindus had pictures of one or more of the umpteen gods and goddesses they held a sect-based loyalty to. Whenever I saw these multifaceted religious symbols I always felt they reaffirmed the pluralism of the country, "enshrined in the constitution" as my Civics teacher in school would say.

When drivers started pasting copies of their licenses as per law I realized that many of them were actually driving rented vehicles. So, often the signs of faith inscribed on the rickshaw were those of the owner rather than the driver. Still pluralist. Mercantile. But pluralist nevertheless.

The guy taking me to my port of call here in Ahmedabad was most definitely Hindu. Two saffron streamers were tied to the rear view mirrors, and a large portrait of the goddess *Durga* impaling a demon with her trident adorned the inside of the rickshaw. He had a large red *tilak* on his forehead and two giant rings on either hand with the pictures of Hindu deities on them.

The rickshaw phut-phutted its way towards the BSC campus, where I was told to go to by a social worker in *Shanthi Samudaya*, the peace and justice movement that emerged when the violence broke out. It consisted of a collection of different NGOs and human rights groups. In Ahmedabad the movement took on the name *Shanthi Samudaya*, while in Baroda, further up north in Gujarat, it went by the name *Insaaf Abhiyan*. The entire state had been torn by the violence for well over a month by the time I was there in April. Most of the carnage occurred on February 28th, soon after the train compartments got burnt in Godhra, and for a few days after. Stray incidents of violence took place in the weeks following. In each city or town, movements comprising a variety of community groups sprung up to combat it, with the ones in Ahmedabad and Baroda being the largest. Some of the movements had a certain degree of structure, others were nothing more than a motley group of brave souls trying their best to deal with an impossible situation.

And it seemed to be an impossible situation indeed. Apart from the sheer amount of time that the violence continued, I never understood how it had spread so quickly; almost spontaneously combusting all over the state, as opposed to being contained in one city or town. Riots, per se, were never this comprehensive.

At that moment however I was more concerned with getting my stuff to some place so that I didn't have to lug it around. I had a dull ache in my shoulder from walking around the airport trying to find an auto rickshaw while carrying a large duffle bag and backpack. More importantly, I really wanted to talk to somebody about what was going on and to

11

get some instructions. I hadn't been told anything when I spoke to the aid-workers working out of the Bangalore branch of one of the main NGOs in the coalition. Only that I was to get my rear end to Ahmedabad as soon as possible and find my way to the BSC campus.

I was however curious as to why a movement like *Shanthi Samudaya* would operate out of an institute called the Behavioural Science Centre. It sounded like the kind of place where monkeys were kept for brain testing, or where mice scurried around in cages pressing buttons for pellets of food.

The auto rickshaw dropped me at the entrance of the campus. I followed the signs for the main BSC office, which was past a large, green sports field with goal posts at each end, pull-up bars on the side, and surrounded by a well-kept cinder track with chalk marks. It had been a while since I had done any serious sports training, but I still kept fit. Nice, I thought to myself. Great that there was a place to run, and maybe even play some football in the evenings, which I was certain there would be time to do. After all, I was just a volunteer. I figured I could even start a team with other volunteers.

As I approached the office, I noticed a shop, already closed for the night and the college cafeteria right next to it. The building was split into three sections, with a courtyard and a gazebo at the centre. There seemed to be lawns in the front and back of the building. I was told to head straight for the large dorm on the ground floor of the building to the left. A small wooden sign, with the paint chipping off, indicated that the bathrooms were on the second floor. The dorm was essentially one gargantuan room, as big as a house, with no partitions. I noticed numerous mattresses on the floor and a place to keep my luggage in the corner. There were also a large number of raggedy pillows and thin sheets stacked next to the mattresses.

I went inside the dorm and threw my luggage down on the floor. It landed with a soft thud. Almost immediately, I heard a gruff murmur. The dorm was quite large and I hadn't noticed that there was somebody sleeping in the corner of the dorm on the other side. Nor did I really expect to as it was barely eight in the evening. He turned around, his navel eyeing me from his ample belly half-covered by his rumpled vest.

"Who are you?" he said with a half snort. His eyes were still red and hooded from sleep, which further accentuated his dark skin. His face sported a scraggly salt and pepper moustache, that hadn't been trimmed in a while. Definitely looks like a Southie, probably even a Tamil guy, I thought, listening to his accent.

"I'm so sorry, I didn't see you sleeping there. Um…my name is Jayram Krishnan. I've come to join *Shanthi Samudaya,* to volunteer in the relief camps and community rebuilding efforts." I said, while cheerfully extending my hand as I walked over to him.

He snorted an acknowledgement and half shook my hand, but more to hold it and help heave himself to a seated position while clearing his throat. He sat on the mattress in a half squat, half splayed manner. His weather-beaten feet and yellow toenails betrayed years of walking everywhere in *chappals* and open-toed sandals. He squinted to get used to the light, as he looked at me.

With a yawn and a scratch, he asked, "So where are you from?"

"From Bangalore, I just got in"

"And you've come to volunteer with the movement?"

"Yes, I'm really excited about it. Just can't wait to get started!" I said with enthusiasm.

He yawned again, "Hmm…so what is it that you want to do?"

"Um…I'm sorry?"

He raised his voice a little in annoyance, "What is it that you want to do here?"

"Umm, I don't know. Whatever's needed I suppose…I really just want to contribute in the fight for justice." I stuttered.

"I see…and how do you plan on fighting for this justice?"

"Well…I didn't really have a proper plan…I was just…"

"It looks like you've come with a plan, you seem to want to get *justice* for all these people." He said sarcastically, yawning again and scratching his belly.

"Well…I…"

13

He interrupted me in mid-yawn while still rubbing his eyes, before I could blurt out something.

"Look, you should know that we don't want any heroes here." he sternly said. "If you're looking to be a hero or think that you've come here to save all these people, then you should just take your bags and fuck off right now."

Ok then. My first lesson.

No heroes. Got it.

He said this without much change in tone or volume, but I was still a little taken aback by his sleepy abrasiveness. I was expecting more of a welcoming attitude towards newcomers. He now reached for his thick plastic-rimmed spectacles, and started wiping them with his soiled vest.

I backed down a little on the enthusiasm.

"I, uh…I didn't mean it that way. I was just wondering what I would be doing here. I'm sorry, I didn't mean to be condescending in any way"

He softened a little bit, but still didn't smile.

"It's all right. Whenever some disaster strikes any region all these outside volunteers come here thinking that they're going to save the fucking world." he said crabbily. "Some even feel like they're going to get something to add to their resume. The same thing happened after the earthquake last year. Anyway, we need all the help we can get here, so even if you're here just to boost your CV, we'll use you."

I smiled and nodded, a little nervously

"My name is Mani by the way." he added.

I asked gingerly, "So what is it that you do here sir?"

"I'm essentially coordinating the health unit of *Shanthi Samudaya*. But I also coordinate other efforts. Professionally I'm associated with the NIMHANS Hospital in Bangalore."

Aaaah, so he was from NIMHANS. The National Institute for Mental Health and Neurological Sciences. During my school years we knew it more pejoratively as the local loony bin.

I asked, "What's the work like?"

He talked a little bit about the need for counselling victims of violence, ones who had lost their loved ones, seen them butchered before their eyes and burnt. It seemed like he had no problems talking about his work. I soon realised that it was probably also a way of venting.

"What kind of counselling is given to the victims?" I enquired, trying desperately to sound as sincere and humble as possible.

"You see, after the violence, bodies were so charred that one couldn't make out whether they were men or women." he said, as he continued scratching himself. "Hundreds of thousands became homeless as their houses were destroyed, and they're now living in relief camps around the city. Mainly in and around the Gomtipur area, Shah Alam mosque, Naroda Patiya, and Vatwa village. Even that Gulbarg Society...oof, there was so much bloodshed there too."

He shook his head as he thought of it, and continued, "Most of the people living in the relief camps have lost a loved one in the violence. And it's a very brutal loss, not like they've died of old age or some terminal illness or something. You can't even begin to describe the trauma. Almost all have nothing to go back to, no homes, no work, nothing."

He paused momentarily rubbing his face to get rid of sleep, and cleared his throat again, this time coughing a little. From the cough I could make out that he was a smoker. After another yawn, he continued narrating.

"Hmm....of course, the camps were completely abandoned by the state government. They were in a bloody state of mayhem to begin with...absolutely inhuman living conditions. Filthy, and now soon the rains will come and then it will be really bad. What kind of counselling can be given to them?" he asked rhetorically. "It's very difficult, yet mental health is of huge importance. These people have been through so much, and have lost so much hope. It's tough, but we need to keep doing something."

Mani talked almost like the work was too overwhelming for the movement to handle. His last sentence – we need to keep doing *something* – struck me as coming from someone who was still coming to terms with the brutality; not the head of a unit in charge of something as important as the health of survivors. I expected something more poised, something more commanding, a strategy, a plan that was being put to action, a plan that *I* could follow.

He then stopped describing the carnage and made to get up.

"Have you had dinner?" he asked me as he started standing up. "You must be quite hungry after your train journey."

"Um...yeah." I said, slightly embarrassed. "I'm quite hungry after lugging my bags all over the place. Definitely wouldn't mind having some dinner."

"There's a nice South Indian place just down the road from the entrance of the campus. Great *masala-dosai.*"

His stellar pronunciation of one of my favourite dishes confirmed his obvious Tamil roots. I felt a strange chauvinism in knowing that a fellow Southie had come all the way to Gujarat to carry out such important work in the face of great odds.

Mani seemed to have warmed up to me a little. The original cantankerousness directed at me had disappeared as we walked past the football field towards the restaurant. Grogginess coupled with a newbie would have riled anyone up I suppose.

~ Chapter 3 ~

The next day I was to report to a *Shanthi Samudaya* meeting as instructed by Mani. The meeting was held on the lawn behind the dorm.

The night before, a few more fairly tired men and women came over and settled in the dorm, each taking a mattress and pillow. They had the self-assured, weary look of folks who had been volunteering for a while, and seemed to know Mani quite well. It was late and they looked ready to drop, so apart from a few pleasantries, I didn't get to chat much with them.

I followed them in the morning to breakfast at the mess hall and then to the lawn where there were many more volunteers seated around in a circle. I noticed that they had not come with those who stayed at the dorm last night and looked like they had arrived in the morning. It was also obvious that they were not English-speaking, middle-class folk like Mani or the others whom I had met in the dorm.

I had found out from Mani the night before that there were two kinds of field-workers involved in relief work in the camps. *Shanthi Pathiks*, aid workers who worked directly under *Shanthi Samudaya*, formed the bulk of the workers and were usually young Muslims from the local areas. They were the backbone of the entire movement, and most of them had seen the violence firsthand – losing relatives, friends, or at the very least, their homes.

Apart from them, there were also volunteers from outside the state, usually young, urban, middle-class youth from all over the country, either as part of a larger college or youth group, or individuals who were basically moved by the news of the carnage and travelled to Ahmedabad hoping to volunteer in the camps. Those who came from outside the state usually ended up volunteering with one or the other of the numerous community organisations that made up the coalition.

The BSC, which I learnt was a very progressive institute, had donated the usage of the dorm for the movement to house the volunteers who came from outside the state. The *Shanthi Pathiks*, since they came from within the community, lived either at the refugee camps or their own homes, if they were still standing.

Mani had also mentioned to me that the *Shanthi Pathiks* were paid a monthly stipend of Rs 2500, while the outside volunteers were entitled to a per diem allowance for food and travel. Hoping to endear myself to Mani, I refused the per diem, stating that I had my own money, to which he gave me an irritated look. I thought he would have been more complimentary of my gesture, so it confused me. But I didn't have time to reflect on it.

I assumed that the folks already seated at the lawn were all *Shanthi Pathiks*. They wore inexpensive shirts and trousers, with cheap sandals. Unlike the outside volunteers who wore fashionable *khadi* shirts or t-shirts and jeans, with nice sports shoes.

Mani started the meeting by asking everyone to introduce themselves. Once we had all introduced ourselves in quick fire fashion, Mani took out a notebook and started addressing the entire gathering in Hindi. He looked like he had been doing this sort of thing for a while.

"Thank you brothers and sisters for coming." he said. "Today we're going to discuss shelter construction, especially keeping in mind the coming monsoons."

From the manner in which he conducted the meeting and the way everyone responded, I realised that these meetings were a fairly regular thing. I also suspected that I would just have to join in and do whatever I was told without any real initiation or training.

He continued in very correct, but strongly Tamil-accented, Hindi, "The main items we will need are large wooden poles for the sides and the roof, strong rope to tie the poles together, as well as rubber and tarpaulin sheets to cover the roof and floor. We'll also need to build one-foot high brick walls around the shelter in order to prevent water from coming in."

He drew a crude diagram giving a basic idea of what such a shelter would look like, and lifted up the notebook for everyone to see.

"Whoever is working in their respective camps will need to procure these items from local shopkeepers and get clear invoices so that *Shanthi Samudaya* can pay for it. For the construction it is important to follow proper procedures," he said, waving a warning forefinger, "else it will be of no use when the monsoons start. It is particularly important to ensure that the shelters be made as water proof as possible because quite a few of the people at the camps will stay there during the nights while their houses are being reconstructed. You will also need bricks and cement for the one-foot high walls. For that you have to measure the perimeter of the shelter and calculate how many bricks and how much cement you will need."

I was taking down notes furiously as he spoke, trying my level best to keep up with the Hindi. I looked up and realised that nobody else had removed their notebooks and were merely nodding along and listening.

Mani went on, "Please make sure that you get invoices, otherwise we will not be able to pay for the items, and then the whole thing becomes a big mess for our accounting departments."

He specified the likely cost of each item so that the volunteers didn't get cheated in the process.

The volunteers asked a couple of questions regarding a potential timeframe to ensure the shelters were up and ready before the monsoons.

One of them, a wiry young man with a wisp of a moustache, asked in Urdu-laced Hindi, "Mani sir, when are the livelihood schemes going to start for the people living in the camps?"

Mani interjected with a smile, "It will take a little more time Nasir, but not too much longer. Basically we're trying to get different NGOs in partnership with the government to procure the required items like carts, sewing machines, a little seed money and all. Some have come and some have not come, so we also need to find out which victims get the first batch of livelihood items. Only those with the highest need should get them, since all can't get them at one shot."

Nasir continued earnestly, "That is the biggest need sir. More than anything people want to get back to work and start earning..."

"Of course, of course Nasir." Mani softly interrupted

him mid-sentence with a smile. "Don't worry, something will come along soon. See, whatever we do we should do it properly, and not in a haphazard manner, even if it takes a little longer."

Nasir quietly acquiesced with a compliant sideways nod.

Mani finally said, "Ok, if there are no more questions, then let's get started. All of you start with the shelter construction in your respective camps."

He then looked at me and said, "Jayram, you go with Nasir and Vijay."

I got up, walked towards Nasir and smiled. Extending my hand, I introduced myself in Hindi, "My name is Jayram."

Nasir smiled wide showing teeth that had red stains from chewing *gutka*. His wide mouth and prominent jaw line stood out against the gauntness of his face and rail-thin body. He bowed his head a little, shook my hand and then touched his chest. His bony palm was completely enveloped by mine, but his handshake was firm.

"Jayram*bhai*, my name is Nasir Khan."

A young man next to him also smiled at me and extended his hand. He was more sinewy and straight-backed than Nasir, and a little fiercer looking. He had powerful reddish eyes that were set in contrast against dark skin. He too shook my hand and then touched his chest.

He introduced himself with a slight nod, "Vijay."

Vijay was an obviously Hindu name, which I found a little surprising. I had thought that all the community-based volunteers were Muslim, and was evidently wrong. Vijay was leaner than me, but I could feel the tensile strength in his handshake, and the raw power in his grip. I had found many times in the past that physical strength in connection to a person's actual physique was often deceptive. I'd met urban, college-going, gym rats with broad chests and massive arms often displaying lesser actual strength than much leaner, labouring folk for whom physical exertion was a way of life. The lean, sinewy arms of the farmer or the manual worker could often exert with greater strength and stamina than the bulging biceps of the dumbbell-lifter.

After our brief exchange, Vijay indicated with a slight

twist of his head that we should leave. Neither of them felt particularly awkward with me or that I needed some sort of primer on what we were doing. It seemed like the most natural thing to them that I was there and accompanying them. I didn't feel any of the arms-length distance that one normally felt when meeting people for the first time, especially in some of the social circles that I had back home in Bangalore.

I looked at Mani and indicated that I was going with a wave, probably because he was now my closest friend in the entire group. He smiled and nodded back, which gave me more confidence.

As the three of us walked along the path towards the entrance of the campus, I asked, trying hard to keep my Hindi grammatically correct, "So where are we going now?"

Nasir answered, "We're going to Gomtipur Jayram*bhai*. The two or three camps that Vijay and I work in are in that area. We need to build shelters there."

"And how will we be going there?" I asked, hoping to offer to pay for the rickshaw and ingratiate myself with my new found friends.

Vijay replied matter-of-factly, "We have to take a bus to the main terminus and then from there take another bus to the Old City."

~ Chapter 4 ~

The central bus terminus in Ahmedabad on a week-day morning was like any central bus station one would find in most Indian cities – dusty, smoke-filled and spilling over with life, human and non-human. One waded through commuters, stray dogs, and vendors to catch the bus before it left the station, while deftly avoiding being bumped by one of the other numerous buses trundling in and out. Often the only way to differentiate between bus stations in different cities was the language and the comestibles sold by the vendors. Peanuts, fried peas, and *bhel* were fairly common to bus stations across India, but in Chennai you would also find *molaga bhajji* and packets of *idli-vada-dosa*; in Bangalore there would be cucumber sandwiches and *bhutta*; in Mumbai there would be *vada-pav*; while in Delhi there would be oily *kachoris* and *paneer-patties* swimming in a spicy brown gravy. The singular purpose of that gravy, I unfortunately realized one time, was to toughen the stomach lining.

In Ahmedabad, apart from the standard fare, you got sweetened *aloo-bondas*. I tried these the previous day in the airport and it was inexplicable to me. The potato-filled fried snack that I had consumed with afternoon tea growing up in Bangalore was a Southern speciality and was supposed to be salty, maybe even a dash spicy. This sweetened version was a travesty that I, quite literally, couldn't stomach. Apart from this gastro-abomination, vendors also sold other, more agreeable, local specialities like *dhokla* and Gujarati sweets.

Vijay, Nasir and I were waiting for the bus that was to take us to Gomtipur. Nasir was quite chatty, describing what needed to be done over the next few days. I found myself needing to concentrate to keep up with his quick-fire Hindi that had liberal sprinklings of Urdu words.

"There has been a lot of loss in the Gomtipur area. Many houses were burnt. All of the people who lost their homes are living in the camps there. If we don't construct the shelters soon, there's going to be real problems. The rain is just going to wash over the ground and there won't be any place for people to sleep or cook."

I asked, "Where do people get food from?"

"From rations distributions mostly." Nasir replied. "We have to do that at least once or twice a week. Right now, most of the people in the camps don't work, so they don't have money to buy food from the market. They're completely dependent on the rations."

Vijay interjected with a hint of anger, "That's the biggest problem in the relief efforts. We need to start working immediately on getting people's livelihoods back. At least then, they'll be able to work and not feel completely useless."

He paused to spit, and then continued, "Also, how long will these relief supplies last? Some week or the other, there will be a problem and then rations won't arrive at the camp, which will then cause a major commotion because the camp residents get frustrated. People become angry and then we'll have even more problems with quarrels and fights. I wish we can start working on helping people with their livelihood. Otherwise all this is no use."

We stood for about five minutes waiting for the bus that was to take us across the river to Gomtipur. Nasir soon spotted it from a distance, pulling away, and he told us to make a run for it. I thought he was out of his mind. They acted like it was the most natural thing to do however and took off without the slightest hesitancy, with me in tow.

I had always been told by my parents not to get on or off moving buses as a child when the school bus would come and pick me up. I really couldn't believe that I was attempting this.

As we rushed towards the bus, both Vijay and Nasir helped me on the run to get on the bus first before getting on themselves. By the time Nasir got on, he was nearly sprinting to keep up with the fast-accelerating bus and then, with consummate timing, jumped onto the footboard.

It was not very crowded, but neither of them wanted to sit, so I stood with them. They both had bus passes, while I bought a ticket for which I had the bus conductor give me change for a 50 rupee note. He was visibly crotchety about it. From the way that Nasir and Vijay looked at me, it was clear that this was not a normal practice.

As the bus continued on its journey, Nasir talked to

me about the ghettoization of the city and how most of the Muslims lived in the Old City just across the Sabarmati river, which was where we were heading. I noticed that he spoke in a slightly more hushed tone now, as if he was revealing some deep, dark secret to me.

"Most of the killings happened there Jayram*bhai*. They came armed with weapons, and kerosene cans. Many came behind the police shouting slogans." he said animatedly. "They would kill and then burn the bodies. We saw many bodies where we couldn't make out whether it was a man or a woman. They came in such huge mobs shouting 'Jai Sriram' or many times slogans directly insulting Muslims. The police fully supported them. But nothing happened here in the new city. Here it was completely peaceful."

As Nasir spoke, Vijay looked on with serious contemplation.

En route, I could see that we were leaving the slightly richer areas of Ahmedabad, which both Nasir and the auto-driver during my first night had described as the New City. As the bus trundled on, we approached the Sabarmati river.

Vijay got my attention and pointed out to a small campus some distance away on the side of the river, with some simple, pleasant-looking buildings.

"Jayram*bhai*, that's Gandhigram." he said.

I peered over to see Gandhi's famous ashram. The place where he wrote, prayed, held meetings, planned political mobilizations against the British, and lived his ascetic life. It was only after seeing Gandhigram that it hit me that Gandhi was, in fact, from Gujarat. I knew it as a vague piece of trivia, but never internalised the fact that the man most of the world considered to be the apostle of non-violence, an ardent advocate of a strange religo-political secularism, was actually from this state.

I asked whether Gandhigram did anything to help the victims during the riots.

Vijay replied with a huff, "What could they do Jayram*bhai*? They issued some statements to maintain calm, but other than that nothing. They didn't even help much with relief efforts. The government will crush them. They're too scared of the government."

I innocuously asked, "Too scared of the government? But Gandhi *was* Gujarati. Why would the Gujarati state do anything to harm the ashram of the most famous Indian, that too when he was from here?"

Nasir laughed, while Vijay gave a sardonic grunt.

"All that is old India Jayram*bhai*. In Gujarat, the old India doesn't exist." he replied with a huff.

As the bus passed Gandhigram we got to the Ellis bridge and started crossing the Sabarmati. It was a wide river, but not too rough. The monsoons hadn't started as yet and the water didn't seem polluted. It was quite beautiful. Not as beautiful as the Kaveri though, I thought to myself.

The bus trundled over the bridge, and soon Nasir and Vijay indicated to me that our stop was coming up.

We stopped at a dusty, crowded road with open drains, and numerous small shops lined along the sides. Unlike the roads from the other side of the river that we had just come from, there were no sidewalks. A couple of men were moving slabs of wood on a bullock cart. A few stray dogs loitered around. It was warm, and the fumes from the auto rickshaws and scooters added to the dusty heat. I immediately spotted some of the principal markers of a poor Muslim colony – a mosque and a butchers shop. Usually it would also include shops for auto-repair, waste-disposal, furniture-making, stone-carving, and a small eatery or two that sold biscuits and sweet buns with tea. I spotted a furniture-making shop a few meters away from the bus stop, as well as a small restaurant with a giant *tandoor* in the front. A heated argument between two young men was going on near the butchers shop. They were shouting at each other in rapid-fire Urdu. It didn't bother any of the others on the street and, while fiery in tone, the disagreement didn't seem like it was going to result in an exchange of blows.

Next to the mosque was a huge graveyard with numerous modified shelters, and tarpaulin sheets tied to act like large tents. Vijay and Nasir beckoned me towards the entrance where there was a small shop selling cigarettes, sweets, chips, and soda.

The three of us got off the bus and I followed Nasir

and Vijay as they made their way towards the mosque and graveyard, navigating past a couple of stray dogs. I stood out like a sore thumb in my Adidas tennis shoes, khakis and denim shirt. I was also carrying my notebook in hand, with my backpack slung over my shoulder. I probably looked like a journalist. As we passed what looked like a tailoring shop, a rotund man with red *paan* stains on his teeth called out gruffly to Nasir.

"Who is that?" he asked with a grimace pointing at me.

We walked a couple of steps towards him, and Nasir said quite nonchalantly, "He's here to work with us in the camps. He's from outside. Recently came to BSC. Mainly he's doing surveys on the losses and helping with rations distribution and all."

I had no idea that I was supposed to be doing any of that, but smiled as sincerely as I could.

Not changing his expression, the man replied, "Ok, then tell him to take down all my details."

He then crudely called me to step closer and, without pausing, said, "You have your notebook? Good, then write down all of this...I lost one of my shops entirely in the *dhamaal.* They burned everything, including all my tailoring machines and cloth. In addition, I lost a lot of money in the fire. I have to get compensation. I say, why aren't you writing any of this down? Write, write!"

He poked at my notebook roughly with a hammy finger, at which point I started fumbling around for a pen and tried to note down everything he was telling me. I didn't know what he mistook me for, but it didn't seem to matter. I looked vaguely like someone with access to institutional power. As far as he was concerned, I was someone who could help. He continued listing in detail all the things that he lost.

Finally he asked, "Did you get all of that? So then what are you going to do about my compensation?"

I had no idea what to say and was about to mumble some useless platitude before Vijay interjected with some authority, "Don't worry uncle, we've already taken down all your details. Compensation is not going to come easily. We're still working on it. But don't worry, we're doing all we can."

The man didn't appear too convinced and indicated his obvious displeasure with an upset sigh and dismissive wave of hand. With that, Nasir and Vijay hurried me along towards the mosque and the entrance of the graveyard.

At the entrance of the graveyard was a small shelter made of corrugated tin sheets with a table and a few chairs. A young man was sitting on one of the chairs leafing through a worn-out register, chewing *gutka*. When we approached he let out a friendly grunt to Nasir and Vijay extending his hand to both of them, and then in a more exaggerated manner to me. Vijay introduced me while the guy was still shaking my hand and he smiled widely showing a set of teeth heavily darkened by excessive *gutka* chewing. His hand was rough and calloused from a living of hard physical labour. Like Vijay, he too was lean and muscular, but more squat. After shaking my hand he touched his chest and immediately offered me a chair, beckoning me to sit down.

We exchanged pleasantries. Vijay then said, "We've come to show the camp to Jayram*bhai*. He's just joined us in our work. He's from outside."

It seemed like the fact that I was from "outside" mattered a bit in terms of my credibility. Nasir too described me that way to the rude shopkeeper a few minutes back. The young man nodded his head vigorously and indicated for us to go inside. I concluded that he was some sort of quasi-administrator for the camp. We entered through a partition in the compound wall of the grave yard and I was able to get a full view of the camp.

What I saw matched the despair with which it had been described to me earlier.

Makeshift tents were made by tying tarpaulin sheets to giant wooden poles, with one giant open-air tent serving as the main shelter for the bulk of the people there. Men, women and children wandered around, some of them in bandages. A group of women sat huddled in a group, pacifying a sobbing friend. The area was horribly overcrowded with kitchen utensils, household items and straw mats strewn on the ground. There was the strong, pungent smell of food being cooked with strong spices on kerosene stoves. The smell added to the dusty heat. Some children played a short distance away where there was a small patch of land. Just outside the graveyard on a small side road, I spotted a few blue portable toilets with *Action Aid* written on the doors in giant white letters. I wondered how such a small number of toilets catered to the needs of the population in the camp. It seemed dreadfully inadequate. Next to the giant tent, was a small concrete room of sorts that looked like the camp office.

Nasir and Vijay headed towards there, and I tagged along. Inside was a large, beefy man sitting at a broken wooden table writing carefully in a long notebook that looked like a ledger. There were a few old files on the table, along with a small fan and a glass half-filled with tea. As we entered, he smiled widely showing a set of, by-now-expectedly, *gutka*-stained teeth and got up to greet us. As soon as he saw me, he barked to a couple of kids standing nearby to get us some chairs. He offered his own to me while we waited. I tried refusing, but before I knew it he along with Nasir and Vijay had already gently pushed me onto the chair while the three of them continued standing.

He asked me, "Shall I get some tea *bhai*?" And before I could say anything, ordered another kid to get some tea from the local shop shoving a five-rupee note in the kid's hands.

Nasir introduced him to me, "Jayram*bhai*...this is Zubaan*bhai*. He is one of the main coordinators of this camp."

I smiled and extended my hand. He shook it vigorously, bowing a little, still smiling widely and then touched his chest.

They started chatting about the shelters almost immediately, while I looked around the bare office, feeling a little awkward to be the only one sitting.

Nasir asked, pointing at the main tarpaulin tent, "So what do we do about the shelter? This is hardly enough for the coming monsoon. People will get really wet."

Zubaan replied, "I know, I know. We have to start building a small brick wall around the shelter to prevent the water from coming in. Also the tarpaulin sheet needs to be changed. There are too many holes in this one."

Vijay said, "It will take a little time to construct, but I think if we can get some of the young guys together, we can finish it as soon as possible."

"Of course we'll get them boss. What are they doing anyway?" Zubaan said confidently. "They don't have any work to do. They're all still waiting for the shops to get reconstructed. They'll all help."

Vijay asked, "So shall we at least see if we can check prices and order the material now? Jayram*bhai* is with us now, so we can go and do that."

I got curious and craned my head forward when I heard my name; both Nasir and Vijay then looked at me. Vijay said to me, "We need to go get materials now Jayram*bhai*. What do you say?"

I was a little surprised that I was being asked this like I was some kind of decision-maker, when I had no idea what to do. I nodded my head, hoping to look confident, but had no clue as to what I was nodding my head for.

Nasir then said, "*Chalo*, let's go then. We should order the bricks and cement and stuff. God knows how long it will take for the shopkeeper to get the material. He'll ask for an exorbitant price, so we have to bargain."

Some kids then came in carrying three chairs. Zubaan said, "Wait, wait. Drink some tea and then go. I've already asked the kid to get some."

Nasir and Vijay then sat down. They chatted a little bit with Zubaan about the camp residents and some of the problems that they were going through. Soon the other kid came carrying four small glasses and a small tin kettle. He hesitantly made to give the change back, which Zubaan told him to keep with a wave of his hand. The kid smiled widely and ran back to join his friends playing by the gravestones. Zubaan took the kettle and poured a full glass of tea and gave it to me. He then divided the remaining tea among the three of them, with each of them getting barely half a glass. While I blew at the steaming tea trying to cool it down and drink it sip by sip, they gulped down the tea in one swallow. I realised that we would have to leave soon, so I did the same, scalding my tongue and throat. We said our goodbyes and I followed Nasir and Vijay out of the camp office.

As we left, little did I realise that this camp, the surrounding areas, and particularly Nasir and Vijay were soon to become an integral part of my life.

~ Chapter 5 ~

Nasir, Vijay and I made our way out of the camp, but they took a different route than the one we came in. We cut right across the graveyard to another pathway that led to a road on the other side. This one was smaller than the main one that had the bus stop. As we walked along the road, I saw what I thought I was going to see when I first stepped out of the airport.

Along the entire stretch of the road were the charred remnants of houses burnt down. Most of the houses had been reduced to rubble, with the roofs having caved in, and the walls broken and blackened from the fires. It looked like a mini war zone with piles of debris and ash in the place of houses. Most of the homes were no more than a couple of rooms, sharing walls with neighbouring houses, typical of poor urban ghettos in India. They directly opened onto the street, which was no more than fifteen feet wide.

Alongside the piles of debris, I saw the burnt bits and pieces of various household items. Parts of smashed doors, beds, picture frames, kitchen utensils, torn mattresses, ripped books, melted children's toys – remnants of the sparse belongings in toiling households who struggled even at the best of times.

I instinctively fished into my backpack for my small Kodak camera. Before coming, I had decided that I would detail everything that I saw as best as I could through journals and photographs. I asked Vijay and Nasir if it would be ok for me to take a couple of pictures, and they were more than encouraging, even pointing specific homes that had been destroyed telling me the names of the inhabitants, and whether they had been killed or survived the carnage.

I shot a couple of photos, and then stopped dead in my tracks as I spotted something in one of the houses. A small light blue shoe no more than three or four inches long, obviously belonging to a toddler, with dark brown blood stains on it. I stared at it for a couple of seconds.

Nasir asked me, "What happened Jayram*bhai*?"

I shook myself out of my reverie and said, "Nothing, nothing. Just seeing that shoe gave me a bit of a shock."

Vijay responded sardonically, "That's nothing Jayram*bhai*, if you start getting affected by all this, then you'll spend the rest of your life just thinking about it. And then no work will ever get done."

I nodded, and took a photo of the shoe.

Vijay then pointed to the metal door of one of the houses. The door and the wall that held it was still standing, but the roof had caved in along with another wall.

"Look Jayram*bhai*, you see these holes at the bottom of the door?"

I took a closer look and noticed three small holes in a straight line.

He continued, "When the *dhamaal* happened, the family locked themselves up in the house. The Hindu rioters came and tried to open the metal door to kill them, but they couldn't. They even tried to ram it with a *trishul*." he said, while miming the ramming action. "That's how the three holes came on the door. When they realised that they couldn't unlock it. They put a big stone outside to prevent the people from coming out, then poured kerosene through the door and outside it, and lit it on fire. All the family members died in the fire."

I remembered book-drawings of a *trishul* being held by the Hindu mythological goddess Durga. As a kid, I had read in *Amar Chitra Katha* comics about her heroic exploits, killing demons with her divine trident. I had even seen a few in the hands of temple idols when the family went to pray, but those were mostly statuesque, and probably couldn't cut butter. It always seemed like such an awkward weapon, more symbolic than deadly. Never thought it could actually cause much damage.

I shook my head, and stared at the house for a few seconds. Nasir then mimed the action of taking a photo, so I stepped back a bit and took a photo of the house. I tried to stop thinking about the story behind each of those destroyed houses. I felt a sensation in the sides of my stomach like it was turning over. I countered it by digging my thumbs into my kidneys, which stopped my digestive system from flip-flopping and curbed the nausea that was building up.

We walked along the street. I put the camera back in

my backpack, not wanting to attract attention from folk who were passing by. As we continued walking, Nasir pointed to another destroyed house.

"This is Zubaan*bhai*'s uncle's house. His uncle and aunt died in the *dhamaal*, but luckily his two cousins were away at the time and managed to escape." he said with a sigh.

I thought back to the beefy Zubaan*bhai* I had just met at the camp office and wondered what other traumas were hidden behind his cherubic smile.

Vijay then indicated for us to quicken our pace.

"Let's walk a little faster. We have to get to the hardware shop to order the supplies for the shelter."

We quickened our pace a little bit, and the running commentary on the destruction that lay on either side of the street also stopped. Soon we reached a much larger road, much like the one that had the bus stop, and turned onto a corner.

I followed Vijay and Nasir to one of the larger shops where there were a couple of young men working on some carpentry in the front. It looked like a hardware store that doubled up as a furniture-making workshop as well.

We stepped into the store. It was warmer inside and quite muggy with the strong smell of paint-thinner, oil, and sawdust. A large man with a big belly came out to greet us.

Vijay and Nasir nodded in acknowledgement, and the man shook my hand without any introduction.

Vijay then said, "Wasim*bhai* we need supplies for building a shelter in the camp."

The man replied, "No problems. What do you need? I'll give you a good price for it. It's for the camp no? I'll give a solid discount."

I felt a little repulsed by the man engaging in crude mercantilism at a time of such devastation. Nevertheless, we negotiated the prices for tarpaulin sheets, wooden poles, bricks and cement. The majority of the time was spent in arguing with the shopkeeper on a timely delivery.

Vijay raised his voice a little as the argument went on, "Listen Wasim*bhai*, we need the materials much sooner than what you're giving as the delivery date. If the rains come then what will the camp residents do? You have to deliver it much earlier. We'll give you a deposit and then tomorrow we'll give you exact estimates of how much we need."

Finally we reached an agreement on the delivery date after some more emotional blackmailing of the shopkeeper. When the shopkeeper asked for a five-hundred rupee deposit, both Nasir and Vijay looked at me.

When I looked back a little quizzically, Nasir leaned towards me and quietly said, "Jayram*bhai*, you can pay the deposit and then keep the receipt to give to the accountant at the BSC office."

I was not told about this by anyone so was a little taken aback. But I realised that neither had they, so didn't ask any questions. I hadn't been given any official spending money by Mani. Luckily I had my own, so fished out five hundred-rupee notes and paid the shopkeeper. I then took the receipt and tucked it into the notebook I had in my backpack.

I later asked Nasir and Vijay whether this was something I was supposed to do in general. They looked at me a little puzzled, obviously thinking that I had been informed of this, and then replied that it was, without giving any further explanation. It seemed almost a given that I should be the one handling the money in the relief efforts that the three of us were engaged in.

I then realised that one of my functions was probably to act as a bridge between *Shanthi Pathiks* like Vijay or Nasir and the main coordinators of the movement. I wondered why I needed to act as a go-between for transacting money between the main NGOs and procuring materials for the relief work. The *Shanthi Pathiks* were the ones slogging it out to get the work done. The money could well have been given in advance to them and they could have handled the receipts without me. I had no idea what my utility was in this process.

I didn't bother dwelling on it much though. I was just happy at getting some work done, and feeling a little useful. For the first time in my interactions with Vijay and Nasir, I had actually *done* something as opposed to just learning about the violence and engaging in carnage-tourism. It actually felt like I wasn't a complete waste of space, even though the task I had just completed could well have been done by a moderately well-trained monkey.

Vijay, Nasir and I then left the shop and headed over to a small eatery to get some lunch. I hadn't realised it was late afternoon by the time we sat down to eat. Time had flown, and I was surprisingly hungry with all the walking we had done, completely unaware of the physical exertion.

We ordered some *tandoori rotis* and mutton curry, which consisted of pieces of mutton cooked in an oily brown gravy. We had this with slices of onions, cucumbers and green chillies. Vijay and I tucked in with gusto, while Nasir ate with a little more reservation. He had only one *roti* to the three each Vijay and I consumed. Both were concerned about whether I was eating well, and would ensure that the server placed the *roti* on my plate first and gave me the meatiest mutton pieces. We didn't talk as much, and concentrated more on the food. They told me that this was more or less a staple diet in the area. After we finished, I paid the bill and it came to a paltry twenty-five rupees, which was what I would have paid for an utterly tasteless cup of coffee in one of the upscale coffee shops in Bangalore.

I was used to a very different diet in my Tamil Brahmin house with my vegetarian parents. I usually only ate meat with my friends when we went out. But it was middle-class restaurant fare, often had with beer or rum – chicken *tikka*, fish cutlets, *shawarma* rolls, mutton *biryani*, *kababs* – not what I was eating with Vijay and Nasir. What we were eating was exactly the kind of food that my friends and I made fun of as a meal for truck-drivers or blacksmiths – food for working class folk with little means and hardy stomachs; not the kind of stuff that people like me ought to eat for multiple reasons. As I tucked in, I could picture the looks of revulsion I would have received back home had they seen the meal I had just partaken in.

~ Chapter 6 ~

I was writing in my journal that night lying on one of the mattresses in the BSC dorm. I was keen on translating my experiences into a book of sorts after I finished my studies. I lazily dreamt that it might even make me famous as a swashbuckling activist-writer who would be called in for interviews and conferences.

Like I mentioned before – I had it all planned out.

On the other side of the dorm were a few of the volunteers Mani had briefly introduced me to the previous night. When I came in, they were engaged in a fairly animated discussion, so didn't want to interrupt them. I smiled at them, and sat down to write. As I was scribbling down notes, a strapping young man with an impish smile, and well-proportioned shoulders, knelt in front of me with a small plate of *pooris* and a cup of *aam ras*. He seemed no more than a few years older than I at the most, with handsome features and curly, dark brown hair.

"Here man, have some *pooris* and *aam ras* with us." he said, thrusting the plate towards me.

Not wanting to appear too enthusiastic, I politely declined even though they looked enticing. But I smiled back at him as I turned down the offer, hoping that he would insist.

He thankfully shook his head immediately with purpose.

"No, absolutely no refusing. Have some *yaar*...it's really good stuff."

I was grateful for his insistence because the food looked good and I was starting to think about what I would do for dinner anyway. I took a couple of *pooris* and proceeded to dip pieces of the fried dough into the thick mango gravy that he had in the small plastic cup. I took a bite and it was delectable. He squatted down on the floor in front of me and started doing the same. He asked me where I was from.

"Bangalore. I just came in yesterday actually." I replied, mouth full of food.

"Really? That's great man! I grew up there, and did my B.A in Bangalore University. My mother still lives there. We're from the coastal regions of Karnataka."

For the last few words he shifted into a slightly broken Kannada. I replied a vague affirmation, in an equally shaky Kannada. Having established a sense of regional familiarity, we soon realized that it was easier for both of us to communicate in English. I found out that his name was Abhay.

"Where are you based now Abhay?" I asked him.

"In Mumbai. I'm doing my PhD in Political Science there."

"What prompted you to come over here?"

"Heard about the violence and just came. I can't exactly say why." he said, shrugging his shoulders. "I thought that I would only come for a few days, and now it's been a few weeks since I got here. I think I will stay for at least 6 months. I'm working primarily in the big camp in the Vatwa region with some *Shanthi Pathiks* there. I don't know...I feel like I'm at least doing something here rather than just wasting my time in the UK."

"UK? I thought you were doing your PhD in Mumbai?"

"Oh yeah, I'm doing it in partnership with a university in Mumbai. But mainly I'm based in the UK while I finish my studies."

"Which university?"

"Oxford." he replied nonchalantly.

It was almost like he was embarrassed to say it.

He continued, "Yeah. I don't know what I'm doing there to be honest. I came here, and then decided to take a year off from my studies while I was here. They weren't very happy about it. Don't really care what they think anyway. Bunch of elitist fools."

I took an instant liking to this guy. He didn't seem like others I had met in my social circles who went to elite universities and couldn't stop bragging about it.

It also turned out that both of us shared an abiding love for cricket. Found out that he was an Oxford Blue ("Yeah I play for their cricket team."), and a bloody Rhodes Scholar to boot ("I'm so glad I got a scholarship for my studies, otherwise I would not have been able to afford it.") This guy was incorrigibly over-achieving, and even more humble at that, which irritated the hell out of me because it just made me like him even more. My ego got a thankful, if somewhat irrational, break from the whipping it was getting when I found out that he was five years older than me.

If he had been my age, I would have wanted to punch myself in the face.

We talked about Bangalore too; revelled chauvinistically about the pubs, the mouth-watering *masala-dosa* at *Vidyarthi Bhavan*, Karnataka contributing more players to the Indian cricket team than any other state at the time, the militancy of the farmers' movement, and – surreptitiously – the belief that Karnataka would never become like Gujarat.

"Say what you want about South India man," I proudly expressed, "but at least there, they are so concerned about their regional identity that this bloody religious crap doesn't play in as much. If you meet a Tamil guy, he's more concerned about his fucking language and *vada-sambaar* than anything else. You'll never see this sort of bullshit there."

Abhay laughed, humouring me. I'd said what I said more with hope than any conviction, and I figured he knew that. I just couldn't imagine the events that had transpired in Gujarat happening in Bangalore. The very thought scared the daylights out of me.

Abhay and I chatted for some more time before we decided to call it a night. I was starting to feel more at home in the BSC dorm, and a certain familiarity with the other volunteers staying there in all of one day, despite barely knowing them. There was no awkwardness, no feeling of newness that one had to overcome. The atmosphere was pleasant and welcoming without being overbearing.

~ Chapter 7 ~

Nasir and Vijay had told me to meet them at the same spot near the entrance of the camp the next morning. I had woken up late so decided to take an auto rickshaw to the spot. I washed up, had some tea at the shop next to the dorm, and walked across the BSC campus to an auto rickshaw stand by the road. After experiencing the smoke-filled dustiness of the central bus terminus the previous day, I was loath to try it again when I could afford to take a rickshaw instead. I went up to the nearest one and asked him if he could take me to Gomtipur. He nodded affirmatively and I got in as he started the vehicle.

The ride was less bumpy than Bangalore roads in the new city. As we made our way to the main road, I noticed that this guy didn't have any religious symbols anywhere on his rickshaw.

"What is your name *bhaisaab*?" I asked, trying to sound as friendly as possible.

He didn't answer, but just nodded his head a little and asked, "Where in Gomtipur should I drop you *saab*?"

"There's a large graveyard near the mosque after we cross the river. If you could drop me there, that would be great." I replied.

"Oh, so you're working in the relief camps!" he exclaimed with a smile.

I nodded and said, "Yes *bhaisaab*, I'm a volunteer with *Shanti Samudaya*. I just came here from Bangalore."

"That's really good. It's wonderful work you're doing." he said, the smile growing even wider.

There was a pause in the conversation as he negotiated some traffic.

His face then changed to a more serious expression.

"This government doesn't care about us at all *saab*...corrupt bastards they are. Violence keeps happening in this city. It's not safe for good people like us anymore." he said angrily.

"Have you faced any violence?" I ventured.

"Me, my friends, my family...all of us are scared. My family and I are planning to leave. My cousin has a tailoring shop in Mumbai and he offered me a job there. It's better than having to deal with all this nonsense." he said.

As he spoke, I saw college-going kids hanging out near coffee shops and *chaat* vendors, seemingly quite oblivious to happenings across the river. Looking at them laughing and going about their daily lives, I felt a deep anger well up in me. They looked no different than my own group of friends in Bangalore. They *weren't* any different than my own group of friends in Bangalore.

I looked at the Sabarmati below as the auto rickshaw rode over the bridge into the Old City, and the roads started getting bumpier and dirtier. I saw wisps of smoke rising from the charred remains of a small row of one-room houses that had been burnt down by the mobs probably a few weeks back. I was beginning to wonder if the river in this city was quite possibly the world's worst portal. Whichever side you crossed into, the other side was worse.

As the auto rickshaw trundled to a halt, I wasn't able to immediately spot Nasir or Vijay at the side of the road near the camp. I stepped out of the vehicle, paid the driver, and sauntered towards the entrance where the same guy with *gutka*-stained teeth sat on a small metal chair, chewing on a ball-point pen. He greeted me with a large smile, beckoned me to sit and then offered to get some tea. I hesitated at first. I was keen on getting started with the shelter-construction work but relented when I realized that it was not so much a request as much as an assumption that I would sit and have tea with him. He ordered some and, of course, gave me most of it. As I was sipping my tea, I asked him whether he had seen Nasir or Vijay, and he said they were inside the camp. He told me to go inside to meet with them.

I finished the tea, and made my way into the camp. People were squatting on the floor beside the small mosque in the courtyard, with children playing near the gravestones. They stared at me as I walked past them. One of them recognized me from the previous day and I smiled at him. He smiled back with a cheerful, sideways head-bob. I entered the camp office where Nasir and Vijay were sitting on a couple of chairs, talking about the shelter materials. Nasir immediately got up as soon as I came in, shook my hand, and offered me a chair to sit on.

I asked, somewhat officiously, "So have the materials for the shelter arrived?"

Nasir replied, "No, not yet Jayram*bhai*, it will take a little more time. Remember…we still have to give exact amounts to the shopkeeper?"

I nodded in realization, feeling like a moron for asking the question. Nasir was still generous in his tone.

I then asked, a little less assuredly, "So, um….what's the plan for today?"

"Well, we need to plan for the shelter construction, no?" Nasir said, like he was explaining something to a child. "So once we do measurements, we can get estimates to give to the shopkeeper for how much supplies we need. What do you think?"

I was a little uncertain about what to say. I was being asked more out of politeness than anything else. It was evident to all of us that they knew what they were doing and I, very clearly, didn't.

Vijay then said in slightly more commanding fashion than Nasir, "Today let's go to the camps here in Gomtipur and see exactly what types of shelters are needed in each camp. Each is different and also in different locations, so they will need different types of shelters. What do you say Jayram*bhai*?"

Nasir nodded along as if it was the most obvious thing, and then asked me, "Do you think that's a good idea Jayram*bhai*?"

I wondered why they needed my affirmation to this plan, despite the fact that it was obviously redundant. It seemed perfectly natural to them that they should ask me, even if nominally, for my opinion, when yesterday I had essentially felt like a glorified middle-man, if that.

Nevertheless I said vaguely, but acting like I was quite sure of myself, "Yes, that sounds really good. It's definitely important to understand what we need to build before we actually build it."

Both of them smiled, Nasir widely, Vijay knowingly, as if he saw right through what a bloody faker I was. I was beginning to really like him for that reason. There was a realness to Vijay. Nasir was endearingly nice, so it was natural to like him, but Vijay had a bit of an edge that was rough on first contact, but appealing in its honesty.

We first inspected the camp that we were already in. Walking around the perimeter, we figured out how many bricks and bags of cement we would need for the shelter. No real measurements, just broad but – judging from Nasir and Vijay's understanding – fairly educated guesstimates. We also calculated the number of tarpaulin sheets, and the number of bamboo poles to hold up the sheets. As we went around the camp figuring this all out, young or middle-aged men would come and offer their advice, which Nasir and Vijay willingly took.

We did the same for the second camp, which was basically an extension of the first, but on the other side of the graveyard. While inspecting the camps, we even debated about whether we could build one giant shelter for the residents of both camps, since they were, for all practical purposes, one big camp. We soon realized that this would put the residents in a bit of difficulty. Most of the camps were established on the courtyards of the mosques in different localities, and in the adjacent graveyards.

The third camp in the Gomtipur area was a short walk away. It was set up in a giant playing field at the corner of a busy junction, and was smaller than the first two camps. When we got there, I saw a table and a few plastic chairs set up in the middle of the camp, where Zubaan and a couple of other elder men were seated. As soon as he saw us Zubaan got up and shook my hand, followed by the now-expected touching of hand to chest, which I too adopted as a greeting mechanism. He then offered a chair to me. All three of us sat down around the table, and I realized that many of the camp folk were squatting on the floor around us.

It was a little unnerving to be spatially positioned in a way that reflected actual power-relationships.

Nasir started to talk amiably, "Zubaan*bhai* we need to take measurements for a shelter, so that we can estimate how many bricks, bamboo poles, rope, tarpaulin sheets and things we need."

"Man, why do you need measurements and all...I'll tell

you how much you need. It's easy, I used to be a mason before the *dhamaal.*" Zubaan replied knowingly.

He then proceeded to give us estimates for shelter materials for the camp, with interjections from Nasir and Vijay. They tried to involve me, and asked me what I thought.

I drew a picture of the shelter based on their descriptions and asked, "So is this what it might look like?"

Zubban smiled, "Very good! This is exactly what it will look like. You must be an engineer or architect or something. I can't draw all of this, I can only build this thing."

I almost blushed at the compliment while realizing that the drawing was superfluous.

As we were finishing, a frail, old man squatting on the floor next to me, cooling himself with a hand-held fan, asked somewhat irritably, "*Bhaisaab* what are you doing?"

His face was shrunken with what looked like despair.

I replied reservedly, "We're trying to build a shelter here so that people aren't affected by the monsoon."

Without warning, he exploded with rage, "What's the bloody use of a shelter! Will it help get back people? Do you know what happened to all of us?"

He was now quivering with rage.

"These Hindu mobs came and killed all of us. Even pregnant women and children. What do you people know? This is how they killed us!"

He then aggressively made a cutting motion with a thin, crooked finger across my torso and abdomen. It sent a shiver down my spine. I didn't know how to react, staring at him somewhat dumbfounded. I felt my stomach turn again and dug my thumb into my side.

Nasir, Vijay, and Zubaan weren't in the least bit shaken or perplexed.

Vijay said, raising his hand reassuringly, "Don't worry uncle, the entire movement is working to get justice. We're also trying to ensure that the camps are in better condition. So we're doing the best we can."

Zubaan then turned to me, almost as if on cue from the old man, but in a much calmer voice said, "The Gujarati newspapers here are the biggest culprits Jayram*bhai.* Even if a hundred Muslims were killed in one locality, they would not report on it. If one Hindu got killed, even in a police-firing, they would rant about it saying 'It's the Muslims' fault! It's the Muslims' fault!' And they would keep saying that the government is doing everything to stop the violence. Bloody hell! It was the government that did all of this."

Nasir then interjected, "And no one even helps us in this city. When the earthquake happened in 2001 in Bhuj, so many Muslim relief organizations gave money, blood, materials. Nobody came to help us when this happened to us. All these camps are run privately…they are state-run camps only in name. The Gujarat government hasn't given us anything."

I didn't know what to say or do, except try and maintain eye contact, while preventing my stomach from turning over.

The old man looked at me again, this time with tenderness in his eyes, and said, "I must have scared you when I crossed my finger across your chest, no? Don't be scared of an old man my son, my anger was not directed at you."

It was only then that I realized he had been fanning me while the conversation was going on. I felt like an ass. I removed my thumb from my kidney and made to sit on the ground next to him.

"What are you doing *bhaisaab*? Please continue sitting on the chair." he said worriedly.

Nasir too expressed his concern, "Jayram*bhai*, why are you sitting on the floor? You'll be much more comfortable on the chair."

I replied, trying to find an excuse without making them feel bad, "No, no, it's nothing. I'm not able to hear this man properly from where I'm sitting, that's all."

I sat next to the old man and hesitantly made eye contact with him. He smiled at me a little and continued fanning me.

"The main problem right now son is getting shelter from the monsoon", he said. "I'm just worried about that. We'll worry about the other problems later."

~ Chapter 8 ~

As I crossed the Sabarmati and made my way to the BSC campus, I was starting to feel a small, but gnawing numbness in me. I could feel my mind getting a little colder to the violence after being there for a mere couple of days. All that concerned me now was getting the shelters up and ready before the monsoon. It was easier. It was actually something achievable in comparison to engaging with the behemoth of oppression that blanketed this place. I felt helpless and scared, and then immediately guilty for feeling like that.

I trudged to the BSC dorm. There were a few young men playing football in the field nearby. They seemed to be part of the college team as they had similar jerseys on. Normally I might have stood and watched. Now, all I could think was: How many of those kids supported those who conducted the violence? How many participated in it? Were there killers among the footballers? They looked no different than the guys I used to train with at my sports club in Bangalore – lean, fit, enthusiastic. The thought was difficult to stomach.

I entered the dorm, dropping my backpack on the floor. No one was there, and I started feeling lonely. I washed up in one of the adjacent bathrooms and puttered around the dorm, not knowing what to do. Did some push-ups and sit-ups to blow off some steam, but didn't have the energy for a full workout. The loneliness was starting to wash over me and I started missing Bangalore immensely. Yet, the thought of returning to Bangalore didn't seem to make me feel better. It was weird. For a moment it felt like that longing for my hometown was completely fake. Like it was a façade, a residual longing that I ought to have felt.

I started getting a little hungry and wondered what I might do about dinner when Maria walked in. I had met her briefly during my first night at the dorm, which now felt like it was a lifetime away. I knew that she was a journalist or film-maker or both. I saw her interacting with Abhay the night before, and was mesmerized by her way of being. She had a luminous look. A gorgeous, dusky face with wavy hair, and an infectious laugh. She didn't wear any makeup, save for a hint of eyeliner, and seemed to always be in *kurta* and jeans. Within a day I was headlong into my first crush in Ahmedabad.

I smiled as she walked in. She smiled back and, trying to remember my name, cheerily asked, "Um…Jay…you just got here right? How have you been so far?"

I replied, "Not bad. It's a bit of a shock. Have been hearing some crazy stories, and I've only been here two days. It's like being punched in the stomach."

"Ya, I know man." she said, as she put her backpack down on the floor. "It's tough to think about what happened here. The blood boils, but then we have to find a way to come through it to get the work done."

Maria had a soothing voice. It had a therapeutic effect on me. I immediately felt more alive in her presence, and couldn't look away from her *kaajal*-lined eyes. She wrinkled her nose when she smiled, almost mischievously. I was smitten, but tried my best not to make a complete ass of myself. I was also quite thrilled that she was from Kerala, surreptitiously finding that out from Abhay the previous night. I was one of those semi-Keralites, those who spoke Tamil rather than Malayalam, and only on my mother's side. Yet, I would claim a Kerala identity quite glibly, even though I didn't speak a wisp of the language.

"You're from Kerala right?" I asked. "My family is from there too."

She replied, "Oh really? Where are they from?"

"From Palakkad, but most of them live in Trivandrum."

As soon as I said Pallakad, I knew she would have identified me as a fake Keralite.

"Aaaah, so you're a Tam Bram? You don't look like one…plus, aren't you a Bangalore boy? That's what Abhay told me." she retorted with a chuckle.

I laughed at her usage of the pejorative for my privileged roots, secretly thrilled that they had talked about me.

I replied, using myself as comedic bait, "Why, because I don't have the sacred thread on? Bloody stereotypes...do you know that I eat meat and drink too? How's that for being a Tam Bram?"

45

She laughed again.

"Oh God! Someone is getting very touchy about their roots eh? Such chauvinism you can find only in a Tam Bram from Bangalore." she said with a twinkle. "I bet you sang in some silly college rock band. Probably listened only to Led Zeppelin or Nirvana thinking you were way cooler than the rest of the crowd. Did you also wear your cap backwards thinking you were stylish?"

I burst out laughing at her accurate assessment. She was cheeky and adorable. It further drew me to her. We hit it off immediately, and I noticed that we were standing a little closer to each other as we spoke. Her hand even touched mine a couple of times as she teased me. It was scintillating.

We talked a little more, squatting next to each other on the mattresses. Turned out that she had worked on quite a few documentaries of note.

"I edited a film on Hindu fascism for this film-maker a couple of years back," she explained, "and that was when I realized what was going on with these groups. So, when I heard about the violence, I decided to come and volunteer with the movement here."

I knew that she and Abhay worked together in the camp in Vatwa, way up in the northern outskirts of the city. I asked her if she was planning on making a film about it.

She replied intently, "No boss. I didn't come here to do any of that. Just came here to volunteer. I'm not interested in that sort of work right now. Also I've just finished two tiring film projects."

"What are they about?" I enquired.

"One is on the plight of villagers along the Indo-Pak border for this peace movement I've been working with in Mumbai, and the other looks at the Dalit liberation movement in Maharashtra. But I'm quite tired of social reform documentaries…they're so draining."

She paused to put her notebook into her backpack.

"Anyway," she continued, "I was in between projects when the carnage took place here, so packed my bags and came. I just want to work here in the camps for as long as I can before I take my next step."

I was starting to feel really small in the company of

people like Abhay and Maria, with my lack of accomplishment. Them being older than me didn't help my ego any more.

As I had that fleeting thought of under-achievement, Abhay walked in, and without acknowledging us, put his bag down and pulled out a bottle of whisky from it.

He held up the bottle high and, smiling widely, exclaimed, "Time to drink comrades!"

Maria asked incredulously, "Wow...how did you get it? I've been dying for a drink all week man!"

I asked, perplexed that it was such a big deal, "Why are you so surprised that he's got a bottle of whisky? There must be a booze shop in every corner of this town."

"You fool...Gujarat has prohibition laws in place", Maria replied teasingly again, "The sale of alcohol is banned here. You didn't know that? You should get out of Bangalore more often and open your eyes once in a while."

I laughed some more, happy to be made fun of by her, as Abhay opened the bottle and proceeded to pour it neat into three small plastic cups that he had brought with him.

~ Chapter 9 ~

Over the course of the next few days, Vijay, Nasir and I frantically worked on getting the shelters up in time before the monsoons. I would take an auto rickshaw every morning across the river and meet them at the entrance of the camp. We would then plan the rest of the day, with shelter-construction being the top most priority right then. But the going was never smooth. We often had to deal with some non-shelter-related problem or the other every day at the camps. Most often they had to do with the timely delivery of rations, government compensation, and medicines. But the more immediate problem was that the shelter materials got delayed a couple of times, and when they arrived they got the quantities wrong. It was a constant hassle that made our progress move in fits and starts.

"Jayram*bhai*, it might help if you spoke sternly to the shopkeeper." Vijay suggested. "When we yell at him, it doesn't make much of a difference since we all come from the same locality. You've come from outside, and you interact directly with the higher-ups in the movement, so he might listen to you more."

"Ok." I said, happy to be of use. "Let's go talk to him."

So saying, we proceeded to the construction materials shop for the umpteenth time. Egged on by Vijay, I contrived to lose my temper and screamed at the shop-keeper.

"What's this bloody nonsense?" I shouted, gesticulating rigorously with my hand. "We had set the date so many days back, and they still get delayed! And then you get the fucking order wrong...what do you think we're paying you for? If we don't get the shelter ready, then what will the people in the camp do?"

The shopkeeper was not particularly perturbed, which infuriated me even more. Both Vijay and Nasir looked sternly at him, and supportively towards my outburst, nodding as I shouted at the shopkeeper.

My yelling did, theoretically at least, have its effect. The shopkeeper promised timely delivery of the rest of the materials. I wasn't repulsed any more by his business-like attitude when it came to the materials; just his delay in delivering them. I realized that I was able to take a more self-righteous stance with money simply because I had quite a bit of it relative to those around me at that time. The realization didn't prevent me from yelling at him again though, to reiterate that we would not tolerate any more delays.

With each delivery of the materials to the shop, we took them over to the camps in a small rented truck belonging to Nasir's distant cousin. Vijay drove as Nasir and I sat in the back with the materials. Through Vijay and Nasir, we often got young men to help us unload the items and start construction of the shelters.

Volunteers also arrived from other parts of the country in solidarity with *Shanthi Samudaya*. A militant peasant and farm-workers union from Rajasthan sent a team of volunteers that I managed to convince Mani to send to help with the shelter construction in Gomtipur. They were a political movement, and staunchly secular. That week was an interesting week with Vijay, Nasir and I coordinating a team of rural Rajasthani activists; Hindu ones with red *tilaks* on their forehead, and Muslim ones sporting long beards. It served to partially undo the cut-and-dry assumptions I was starting to build in my head over the last couple of weeks.

We also coordinated with the volunteers of the large Muslim organizations in the region, like the *Jamaat*. Many of the *Shanthi Pathiks* also volunteered for those groups, though unlike the large NGOs, most of the local Muslim organizations couldn't pay a stipend.

Work was moving along bumpily because of the staggered delivery of materials. Finally one day, we received the bulk of the materials we needed, and planned on finishing the shelters in the next couple of days. The monsoon was supposed to be arriving soon after the planned completion date. That evening as I made my way to the BSC dorm, crossing the campus, Abhay walked over to me from the other side of the football field. He waved at me to stop, before I could make it to the dorm.

"Jay...Vijay and Nasir called the BSC office line and asked that you come back immediately to Gomtipur." he said, a little worriedly. "Mani found out that there're going to be showers tomorrow afternoon, so the shelter in the main camp needs to be constructed as soon as possible tonight."

I thanked him, and immediately turned around and jogged back to the main gate of the campus to get into an auto rickshaw. I reached the camp and made my way through the entrance to the middle of the camp where construction was frantically going on.

Vijay and Nasir, along with a bunch of other young men, were in their vests and shorts working hard, laying bricks and cement, erecting bamboo poles, and tightly tying them together with gunny rope. The new tarpaulin sheets were on the ground next to a pile of bricks. Many of the camp residents were gone, probably to their charred homes, and would spend the night there if the shelter wasn't ready by then. They would have needed to drape old tarpaulin sheets over the burnt structures to shield them from the rain, since the roofs of most of the houses had completely burnt down. I put my backpack on the table next to the area where the construction was taking place, and removed my shirt to join Vijay, Nasir and the others.

We worked the entire, exhilarating night constructing the shelter. We would take five-minute breaks every couple of hours to have tea or water. Vijay had been offering me cigarettes, which I always declined. Having been an amateur athlete, smoking was anathema to me. I couldn't imagine doing something like that to my body. But this time, during one of the later breaks, when we were close to being done, I asked him if I could bum a cigarette from him when he took out the pack to smoke one with his tea.

It felt awesome lighting up. For a brief moment as the nicotine got into my blood stream, the stress of the night seemed to evaporate.

We sat drinking tea and smoking during the wee hours of the morning, our muscles starting to ache. We didn't talk much, barring the odd word or two to reiterate what more needed to be done. I felt an immeasurable feeling of comradeship with Vijay and Nasir.

We were done at the crack of dawn. It took nearly twelve hours through the night, but it felt good to see the finished shelter. We were exhausted and, on Nasir's prompting, decided to get breakfast and tea at the local eatery that served *parathas* with spicy omelettes in the morning. We washed up in the sink that had been set up right outside the shop, and sat at a table. The sun was just starting to rise as we sat down, and people were getting their days started, with the *kabaadiwala* carrying junk in his cart to be recycled, and auto rickshaw drivers starting their engines. The butcher's shop diagonally opposite the eatery opened his shutters, and we could see the red hunks of meat hanging from the hooks.

Vijay called to the server, "*Bhaisaab*, bring us three teas, along with some *parathas* and omelettes please."

And removing his pack of cigarettes, he asked, "Also, smoking inside...yes?"

The server nodded in affirmation. He quickly brought three sweet, milky teas in glass tumblers. I took a sip and it tasted delicious. Vijay offered me another cigarette, and I promptly took it without a second thought. I had probably smoked all of two cigarettes my entire life, and here I was smoking two in one day.

It felt good to sit at the table with Vijay and Nasir, smoking and drinking tea again, this time having finished the construction work completely. The second cigarette didn't give me the same high as the first one did though. I remember thinking that this was probably how folks got addicted, but scoffed at the prospect. Nevertheless made a mental note to not smoke any more during my time there.

We chatted a little bit about the shelters, and what more needed to be done to ensure that they could withstand the entire monsoon. Soon though the topic drifted slowly into our personal lives.

I asked Vijay, still having not fully addressed my earlier surprise at his Hindu name when I first met him, "So what is your full name Vijay?"

I wanted to know what his religion and caste was, but was too shy to ask directly.

He replied, "Vijay Christianbhai."

"Oh, so where are you and your family from?"

"We're from here Jayram*bhai*, my family is Gujarati."

I turned to Nasir, and asked him, "You're family is

Gujarati too, right Nasir? Or did you migrate from some other part of India?"

Nasir replied, "No, no. We're fully Gujarati...we're Gujarati Pathans."

"And did you lose people in the violence?"

Nasir looked away, and said, "My family *Inshallah* was spared Jayram*bhai*. But I lost some close friends, either killed by the police or the mobs."

There was a pause as he thought of his friends. He then shook himself out of his momentary reverie, and said with conviction, "Our lineage is Pathani Muslim. We come from a long line of very great warriors Jayram*bhai*, so we will come through whatever problems there are."

He said this with a pride that belied his amiably accepting personality. I hadn't heard him speak about his identity like this before. I was still curious about Vijay's religion though.

"And are you Hindu, Vijay? That's a Hindu name that you have, no?" I asked innocuously.

He snickered a little bit, "Haha. No, no Jayram*bhai*...well, actually about half of my extended family is Hindu. But many of us are Christian converts, which is why my last name is *Christian*bhai, but many of our first names are Hindu names."

He emphasized the vernacularized version of his converted surname.

He continued, "We're Dalits Jayram*bhai*. Both Hindus and Christians are there in our family."

I remembered reading how the groups who conducted the pogrom had often used Dalits as their foot soldiers in carrying out the carnage against the Muslims.

An overwhelming feeling of love, not just for Vijay and Nasir as individuals, but also for their friendship with each other, was welling up inside me. It was tempered by a fearful sense of fragility. How would they survive the forces that existed to divide them? But then again, they had survived the most violent manifestation of those forces. So surely they would survive its aftermath, right?

Nasir, almost as if reading my mind, said, "Dalits and Muslims would always be together in the past Jayram*bhai*. We would be invited for Christmas or Diwali, while they would be invited for Eid celebrations and feasting. Now look at the way they're tearing up our communities."

Vijay nodded and said, "There were never any problems between our communities Jayram*bhai*. Even when the *dhamaal* happened, there were Dalit-Muslim colonies that remained united. One has been called Ram-Rahim Nagar for a long time, and the Hindu Dalits came out when the killings were happening and made sure no violence occurred in that colony."

He paused to take a drag of his cigarette, and shook his head with conviction, wincing as he exhaled smoke.

"They've been trying to divide us for a long time Jayram*bhai*, but even with this carnage, I feel we will still somehow try to remain united, at least in other parts of the country, and even in Gujarat. Because whatever they do for their profit, ultimately makes both of us suffer."

As he spoke, I wondered where he placed me in this analysis.

I asked them who their political influences were.

Vijay replied first, "One of the leaders who has really inspired me is Ambedkar. He was a legendary Dalit revolutionary. If it weren't for him we wouldn't have the kinds of movements we have today to fight for our rights. He wrote our constitution too, which is an amazing source of pride for Dalits. His writings were what politicized me at a young age Jayram*bhai*. I probably have his entire collection of writings in my home."

I nodded and smiled. I could tell from the way Vijay talked about Ambedkar, that it was not just a casual influence. Nasir then turned to me.

"I read a lot of Gandhi*ji*'s writings in college Jayram*bhai*. He was great because instead of distrusting religion, he used it in the freedom movement." he said, with deep thought.

He continued, "I think it's impossible to stay away from religion in India, so it's better to use it properly. Gandhi used Hinduism to start a peaceful, secular politics in India and drive away the British. Since he used his religion for a politics of peace, it can be a very useful tool against the fascists."

53

I was impressed. I also found out with much joy that both of them adored my own single greatest hero figure, Bhagat Singh, the socialist revolutionary who fought the Brits.

I was thrilled to be engaging in this conversation with them. While working with Vijay and Nasir, I had always wondered whether we would be able to have conversations about things other than the work on the ground, what with the vastly different backgrounds we shared. It was uplifting for me to be talking about people who were immense influences on me growing up. I was a huge fan of all three revolutionaries myself in college, devouring some of their more mainstream works, the ones that the Indian elite accepted. I often found myself questioning my nationalism when reading them, but irrationally rationalized their anti-colonial rhetoric as consistent with my privileged jingoism.

We sat and ate one of the most delicious breakfasts I had ever eaten. Had another tea with another cigarette, this time Vijay and I sharing one, and then I decided to head back to the BSC campus.

"Why don't you stay with one of us Jayram*bhai*? You can have dinner with us too and leave the next day." Vijay suggested.

"Yes, that way you don't have to go all the way back to the BSC campus. You can also meet our families." Nasir added.

It sounded like a good idea but I really wanted to hang out with Abhay and Maria after such a long night.

"I would love to, but I think it might be better for me to leave. I have some work with Abhay and Maria that I need to complete." I said, not wanting to give my desire for drunken merriment as an excuse.

"Before I leave however, do you mind if I asked you another question?" I asked.

"Not at all, go ahead Jayram*bhai*." Nasir said.

"I've noticed that all you guys from the area touch your chests after shaking hands. What does it mean?"

Nasir laughed a little.

"It's nothing Jayram*bhai*, it's just a way of greeting each other...all it means is that we're accepting you into our hearts as we greet you." he replied, smiling wide.

~ Chapter 10 ~

I was starting to get increasingly comfortable with the way things were going, both with the work in the camps and the evening hangouts with Maria and Abhay. I looked forward to those evenings after a hard day at the camps. They were filled with hilarity and good conversation.

And I thought a touch of live music would be the perfect addition.

I loved playing the guitar. I wasn't very good at it – was a better singer – but learnt enough open chords to be able to play basic rhythm to complement my singing. I had formed a rather mediocre cover band in college, with a few of us getting together and playing in a couple of different college festivals. More often than not, the crowd would only want the popular Bollywood songs that most of the other bands used to specialize in. The "Western" music bands were always shunted to the end of the show, after the Bollywood songs were done. Couldn't really blame the organizers though; the music we covered wasn't that popular unless it was a really well-known song. The crowds would leave when bands like ours came along, and only some of the more Westernized kids would remain to listen to us. We also never performed, or even attempted, our own music. It was tough enough getting crowds to listen to well-known covers, pretty much no one wanted to listen to our own compositions.

I had a rather old, but beautiful-sounding rose-wood acoustic in Bangalore that I hadn't bothered to bring with me to Ahmedabad. I was now starting to miss it. I wanted to perform for Abhay and Maria on the nights when we would drink boot-legged whisky and laugh together, which was now a daily ritual. One evening, after returning from the camps, I asked some staff members at the BSC office for directions to some decent music shops. I took an auto rickshaw to one of the shops I was sure would have a good collection of acoustic guitars, based on its location in one of the major business areas of Ahmedabad, not too far from the BSC campus.

I withdrew some money from my bank account. The per diem allowance I was getting from *Shanthi Samudaya* (that I had decided to take eventually) was not enough to sustain the

periodic drinking and eating out that I did with Abhay and
Maria. So I would often dip into the savings account my
father had set up for me. It only marginally occurred to me
that Vijay and Nasir had to make do with a meagre stipend
without a safety net. Not just for their individual sustenance,
but also contributing to that of their families. It didn't really
bother me though at the time. I wanted an acoustic guitar to
serenade my friends. I had the means to get it and I was going
to get one.

The music shop was in a shopping complex a couple
of kilometres from the BSC campus. Multiple folk were
walking milling around the many small malls that had sprung
up in the area. Again, I couldn't get over how eerily similar it
was to other shopping centres in Bangalore and, by now I
realized, every other major city in India. College-kids hanging
around, having a good time, men and women shopping with
their kids, families eating out at the different restaurants, street
vendors selling their wares at the mercy of the cops who
would often threaten to drive them out unless they paid a
bribe, auto rickshaws lining the stands, and multiple vehicles
weaving their way through traffic. In general, Ahmedabad, on
this side of the river at least, was much cleaner than
Bangalore, which was notorious for its pot-holed roads. But
that was the only difference. For the most part it felt no
different than the innumerable number of times that my
friends and I would cut class and loaf around the city.

I went inside the shop, which was big and well-
stocked with a variety of good-quality musical instruments. I
asked the shop-keeper for the range of prices on acoustic
guitars, hoping that the money I had withdrawn would not get
me only the crappiest of the lot. He said they ranged from five
hundred rupees, for some cheap Indian guitars, to well over
twenty thousand rupees, for high-quality imported guitars,
either from the UK and Spain. I had withdrawn eight
hundred, so told him that my price range was limited to that.
He wasn't particularly thrilled, but showed me a few guitars
within that price range. He couldn't complain really, because
there weren't any other customers when I walked in. I
borrowed one of his picks, and strummed on a few of them.
They had a decent sound, though nowhere near as good as the

one I had at home.

I finally chose one, after inspecting the fret board, the seasoning of the wood, and the sealant for the box on all of them. I also asked him for a cheap guitar case made of rexin, a few picks and a couple of extra sets of strings. Overall it came to a little over eight hundred. His earlier nonchalance had disappeared and he was now quite friendly to me.

"What's your name? You speak very good English and seem to know a fair bit about guitars. Most people can't tell the difference between a good or bad sound." he said.

"Um, thanks." I said with an awkward smile. "My name is Jayram...Jayram Krishnan."

His own English was far better than what I normally heard. He was probably educated at an English-speaking school and college.

"So, where are you from and how did you get so interested in music?" he asked.

I replied with a smile, "I'm from Bangalore...we had a band in college that I played rhythm in and also sang lead vocals."

"Really?" he replied excitedly. "I play in a band too. What kind of music do you play?"

"Just some covers...you know famous ones, mostly Classic Rock, or Rock 'n' Roll. I'm not that good to be honest."

"I'm sure that's not true." he responded with a warm smile. "In any case, it's tough to make it big in music nowadays even if you're really talented. Maybe in Mumbai or even Bangalore one can, but here it's tough."

I nodded with a sigh. He was easy to get along with and I felt bad for misreading his earlier aloofness.

"And...what are you doing here?" he then asked, while packing the guitar into the case.

"I'm volunteering in the camps, doing some relief work and human rights campaigning. I'm working with *Shanthi Samudaya*."

"What camps are you talking about? There was some rioting I know, but there aren't any camps here in the city are there?"

I was a little surprised at how little he seemed to

know.

I replied, "Well, they're all mainly in Gomtipur, Vatwa and other areas."

He looked a little perplexed.

"Oh…I see…and what do you do there?" he asked inquisitively.

"Mainly relief work, like shelter construction, rations distribution, livelihood generation…also some human rights campaigning. We're soon starting a survey to launch a big legal campaign for the justice of the victims."

He nodded along.

"Very good…it's good work that you're doing." He said appreciatively.

There was a pause as he stuffed the strings into the case and zipped it up.

Then, without batting an eyelid, he continued in the same friendly tone, "It's all because of those Muslims…they're so violent you know. Look at this part of the city where most of the Hindus are, there are no problems at all. I don't understand why they can't just learn to live peacefully like us."

I was jolted by this, but he didn't see it. He shook his head despairingly as he spoke.

"Anyway, I'm sure you know what I'm talking about, since you're working directly on the ground. What kind of work are you doing in the camps?" he then asked, still smiling. "I'm sure the camps are mainly for Hindus, right? Because we were the ones who were worst affected, no?"

I replied with anger, but still in shock, "Um…no, not at all. All the camps are populated almost completely by Muslims. They were the worst affected."

"Hmm, hmm." he replied, his smile disappearing, and briefly looked me in the eye, noticing my visible anger now.

He paused to ring up the cash register.

He then continued, a little more cagily this time, "The English media keep doing this minority-appeasement, saying the Muslims are treated badly in Gujarat, and nonsense like that…"

He was about to say something else when I cut him off, and said curtly, "Listen, I have to get going, so let me pay you and I'll leave, ok?"

He was taken aback by my sudden closing of the conversation, but nodded compliantly and rang up the bill. I paid him the exact amount and, without saying another word or looking at him, walked out hurriedly with the guitar in hand.

On the auto-ride back to the BSC campus, I felt flushed with a helpless anger. I replayed the short conversation in my head and felt like kicking myself for not making a better argument. I should not have bought the guitar from his stupid shop, I told myself. I had no idea how to confront him, so instead chose to avoid it. I couldn't tell if it was what he spouted, or my own weakness that contributed more to my anger. Either way, it was not a pleasant feeling.

I walked sullenly across the BSC campus towards the dorm. Abhay and Maria were inside engaging in an animated conversation. I dropped the guitar on the mattress I had appropriated as my own over the last few weeks, and walked towards them. They smiled at me and then looked at the guitar.

"Oh wow...how lovely!" Maria exclaimed joyfully. "You bought a guitar. You have to play for us tonight."

I replied, "Sure. But not right now."

Abhay asked caringly, "What happened man? You look upset about something."

"Nothing happened to me...but I just had this very brief conversation with the shopkeeper at the music shop" I replied, glad for the opportunity to vent, "He asked me what I was doing, and was really nice to me. I replied saying that I volunteered at the relief camps as a human rights worker. Without blinking an eye he blamed the Muslims for the riots, calling them violent and everything."

I shook my head.

"What an asshole!" I exclaimed in frustration.

Maria nodded with concern, and said, "Listen Jay...this is not a one-off thing. You should be careful about what you say to whom."

I looked at her sullenly.

"And it comes in all kinds of ways..." she continued, "you don't even have to tell them that you're a human rights

59

worker. Just two days ago, I went to buy some eggs from the grocery store nearby. He looked at me so angrily when I asked him where the eggs were...said that he doesn't carry non-vegetarian items. You should have seen the way he talked to me...so rude."

I didn't understand, "Why would he be angry at you for asking for eggs? I don't get it."

"Because here, to be non-vegetarian basically means you're not a true Hindu." Abhay explained. "The people who eat meat are mainly Muslims, and some Dalits. The *Hindutva* philosophy is all about creating differences to show that Hindus, mainly upper-caste Hindus, are superior. That's why most Hindu grocers don't even carry eggs, because they consider it non-vegetarian. And even those who don't believe in the sectarianism will lose business if they don't toe the line."

Maria interjected, "It's a divide and conquer philosophy that ultimately serves elite interests."

I listened in silence and didn't know what to say.

"That's why we have to sometimes switch off", she continued. "If we take it all in and only think about the carnage and the bloody politics behind it, we will be completely immobilized to do anything about it. That's why I say that we should now get a little drunk and you should sing us some songs."

And before I could protest, she removed the guitar from the case and handed it to me.

What a smile she had.

We poured ourselves strong whisky drinks and chatted the night away, smoking cigarettes. We laughed a lot, even at the most inane jokes that were cracked. I played a few songs for them. Simple, easy covers that I knew well. Beatles, Dylan, Simon and Garfunkel; they knew them, and sang along during the choruses. It was fun. Abhay even hugged me warmly after one of them.

I blushed, and drank some more, the whisky helping me forget the day and revel in the evening.

Maria and I touched each other periodically as the booze drove away some of our inhibitions. Later that night, we lay down on adjacent mattresses, holding hands as we drifted to sleep.

~ Chapter 11 ~

With the many frantic days we spent on the construction of
the shelters in the camps, Vijay, Nasir and I had developed an
easy comradeship. We generally backed each other up during
contentious discussions with community-leaders in Gomtipur,
or when we had to approach *Shanthi Samudaya* for extra funds
either for camp materials or rations. In the weeks after the
shelters were constructed, the entire city was enduring a state
of perennial rains. The camps were wet and slushy, and all the
residents had to cook in horrendously cramped conditions
under the one shelter in their respective camps. The structure
itself was not close to being adequate to shelter all the
residents properly. Fights continuously broke out due to lack
of space, which we would have to intervene in. Many of the
camp residents went home at night to sleep, using the old
tarpaulin sheets they had temporarily put up, while waiting for
the corrugated tin roofing sheets that the relief organizations
were soon to deliver as part of the house-reconstruction
project.

Vijay, Nasir and I were consumed with ensuring the
shelters held out for the monsoons until the materials for the
house reconstruction arrived. In addition, we would deliver
rations on a weekly basis, and conduct surveys with the
survivors of the violence on how much they had lost in terms
of family members and material possessions. The rations-
distribution almost never went smoothly while the surveys had
to be conducted on a daily basis since the legal campaign, both
for justice and monetary compensation, was under a major
time crunch. It was hard to manage priorities as we were
dealing with emergencies almost every day.

One day we were told by Mani that we had to
conduct surveys the entire day.

"We are behind schedule with the surveys for the
legal campaign, so please ensure you catch up today, and don't
get sidelined by other issues." he instructed.

But as we got to the camps we found out that one of
the shelters was starting to sway a little bit, because of its
shoddy construction. We spent half the day re-constructing it,
and bolstering its strength with extra bamboo poles. By the

time we were done, it was well into the afternoon and we barely managed a couple of hours worth of surveys before calling it a day. Mani was not happy, but once we explained the emergency situation he calmed down. Vijay, Nasir and I formed a common bond when dealing with people and institutions. Push come to shove, we would always back each other up.

I had transformed a good deal from what I had come in as. Not that I was by any means an expert on relief and human rights work, but getting some hard experience importantly coupled with my class-privilege had me naturally assuming a leadership role along with Vijay and Nasir. It was frightfully clear that they knew way more than I did. But my role as a middle-man between the big NGOs and the grassroots community-workers put me in an important, if highly undeserving, position of leadership for the work in that area. I didn't have time to reflect on the injustice of the whole situation – a middle-class kid from Bangalore coordinating efforts in an area he had barely been in for a few weeks. All I concentrated on was the work with my comrades.

The insidiousness of the carnage was always beaten into me though, and I would continue to spot things that I had failed to notice on previous occasions.

One evening, after completing the surveys in the most faraway camp, Vijay, Nasir and I walked through the same row of burnt houses that we were now seeing on a daily basis. Life was slowly starting to return to those houses, in sputtering fits and starts, with no help from a viciously callous government. As we walked by, I noticed that one of the houses seemed to be untouched. I had never noticed that house before. It was strange, because the houses on either side of it on that row were all burnt down.

I asked Nasir, pointing at the house, "Nasir, why is that one house untouched? All the other houses in that row have been burnt down except for that one."

Both Nasir and Vijay knowingly smirked, but their expressions weren't amusing. Nasir then beckoned me to walk closer to the house.

"I'll show you why Jayram*bhai*. Let's go closer to the

house."

As we walked to the front of the house, I noticed an *Om* symbol drawn just above the door frame. Upon closer inspection, I could see a laminated picture of *Ganesha*, my mother's favourite deity, nailed above the doorbell.

"Jayram*bhai*, before the *dhamaal*, all the Hindu groups came and conducted informal surveys in the predominantly Muslim areas of Ahmedabad." Nasir explained. "They also used their contacts in the government departments for information on the religious makeup of the houses."

Nasir paused as I got a closer look at the markings made on the house.

Vijay continued where Nasir left off, "Before the carnage, they came with the police to the Hindu housholds and told them to put clear markers on their houses so they wouldn't be burnt down when the rioters came. It was all clearly planned Jayram*bhai*. The family in this house left the day before the violence started because they knew what was going to happen."

I stared at the house, and then looked at Nasir and Vijay. They looked at me, a little triumphantly. They knew they had given me yet another piece of knowledge that had opened my eyes to the horrors that had transpired. Vijay nodded as if he knew what was going through my head, and then indicated for us to keep moving on. We walked in silence the rest of the way, and checked in with Zubaan at the main camp to collect the surveys he had done.

I collected all the survey forms and tucked them into my back pack. They were to be given to the *Shanthi Samudaya* office where a couple of volunteers were involved in strenuous data entry for the legal campaign. Vijay, Nasir and I always ended the day with a visit to the tea shop near the entrance of the main camp in Gomtipur, after which I would get into an auto rickshaw and head back to the BSC campus.

We sat at the tea shop and ordered our three teas. By now, I had started buying my own packs of cigarettes, which I would share with Vijay. We lit up after our teas arrived, and I took a long drag of my cigarette. I shook my head in exasperation.

"I don't know what to think any more." I said,

exhaling slowly. "This place is crazy...I've never seen anything like this. I mean, how deep does this poison go?"

Nasir replied, "I know Jaram*bhai*. We've been living with it for so long now. Sometimes my friends and I want to just run away to some other city in India. We might struggle and be poor, but at least we won't have to deal with this sort of nonsense."

"What's the use of going somewhere else?" Vijay retorted, with angry conviction. "What guarantee do you have that the same thing won't happen in some other city, huh? This is my home, boss. If we allow ourselves to be driven out of our homes, then what hope is there for the rest of India? I want to stay here *bhai*. I'm Gujarati, my family is Gujarati, Gujarat is my home. I won't leave. Anyway, many people have tried to do bad things...when people fight back and resist, then it will stop. But we cannot be cowards and run away."

Nasir acquiesced a little in agreement but reacted testily to the insinuation of cowardice.

"I'm no coward." he said, raising his voice. "I'm not saying we should not do something. I'm just saying that sometimes I feel like running away. My family was spared, but I lost friends in the *dhamaal*. How much can we take of this?"

And then, turning to me, he continued, "Our minds also get constantly attacked by this Jaram*bhai*...it's not easy. I'm not leaving or anything like that, but it gets very frustrating sometimes."

The last couple of sentences were said to me, almost as if Nasir was just as much seeking my support as he was replying to Vijay. By now, both would sometimes compete for my support in conversations – Vijay commandingly, Nasir sweetly.

Vijay said, with the same anger, "I too am frustrated, but you don't see me thinking about running away from the problems we face. We all have to face them together, otherwise what's the point of doing this work? Tell me, who will do it then?"

It seemed like Vijay was getting angry at the very thought that Nasir or I would abandon him in the struggle. I couldn't blame him. People like him and Nasir – who stood up to fight the good fight sans glory – were few and far between. It could have been really frustrating for Vijay to see traces of a wavering commitment from others whom he considered his comrades and friends.

I looked at them as they spoke, sipping my tea, taking deep drags from my cigarette. They chatted a little more about it, finally resolving the discussion, as always, with Vijay's strongly-reasoned arguments that Nasir would eventually agree to. I listened to both of them, glancing at them once in a while, but mainly staring out onto the bustling street as they spoke. My bond was growing every day with them. It was a bond that was new territory for me though. Their instincts were a little different from mine.

I recalled an incident a few days back when Abhay came to help with rations-distribution. The four of us went out to a restaurant in Gomtipur after the day's work. As we left the eatery, a violent fight broke out between a couple of young men across the street, and a small melee ensued, with the friends of each youth joining in. Abhay and I instinctively moved backward to make more distance between us and the commotion. Simultaneously, Vijay and Nasir rushed to the scene, shouting at the men to calm them down so that further blows weren't exchanged. Abhay and I stared at them as they pulled the fighting youths apart, getting shoved around in the process, but ultimately preventing an all-out street fight. It didn't occur to me that I ought to involve myself in the situation. They didn't flinch or hesitate for even a second before running into a rather violent situation in order to calm it down. The communitarian way in which they acted was in sharp contrast to the individualistic manner in which Abhay and I behaved. I couldn't help but think that it reflected, in part, our different social moorings. It was the same instincts that guided their work as *Shanthi Pathiks*.

For the first time in my life, I had friends from vastly different class and community backgrounds, who didn't speak English, who lived very different material lives than I did. I felt a deep sadness at seeing two friends and comrades having to live through such madness day in and day out. A moment of cold-blooded fear at the thought of something happening to either of them shot through my spine. I wanted to get them out of there, to have them come back with me to Bangalore, and work with them in setting up an NGO there. But then again, this was their home, as Vijay rightly put it. It had to be fought for.

You know you have deep love for someone when you fear something bad happening to them in your bones.

~ Chapter 12 ~

It had been two months since I landed in Gujarat and, during that time, I had completely lost touch with my family and friends back in Bangalore. A couple of phone calls here and there that my parents made to the BSC office were all that had transpired since I got to Ahmedabad. They would ask me questions and would in turn receive irritated, monosyllabic replies from me. I decided that I had to get back in touch with them. I thought I would do this by writing an email to my friends and family back home. It was a way for me to vent, but more importantly it was also an attempt to reconcile the world I had left behind – a world that was everything to me only a couple of months back – with my new painful rebirth.

However, I don't think I accounted for an empty, confusing anger building up inside me as I wrote this email.

By 2002, the internet had become a way of life in many parts of the country for folks who could afford computers. I had already set up a second email account by 1998. I remember the username that I used to set it up – *soldier98*. Ever since I was old enough to think, all I ever wanted to do was join the Indian army, become a commando, and fight insurgents in Kashmir. I was quite the nationalist, a sentiment which kicked into high gear in the summer of 1998. I had been using a generic email with my name until then, when one morning, on May 12th of that year, I woke up and read the newspaper headlines. The central government led by the BJP, the same party that later orchestrated the carnage in Gujarat, had just detonated multiple nuclear weapons in Pokhran. India had defied international pressure and had become a nuclear power. I felt such a measure of pride that I decided to discard my old email address and create a new one symbolizing what I wanted to be and the year when the nationalism that gripped me was at its zenith. I was only too proud of that decision especially a year later when I wrote a rabidly jingoistic article about the Indian war-effort against Pakistan in Kargil for a friend's online news magazine. I signed off with that email address.

A strange feeling crept into the pit of my stomach now when I thought about my email address. I was confused, and couldn't reconcile with the form my earlier nationalism took. I thought it was an important sentiment because it still emerged from the words of liberation I had internalized from Bhagat Singh, Gandhi, Nehru, Ambedkar and more. But somehow it had a virulent streak in it when I caricatured it into ideological adoption. The terrorists I wanted to kill in Kashmir didn't seem like terrorists anymore; the nuclear tests took on a more sinister hue; the logic or lack thereof to patriotism was starting to feel different, more real, more painful, more heterogeneous. And yet, I still couldn't let go of the sentiment; somewhere deep inside me there was an idea of India that held a temporary truth, a nationalistic feeling that was still present but rapidly evolving. I wanted to reconcile that with what I was seeing here in Gujarat, a place that was just as much a part of that idea as any other region.

The decision to write to my folks was taken extemporaneously on my usual auto rickshaw ride after a day at the camps. Instead of heading towards the BSC campus, I told the driver to take a slight detour and stop at the internet café that Abhay, Maria and I sometimes visited to check our email. I walked into the café, and sat down at one of the computers after signing in at the front desk. Without stopping to think, I wrote to my family and friends.

My dearest kith and kin,

I write to you after a couple of months of being in Ahmedabad, volunteering in the relief camps and the human rights campaign here. I work with some of the most amazing, courageous people on earth. It has been, to put it mildly, a life-changing experience. I know it's only the beginning for me, and I don't know how long I will stay, but I feel like I must, for however long I can. This is an important moment in India's history, and we cannot allow for it to be forgotten, ever. Bangalore is so far away for me right now, almost like another country. I miss Bangalore, but when I return I don't know if I will see the same Bangalore I left. I don't know if I will see the same you either. I certainly won't be the same me.

A lot has happened here. I feel like I am only scratching the surface of a mini genocide. The roots of fascism have been planted. If we don't fight it, we will have only ourselves to blame for the ripping apart of the very soul of this nation and people. The idea of this place we call India, this genius land that is the most diverse in the world, the insane chaos that provides us merry frustration, this land that has fought off colonialism and imbibed every culture and mode of thinking that humanity has to offer...this microcosm of our world itself is in danger of succumbing to a virulent philosophy.

The stories are too many to ignore. People weren't just killed. They were butchered. Women and children were not spared. Shouts of 'Jai Sri Ram!' bellowed as the Hindu mobs conducted their carnage. It was planned; methodical. Muslim localities were specifically targeted, while Hindu houses were spared. Hundreds, if not thousands, have died. Women were raped before being killed. They were killed with swords and guns, and then burnt. The police and state government were fully behind this. This was no riot. This is fascism. I see the venom deep inside society here. The violence happened on one side of the Sabarmati river. The cause is on the other side. This is not India. It cannot be. Yet it is.

I know that most of you are Hindu. I know also that you will not want a rich philosophy of faith and life to be usurped in this way. What they preach is not Hinduism. I'm sure this poison is not something we would want in our beloved land.

As you go about your daily lives, sitting in front of your laptops, eating in nice restaurants, watching the latest Bollywood movie...I ask that you open your eyes...please. I know I'm just a greenhorn, and I don't mean to preach...but please, for the sake of India, for the sake of humanity...open your fucking eyes, say a prayer, fight this scourge. India deserves more. The world deserves more. Do something.

I love you all, but I need to be here, and even when I leave this place, I will never return to what I left when I came here. I hope you will be here with me in spirit.

With love and respect,

Jay

I stared at the computer screen after signing off. I took a deep breath and exhaled. It felt like I had been holding my breath for the entire duration of writing. I clicked on the 'send' button, waiting for the sent message to appear on the screen. It came within a couple of seconds. I took a deep breath and exhaled again. It was like a release I hadn't had for weeks.

I re-read the email in my sent box and realized that there was likely a better way of saying many of the things I said. It was more arrogant than it probably needed to be, especially since my family and friends weren't the people I was angry at. They were just an easier target. I immediately felt a little anxious, and stared at the computer screen after that, looking at the people I sent it to, wondering how they would react, what they would think of me. I decided to try and ease my anxiety with a cigarette outside.

I didn't bother surfing the net or reading any of my other emails, which were all mostly emails from my college friends about celebrating jobs, GRE scores, and admissions to prestigious MBA programs, or emails announcing equally mundane developments in the family. I couldn't give a damn about who was getting a high pay, moving abroad to study, getting married, having a baby, or moving on to a new job. At that moment, they could all have shoved their lives up their asses for all I cared. I logged out, paid the guy at the front desk for my time at the computer, and walked out. I stepped outside the shopping complex that the internet cafe was located in, and sauntered over to a small juice stand in the corner. I ordered a lime-soda, and sat on one of the small stools beside the stand. Took a few sips of my drink and lit up. I sat there, staring into the traffic on the road, smoking and drinking my lime-soda, feeling lighter than I had felt when I walked into the internet cafe. The drag from my cigarette gave me an instant high. I had a lingering smoke, downed my drink, and left to spend the rest of my evening with Maria and Abhay. By now, the time spent with them was the highlight of my every day.

We had decided to move into a large one-bedroom apartment with a couple of short-term volunteers. This also served as a place for other short-term volunteers to sleep in for the time they stayed in Gujarat. It was barely a hundred meters from the BSC campus, so the distance to the camps was the same. Abhay had managed to get it for free from a friend in London, who owned the place and suggested that we live there since it was lying vacant anyway. It was marvellous. We felt like we could live with a little more freedom than having to adhere to the restrictions of the BSC dorm, where booze was forbidden, and we had to be clandestine about hiding the bottles. We had a bunch of mattresses, sheets, and pillows, so folks just slept wherever they wanted to in one of the two bedrooms, or the large living room.

I was thrilled when Abhay suggested we move to the apartment because Maria and I were now falling asleep in each other's arms every night. Each night brought with it a delightfully new level of physical intimacy, testing the social limits of sleeping in not-so-private conditions. We hadn't talked about it, but were starting to revel in it. The evenings I was spending with Abhay, Maria and the short-term volunteers who were present at that time were starting to feel like a heady drug to me; a salubrious oxygen-like fix I needed every evening, culminating with Maria's safe embrace and unmitigated affection.

I walked through the door of the apartment, smiling. A couple of volunteers were hanging around the living room chatting in a lively manner, smoking cigarettes. The whisky bottle had been opened, and a round or two had already been poured. I waved happily at them, took one of the plastic cups and poured myself some. I lit up another cigarette, and went into the kitchen. Abhay and Maria were in there standing next to each other, chopping vegetables for dinner. I went in and put both my arms around their shoulders, kissing each of them on the cheek.

Maria exclaimed, "What's gotten you so happy Jay? Normally you're always so angry with the world."

I shrugged my shoulders.

"I don't know...I just want to have a little fun tonight. And I love you both." I said in faux-emotive tone, smiling surreptitiously.

Abhay chuckled.

"What are you talking about, you soppy ass?" he teased. "We have fun every night...I have never seen you without a glass of whisky in your hand. And now it looks like the two of you have been joined at the hip!"

Maria slapped him on the back of the head jokingly but with some force, and laughingly said, "Shut up man! Who are you to say anything? What about that girl from Delhi that you had that raging affair with...and for all of one week at that!"

I joined in, "Also aren't you bisexual man? That means you have the best of both worlds my friend...the whole world is your oyster."

Abhay laughed loudly, lifting his head high and squinting his eyes.

He was drunk, and Maria was quite inebriated too. I started drinking hard to catch up with them.

We continued joking around while cooking dinner, and then sat down to eat. Dinner consisted of *rotis* and vegetable curry, with yogurt. I ate like I had never eaten before and, for the first time in weeks, felt like I had regained my former gargantuan appetite. We sat up late into the night, and soon it was just Abhay, Maria and I on the veranda of the apartment, drinking and smoking, reflecting on more sombre things. Maria and Abhay would constantly bounce ideas off each other about their work at the camps in Vatwa. Our conversations always started jokingly, but normally ended on politics. I learnt a lot from their reflections.

"It's sinister. We found out today that the state government is handing out compensation to the survivors of the carnage in the form of bonds for the Narmada hydro-dam project." Maria said, shaking her head.

"It's like rubbing salt in the wounds." Abhay responded. "Last year, I travelled with some of the villagers in the Narmada valley who were resisting the project. There was militant resistance against it."

Maria said sardonically, "Huh...pitting the poor against the poor, providing so-called compensation to victims of political violence by handing them bonds of a project that benefits some of the largest corporations in India, in the process screwing the villagers there as well."

"Bastards are killing two birds with one stone." Abhay said in quiet anger. "Capitalist scum and their fascist attack dogs."

Maria replied, "That's how monopoly capital has always worked throughout history though. Use whatever means available for profit...even fascist goons if necessary."

I didn't fully understand what they were saying, but was too ashamed to ask, so listened and nodded along. I knew about the resistance to the Narmada project, the *Narmada Bachao Andolan*, and I was seeing first-hand the carnage perpetrated here, but it would be much later before I made the connection they were making. As I moved on with my life, when my mind started ridding itself of its hitherto dense condition, I often reflected on conversations with them in retroactive realization.

Later that night the three of us slept beside each other, Maria and I wrapped in each other's arms. Abhay was snoring lightly beside me, while Maria was on the other side, her head resting on the nook of my shoulder. Still a little inebriated from the night's libations and hypnotized by the rotating ceiling fan, I thought back to the email I had sent. I reflected on the last couple of months when everything got turned on its head and things stopped making sense.

A tear drop trickled down my cheek. It took me by surprise. I had none of the feelings I normally associated with tears. My face convulsed a little. I tried to control it, but the more I tried the more I wanted to just let go. My head started shuddering softly, and I could feel a dull ache in my temple as another tear drop trickled down. My breathing quickened and my lips quivered slightly as I exhaled.

Maria raised her head a little.

"Jay?" she whispered, a little sleepily, her voice a touch raspy from the booze.

I didn't say anything and continued staring at the ceiling, trying to stop the tears from flowing. Her voice broke me out of my reverie. She saw my eyes welling up.

"Jay...what's wrong?" she asked softly, her warm breath soothing my ear.

I shook my head.

"It's nothing..." I whimpered. "It's just, you know...the last couple of months..."

I trailed off, as another tear drop ran down my face.
"I know." she said with tenderness.

She turned onto her back and slowly guided my face onto the nape of her neck as she embraced me tightly, her soft palm nestling my head. I cried softly into her shoulder as she stroked my hair, well into the wee hours of the night, neither of us saying another word to each other.

~ Chapter 13 ~

The organisations that made up the *Shanthi Samudaya* coalition were all engaged in different sectors of work, but institutionally they could be bifurcated into two types. There were a couple of very large international NGOs that had branches all over India and the world. Their branches in Gujarat were part of the coalition, and wielded disproportionately large influence over the direction the coalition took. They provided most of the relief funds in addition to providing administrative leadership and oversight but weren't very entrenched with the local population that those funds were meant to serve.

Apart from them were numerous, much smaller, community organisations including charities, civil liberties groups, Muslim community organisations and small NGOs who all had strong local networks. They were the ones who implemented most of the relief, legal, and human rights efforts that were planned by the coalition.

Mani acted as one of the de facto organizational heads of the coalition, even though it wasn't supposed to have a leader, per se. There were a couple of others who also had leadership roles, but since Mani was the person I had interacted with first, it was natural to work with him as the primary coordinator. It seemed quite ad hoc, but I soon also realized that Mani did indeed handle a large part of the coordination for the camps in Gomtipur. Abhay and Maria dealt with a different coordinator, who was quasi-in-charge of the camps in Vatwa.

The relationship between Mani and I had grown into a friendly one between experienced warhorse and avid greenhorn. He saw that I was hard-working and willing to learn. Granted, those traits qualified me to be little more than a well-trained sheep dog. But when he realized that I was one of the few volunteers, like Abhay and Maria, who planned on staying for more than just a couple of weeks, he seemed to respect that perseverance despite my blundering first steps. He even hugged me when he saw me come back from the camps a couple of times; patting my cheek with paternalistic affection, the way many elders in India do to young whippersnappers. He seemed to regard the organic team that had developed between Vijay, Nasir and I, quite highly. He mentioned us to newer volunteers a couple of times as people to watch and learn from. I felt proud each time he did that. It was also useful to be on Mani's good graces. He was crucial to ensuring that we got materials ready and work done on time without too many questions or bureaucratic oversight that hampered progress.

We soon learnt how to play the game efficiently.

I found out that in order to get funds for any of the activities we undertook in the camps, we needed to requisition for them directly, either from Mani or one of the financial coordinators of *Shanthi Samudaya*. All of them worked for one of the large NGOs. However, in order to get the work done, we always coordinated it with one or more of the community groups depending on their strengths and the kind of work that was required. This was the most crucial link that folks like Vijay, Nasir and I played – get the materials and funding from the big NGOs, and funnel them to the smaller community organizations that had the best local grassroots networks. One such small organization that I found myself immensely inspired by was a tiny workers' rights group based in the heart of the old city.

Maria had recommended that I contact them for the work in Gomtipur. It was founded and headed by a Muslim woman named Nasreen. It's rather generic name was the Community Development Trust. Vijay, Nasir, and I went to meet her to start a livelihood-generation program that we were trying to coordinate in Gomtipur as part of a larger project of *Shanthi Samudaya*.

We met her at her office. Her beautiful, weathered face radiated strength from behind a worn out desk in a sparse office. She pointed the potential pitfalls with accuracy, and highlighted the issues we needed to be wary of as we conducted the project.

"The main issue is to ensure that those with the highest need get the first instalment of livelihood materials." Nasreen said with poise. "Also, we will need to do some dividing up by trade. So we should cull this information from the surveys that you have already been conducting. Let's ensure that we have a plan for those who will not get livelihood materials immediately because they will justifiably be angry...so make sure you hold a community meeting in all the camps and be very honest about the livelihood scheme, how we're going about it, and answer all questions in a calm manner. It can get quite raucous, so we have to be prepared."

She was intelligent and grounded in a refreshingly forthright manner. I was quite enchanted by her strength. The three of us nodded along as she spoke, while I took some detailed notes. Vijay and Nasir only understood bits and pieces of what she was saying, since she started speaking in English and none of us stopped her to request that she speak in Hindi.

She continued, "Before we do all this of course, we should make sure that we get clear numbers on what materials we need, and the quantity, from *Shanthi Samudaya*. That way we'll be in the best position to bring everything to the community in a forthright manner. Whatever we do, we should be absolutely honest about how much there is, and how long it will take to get the rest of the livelihood materials for residents who don't get anything in the first instalment. This is why we need to also ensure that a proper needs assessment is done."

I asked a few questions on the logistics of the whole project, and we worked on the next steps that needed to be taken. It felt good to know that the project would be in partnership with a person of such ability and honesty. As the meeting wound down, the discussion eventually veered towards, of course, the carnage that had taken place.

The conversation quickly shifted to Hindi. Nasreen spoke about the hell that transpired. Her tone became darker.

"We would get phone calls every minute about this person who got killed or that family that got burnt. It was madness." she recalled, eyes looking elsewhere as she went back to that time.

"My sister and I were so scared, but we still had to do our work. We tried to save as many families as we could, but it was not much." she said with resignation.

Nasir asked, "Nasreen*behen* what was the kind of

work your group did during the *dhamaal*? Is there anything that could be done now after the carnage?"

"What could be done Nasir*bhai*?" she replied. "It was an emergency. The only thing we were concerned with was saving as many lives as we could. Since the *dhamaal* none of our regular projects have re-started. Now all we do is relief work, and also trying to help with the human rights campaign."

Vijay nodded his head in acknowledgment, "That's so true Nasreen*behen*, all the NGOs in the area are only thinking about relief, relief, relief. I hope that once this relief work gets over, we can also do other forms of work."

Nasreen nodded.

"*Inshallah* that will happen." she added, looking up to the sky. "But even then, whatever work we do will move towards rehabilitation. So even if some NGO is working on health issues, their work will now have to cater to the survivors. And with this legal campaign? All of us know how slow the justice system can move here, and that too in Gujarat, these bastards are there even in the courts. God alone knows how long it will take and what sort of struggles will be needed."

I asked, "How do you think your organization will cope with all of this now Nasreen*behen*? It seems like so much for the smaller NGOs to take on."

She replied in English, nodding in agreement, "Very true Jayram. There are multiple spaces that we have to negotiate. For instance, we still have to continue applying for government grants. You see...not all of the state has been taken over by the Hindu fascists, so we have to try to use those avenues to support the work. Also larger NGOs, with massive budgets, need us. Without us, what work can they do? They don't have any field experience, no community networks, nothing."

She looked down at her desk, shaking her head with a cynical half-smile.

"When doing this kind of work, all the romanticism of this work goes away." she continued. "We have to do what we have to do in order to get the work done. The larger institutions have the funds, and they want to show that work is getting done, so need to work with us. We are able to do that kind of work, but cannot access the kinds of international funding that they can and so need to work with them. It might be social work, but it's also a bit like a business deal. If our heads are in the clouds, we won't get anything done, we'll just be talking."

I had seen this resigned rationality in other activists, and it helped ground me. Nasreen was wise and experienced. Like Maria, she had a way of being commandingly intelligent in word and deed without being authoritarian – a quality I'd found almost solely in women anywhere in the world, probably because they hadn't been socialized into domineering masculinity. But unlike Maria, it didn't seem like Nasreen was the kind of person one could joke around with much; she had a hardened edge to her being. She looked like a workaholic, and someone who had seen too much, one of those unsung heroes who did amazing work but buried the trauma of their experiences deep inside them. It was hard not to be drawn to her seething beauty.

The conversation was drawing to an end. We made plans to meet again and reiterated the next steps that needed to be taken. We got up and said our goodbyes to Nasreen with deep respect. We were in the presence of someone who deserved at least that much. As we got ready to leave, I asked her one last question in English, hoping to end our meeting on a positive note.

"Nasreen*behen*...if you don't mind my asking," I ventured, "you had said that you and your sister were so scared when the violence was happening, and yet you continued to work in the community. May I ask where you found that strength?"

Nasreen replied, with the same composure she displayed throughout the conversation, "My sister and I each carried a small vial of poison with us every day. We decided that if the mobs came to get us, all they would get would be our dead bodies and not us."

~ Chapter 14 ~

With the livelihood project underway, I had temporarily forgotten about the email I sent to my folks in Bangalore. It did, however, reignite the connection with my parents and I realized that I needed to do a better job of keeping in touch with them. I called my home from the BSC office a few days later and was finally able to participate in a lengthy conversation with them. One where I actually managed to string a couple of sentences together instead of giving them curt, one-word answers.

"We read the email you sent many times over *kanna*...I don't know what to say, there aren't any words to describe..." Appa said, trailing off, nearly breaking down.

I could sense his eyes welling up. It shook me out of my callousness.

"We saw the news here every day when the riots were happening, but then nothing describes it in as much depth than what you just wrote in your email." He continued, composing himself. "You're doing something wonderful Jay. I just hope others also realize what happened in Gujarat. I think the rest of India is quite oblivious to all that happened there. The news now has completely shifted to other things. People have such short memories."

He sighed, "I don't know…it's so sad…you should write about it sometime, and make sure more people read about it when you get back from your time there."

It was nice to reconnect with my parents. I could hear Amma in the background pestering Appa for the phone. He gave it to her.

"How is your health love? Are you taking care of yourself, you know, eating properly and everything?" she asked with tenderness. There was relief in her voice at our renewed connection.

"I'm doing fine Amma...we eat well, and I have lovely people here who are with me day and night, on both sides of the river." I replied, not bothering to tell them about the infrequent eating, daily alcohol-consumption and cigarette-smoking that was bound to have already taken a toll on my formerly fit body. I knew it would worry them. Amma would have immediately reverted to emotional blackmail to make me quit.

"Anyway," I said, trying to veer the subject away from topics that required me to lie, "how's Akka doing in the States?"

"She's coming back soon with her husband. They're just made for each other, you know. It's wonderful...they're buying an apartment in the same residential complex as ours. We'll be so close to each other. We can hardly wait for their arrival." Amma said excitedly.

"That's great Amma...just great." I said, trying to match their excitement in word, though unable to in feeling.

They asked me more about the work, obviously happy that I was opening up to them after my earlier cantankerousness. I knew my email had also worried them. They tried to hide it in vain, choosing instead to ask indirect questions that they hoped wouldn't irritate me.

Appa asked, "So Jayram...we're just asking, so please don't get angry...um, what would happen if there are some riots with Hindus targeting Muslims, and you're in a Muslim area? Will your friends take care of you? Because some of the Muslims might get angry...and you being Hindu..."

I laughed, not mockingly but in genuine reaction to the ludicrousness of that thought.

"Oh god...don't worry Appa." I replied confidently. "I'm treated like a member of the family in Gomtipur. They will do anything for me, you know, and protect me from any rioters. I'm like a brother to them. Really, I'm not just saying it. There is nothing to worry about in that regard. What's more worrying is what the fascists might do to me if they find out that I'm a Hindu working with Muslims."

I immediately regretted the last sentence as it came out of my mouth.

"What do you mean by that?" Appa asked, his tone getting flustered. "Will they find out? You should be careful Jayram...just get out of there if anything happens. Please..."

I started damage-control.

"*Ayyo* Appa. Don't worry." I said, trying to sound blasé. "I was just saying that sarcastically to tell you that there is nothing to worry about here with respect to my working in the Muslim areas. There are no fascist groups here anyway. Really, I was just saying that in a joking way. You should come and see this place. They treat me like a brother. Vijay and Nasir will do anything for me Appa, so don't worry."

I inserted a little white lie there. There *were* a couple of fascist groups not too far from the Muslim areas, and I wasn't fully joking about what they might do, but didn't feel like dealing with my parents' worries. I knew I had only partly reassured them, but my tone was strong enough to reduce their worry at least a little bit. I didn't have the mental energy at that time to go into a lengthy nuanced conversation. As a way of shifting the conversation from my own personal safety, I told them about the work I was doing with Vijay and Nasir, the conditions at the camps in Gomtipur, and the evenings spent with Maria and Abhay.

The fact that I was spending less stressful evenings with friends from other parts of the country comforted them quite a bit.

"So, who are Maria and Abhay? Have they also just finished college like you, and taking a break?" Appa asked.

"Somewhat, yes." I replied. "They're a bit older than me though. Abhay is doing his PhD in Oxford; he's a Rhodes Scholar. And Maria is a documentary film-maker; she won some major national awards for a couple of her recent films."

I could almost see Appa's eyes widening with amazement.

"That's simply wonderful Jay...I didn't know such accomplished people were also volunteering in the relief efforts there." he said.

I knew this would happen, which was why I ensured I told them about Abhay's and Maria's achievements. If an award-winning documentary film-maker and a Rhodes Scholar had come to Gujarat to do the same work that I was doing, I must have been doing something right.

I found myself getting a little irritated though. I weakly told them that their accomplishments outside of their work in Gujarat shouldn't matter, primarily because I didn't boast of any, but also because it genuinely shouldn't have mattered.

"The fact that they're here is what is truly important,

regardless of their accomplishments." I told them, smarting a little. "Also, there are many more really poor volunteers in the movement from the community, like Vijay and Nasir, who are doing far more courageous work than those of us who come from outside."

They agreed, and Appa immediately acknowledged, however indirectly, my comments.

"Of course, of course, Jay." he said, trying to reassure me. "We're not saying that simply because one is accomplished that it's great to do this work. It does not matter what status people come from. In fact it's obviously much tougher for poorer people to do this. The fact that everyone is doing this work is great. We're just happy that you're doing this with such wonderful people."

I knew that they were agreeing with what I said out of love for me, to spare my ego a little, but I was still happy to hear it. I had to head to the camps, so proceeded to end the conversation. Amma came on the phone again to say bye.

"Ok you two worry-warts," I said, trying to use a casual tone again, "I have to head to the camps now, so will call later. I hope everything is going well in Bangalore."

Amma replied, "Ok *kanna*. We miss you. Please take care of yourself, and keep calling."

"Ok Amma...bye. I miss you too."

I hung up and sighed deeply. I realized that a smile had crept across my face. It felt nice to have an open conversation with Appa and Amma. My parents were among my dearest friends. We didn't agree on everything, but they were making genuine efforts to grow with me and meet me half-way, despite my crankiness; something they would continue to do with heart-warming effort after my return – and rebirth – from Gujarat. This was a relationship unlike what many of my friends had with their parents. Appa, Amma and I always had very honest, engaging conversations with each other. I never realised how sad it would have been for me had we lost that, as we very well could have in the last couple of months. The realization particularly hit me later that day.

I returned that evening and again decided to check my email

rather then head straight to our apartment, so stopped by the small shopping centre that had the internet café. I sat down in front of a computer and logged on. I opened my email account and saw one from my parents that immediately caught my eye. It was entitled *Jayram's activism and current work*. It was a mass-email sent to multiple family and friends. Appa did this on occasion to give updates on what Akka and I did. He sent one when Akka got admitted into a top university in the US, another when I graduated from college and did well in my GREs, yet another when Akka announced her engagement. I was curious to see what he had written about me. Most of my relatives placed value almost solely on monetary and titular achievements. They would not have considered the work in Gujarat of merit or value, other than as a condescending notion of charity. I had long since stopped trying to develop relationships with them, but my parents often still played the game, so I wondered how they would broach this topic with the rest of my family.

The email was moving and uplifting. It was not very long. I knew that Appa had written it, and he never wrote more than what was necessary.

Dear family and friends,

I write this email to inform you all of Jayram's recent endeavours. As some of you may know, he decided to take some time off after his degree to do some volunteer work in Gujarat, working with victims of violence there.

He had always been very involved in issues around equality and human rights, even in Bangalore, so he wanted to get a proper experience on the ground before going abroad for his higher studies. He works in the relief camps, doing shelter construction, rations distribution, and conducting surveys for the legal rights campaign. He's working with some amazing people who have come locally and from all over India to help in this great cause.

Jayram and his friends put in long, backbreaking hours in difficult conditions at the camps and for the justice of the victims. They do this under an atmosphere of hatred that threatens to rip the very soul of our secular nation. It is amazing work that he and his friends do. We ask that you hold him and his friends in your thoughts and prayers as they fight for such a good cause. We speak from the heart when we say that if he had received the Nobel Prize, become the CEO of Microsoft, or won Wimbledon, we couldn't be more proud of him.

With love

Krishnan and Ramaa

I sat and stared at that last paragraph. Tears welled up in my eyes. I was undeserving of this lavish praise, the kind that came only from loved ones in your innermost circle. But it wasn't that which got me choked up. I had turned an important corner with my parents. I realized that one of the main reasons I was so crotchety with them was because I didn't believe that they would attempt this journey with me. But their unbridled love for me combined with their open minds and enormous hearts was a force more powerful than I had given them credit for.

I knew that they were making this attempt to meet me half-way because they loved me and saw that they would probably have lost me had things continued the way they had for the last couple of months. But I also knew that this type of loss had happened before with many radical activists, who came from conservative families, slowly but surely distancing themselves from their families. Both Maria and Abhay told me about how they had moved on from their parents; how they shared empty, polite relationships; how they rarely talked about their political growth with their parents; and how they wished that it was different. That was the norm. So I was expecting it to be the same with my own parents. That expectation caused me to pre-empt it and subconsciously push Appa and Amma away without giving them a chance to grow with me, or even believing for a second that it was possible.

They had proven me wrong. I might have lost much of my extended family, in fact I knew I already had, and I didn't care. But the relationship with my parents was different. I could not brush off losing them the way I could with the rest of my family. As I grew into my late teens and early twenties, our relationship had also grown through honest discussions and arguments. I loved them, not just because they were my parents, but because they were my best friends. My buddies in college constantly talked about how lucky I was to have parents like mine. It would have hurt to lose that and I knew it. I was grateful for that not happening.

I logged out, paid the café owner, and walked out of the shopping complex. I sat on my usual stool by the juice stand, and ordered a lime-soda. I took a couple of sips and lit up a cigarette. I dragged deep as I enjoyed another lingering smoke in contentedness, as dusk slowly descended upon the city of my rebirth.

There would be problems no doubt, clashes from walking different paths while still staying within eyeshot of each other. But I also knew that the fundamentally honest love and friendship I shared with Appa and Amma would still be there even after Gujarat. In the midst of all that I had seen and experienced in the last couple of months, it was a comforting thought.

~ Chapter 15 ~

An important part of the work we were doing included detailed survey forms that needed to be completed through interviews with individual victims and their families, specifying the human and material losses. This was needed for the Public Interest Litigation being prepared by *Shanthi Samudaya* to file for compensation and legal justice. Documentation and reportage was another reason. The forms were designed by one of the bigger NGOs that were part of the coalition. They were meant to provide such a truckload of information in the PIL that the courts would have no choice but to get on the side of the coalition, and hold the government accountable for what happened.

Collecting the information was one of the most mind-numbingly tedious activities we did.

"What is your name?"

"Fatima Bano"

"Who are the family members in your house?"

"One husband, Qasim. Three children. Ahmed, Mohsin, and Ameena."

"And where are they?"

"Qasim was killed in the *dhamaal*. Ahmed is missing. He was lost in the *dhamaal* and we never found him again. Mohsin and Ameena are with me in the camps, and we're now staying with my sister."

"Mmm...and what were the livelihood items you lost in the *dhamaal*?" (Cynically wondering if anything could have survived when the entire house burned down.)

"My husband's bicycle cart was burnt down. All my materials for making clothes were also burnt down with the house."

"Ok, and what other valuables did you lose?"

"I lost all my wedding jewellery, and the clothes. We also lost all the kitchen items."

"Mmm...and what was the value of all them put together?"

"I don't know exactly."

(In slightly irritated monotone) "Just give an

87

approximate value."

"Probably 2-3 lakhs. Yes, I think it would have come up to that much or more actually...um...so, will we actually get some compensation *bhaisaab*? We're really struggling right now, and there's no work either...we're really desperate..."

(In same monotone) "Yes, yes, but we have to be patient. Now...what was the value of the house?"

And so on...

There was a coldness with which I operated when I worked on doing surveys, trying to collect as much information as possible. I might as well have been conducting a consumer survey. I was numb. Shut myself out from the losses and just noted them down on the forms. All I cared about was the accuracy of the information. The humanity interred in it was completely out of my realm of operation; especially if we did surveys all day. I got irritated when people were not able to remember details properly, even castigating them on occasion when they would break down. I was a metronome collecting information.

I didn't feel this level of emotional sterility when we did other activities, like getting rations, running community meetings, constructing shelters, or getting work done for the livelihood project. All those activities were tiring, frustrating, exhilarating, depressing, anger-inducing – in short, they were alive. With the survey forms, I felt none of that. Just numbness. It was mundane work that sucked you emotionally dry. I knew the immense value of the work however. So did Vijay and Nasir. We used to motivate each other whenever one of us got frustrated. Maria and Abhay too had to do this in the camps in Vatwa. On days when all three of us returned to the apartment after a day of surveys, the evenings would be filled with absolute merriment. No talk about work or politics or anything; just drunken laughter and silly jokes.

For those of us working in the camps, the forms also served another, more immediate, purpose of vital importance. They doubled up as a needs-assessment tool for the livelihood project. The livelihood project constituted the procurement and distribution of sewing machines, vending carts, seed money, cycle repair tools, auto-shop tools, carpentry tools, and whatnot based on the most widespread trades that people conducted for their livelihood. These were in short supply because the number of people who had their livelihoods destroyed in the carnage was astronomical. Even the lucky ones, who escaped being killed or maimed, had their lives destroyed in every other way due to the clinical manner in which the mobs wrecked havoc. Every element that might constitute a normal life was destroyed.

We had no choice but to distribute the materials as they came in on a needs-based manner, and wait for subsequent procurements to make further distributions in a staggered way. Mani and a couple of other coordinators of *Shanthi Samudaya* met with the volunteers and community-leaders from various camps around the city to figure this out. It was determined that the highest need was for families where one of the parents had died. Essentially, getting livelihood materials would be based on how many earning family members were killed in the carnage, and how many children were in the family. Children who had lost both their parents were either with uncles and aunts, on the streets, or eventually shipped to residential school-cum-orphanages across the country.

This naturally caused a huge ruckus in the camps when the first instalment arrived. Accusations of favouritism were hurled at us by camp residents who didn't receive livelihood materials.

"I'm sure you all have taken bribes from those families to give them the materials! Otherwise, why are they getting some and us nothing?" an elderly woman shouted.

"Or probably you all have sold half the items in the black market and pocketed the money...you all must be enjoying yourselves at our expense!" screamed a local shopkeeper.

Vijay, Nasir and I had heated arguments every day with many of the camp residents. The harshest expletives and accusations were thrown at Vijay and Nasir. They both took it upon themselves to defend me against any accusations, getting angry at the mere suggestion of wrongdoing on my part.

"Don't you dare scream at Jayram*bhai*...he's come all this way to help us and he doesn't deserve this!" Nasir said agitatedly.

"Exactly! All of us are trying to help the community here, and you all are screaming at us like this...Jayram*bhai* doesn't need to hear all this from you all!" Vijay shouted back.

There was, of course, no logical reason for according me that degree of integrity. The three of us did become tighter as a result, but also had to work hard in ensuring that more people got livelihood materials. The anger of the residents was justifiable. But we were not looking at it as outsiders, and our irritation boiled over on more than one occasion. It was not easy to hear this from people we cared so much about, and we reacted with anger, which wasn't very helpful. The only thing that counted was work.

The accusations and anger reduced considerably when the next batch of livelihood materials was delivered, this time to many of the residents who had accused us of chicanery the first time around. It was satisfying to have come through on promises. We were so close to the ground that we weren't functioning out of any grand political ideal, but just pride in coming through on what we said we would do. It was a personal commitment to the work we were doing, not too different from any other form of satisfaction that people derived from a job well done. The early idealism and zeal for a vague notion of justice was now shunted to the back of my mind. The only time I engaged with it was in inebriated conversations I had with Maria and Abhay in the evenings.

But there were occasional jolts to the backbreaking grind.

One evening after a long day of surveys and rations distribution, I decided to walk across the bridge on a whim to wind down with a smoke. I thought I would get into an auto rickshaw on the other side. I walked along the bridge stopping every now and then to look at the Sabarmati below. It was much fuller and flowing with gusto following the heavy monsoons. It was quite muddy, and a big plunge below from the bridge. I shuddered a little when I momentarily imagined falling in. I might have survived. I was a moderately good swimmer, but it would have been a struggle.

As I reached the other side of the bridge, I realized that I had never been in this area before. It was clearly Hindu dominated, but poor like the Muslim neighbourhood across the river. It was still quite a distance from the glitzy shopping areas and gated residential communities of the city, like the apartment complex I lived in. Materially speaking, it was not very different to the area in Gomtipur that had the camps, except instead of a mosque, there was a temple. There were also no butcher shops, but apart from that, similar businesses and trades. The dusty streets were narrow and the houses were smashed into each other.

I walked around trying to find an auto rickshaw to hail. I generally stood out in poorer neighbourhoods because of my clothes, the way I walked and carried myself. In general people gave me a second look before going about their daily lives. This area was no different. As I was searching for an auto rickshaw, I walked past a small shop that lay along the narrow street adjacent to the bridge. A couple of stern looking young men were sitting by a small table inside the shop. It didn't look like the shop was actually selling anything, but had a sign up in Gujarati that I didn't understand. They didn't look away when they saw me, and muttered a few words to each other, evidently about me.

As I walked past them, they called out to me in Gujarati. I looked back at them, and smiled, but shook my head indicating that I didn't understand the language.

One of them called out to me in Hindi, "Come here *bhaisaab*. Come here."

They didn't seem too stern now, and one of them even smiled a little. I went towards them thinking that they wanted to sell me something or were just curious to know who I was. I was an obvious newcomer to the area.

I stood in front of them and enquired, "Yes *bhaisaab*. What do you need?"

They asked inquisitively, "What are you doing here? Are you from outside Gujarat?"

Something was worrying me now. Their tone seemed friendly enough, but in an artificial way, and their smiles were not comforting. They had an edge to them.

"Yes, I'm from Bangalore *bhaisaab*. Why do you ask?"

"Oh, no reason. Just wanted to know that's all. What are you doing in these parts?"

They had been staring at my chest, and only then did I realized that I had my *Shanthi Samudaya* ID card hung around my neck, as was the normal practice for all volunteers. They spotted it as I approached them.

I said, "I'm here working with *Shanthi Samudaya*. It's an NGO."

"NGO? What does it do?"

"They do good work."

As I spoke I noticed a sharp-looking *kara* on the table, that the guy was playfully twirling with a gnarled finger as he asked me questions. The long blade was a little rusty, but still in good shape. A slight chill went up my spine. They were both smaller than me, and I could probably have fought them off if needed. But if they wanted, things could have gotten pretty bad for me. Their lackeys might have been close by, and I didn't know what kind of goon-power they had in the area. I needed to try and cool things down.

He continued probing, still giving that evil smirk, "What kind of *good* work?"

I smiled innocently and said, "Just good work with people. For the community."

"You people work with the Muslims eh?"

I had guessed right. He stopped twirling the *kara*, and started tapping the blade against the table now. His tone didn't change in volume, but became a little more menacing. I could feel the chill working its way up, but tried not to show it. I wasn't really scared of death. I knew they were unlikely to kill me, but the possibility of getting badly roughed up made me a little nervous.

I continued in my faux-innocent tone, playing the dumb urban brat, "We work with all people *bhaisaab*. I don't know who is who. I've just come from outside, from Bangalore. Don't know this place that well."

"I see...so what are you doing here then? Tell me, what business do you have here?"

I didn't waver in my tone.

"Nothing boss. Just coming to visit that's all. I don't know this place well at all."

I needed to change the tone of the conversation. I looked around the area pretending like I was searching for something.

"Anyway," I said, sounding inquisitive, "tell me *bhaisaab*, where can I get an auto rickshaw to the new city?"

He continued staring at me and gave me a once over, but his eyes lost some of their malevolence. It was working. The question changed the mode of the conversation.

"Hmm...ok...you'll get an auto around the corner from that shop over there." He said, now losing interest.

His tone lost its menace, and instead became indifferent, even a touch irritable. I had re-established the paradigm of middle-class man in a poor neighbourhood seeking information from person residing there.

To hammer in the idea that I would be a waste of his time, I asked, "Will they go according to the meter, or will I have to set a price beforehand."

He shrugged his shoulders slightly, and said, "You have to see. Just ask them. They will probably come according to the meter."

"Ok *bhaisaab*. Thanks."

I then waved my hand to bid them goodbye. The man waved me off lazily, like he was brushing aside a pesky kid.

I walked away before giving them a chance to restart another conversation. I walked normally so as to not seem like I was trying to run away, but still took long strides to the auto rickshaw stand. I lit a cigarette, and could see my hands shake a little bit as I struggled with the matches. I took a drag and coughed violently, like I had just inhaled the fumes of burnt plastic. I looked at the cigarette and realized that I had lit it the other way around. I threw the cigarette on the ground and hailed the first auto rickshaw I could find, taking deep breaths on the ride home to calm my nerves.

~ Chapter 16 ~

My brief interaction with those two goons made me realize that I needed to be a touch more vigilant than I had been until then. There was little time to reflect on the experience though, because we had another problem just around the corner. One we hadn't really accounted for when we started working in the camps.

The annual Rath Yatra was to take place again with all its pomposity in Ahmedabad. The chief minister of the state, the same man who orchestrated the bloodshed, had been facing immense pressure from the media and central government to prevent an outbreak of violence during the militant Hindu parade. His own party in the centre was pushing him to ensure it would be a low-key affair, at least ensuring a modicum of peace. It would have looked bad for more violence to occur when the state was simultaneously seeking more private capital for investment.

The buzz around the camps and communities in Gomtipur the day before the *yatra* was one of adrenalin-fuelled fear and angry anticipation. Zubaan told us that the young men in the camps were not going to tolerate any more violence.

"They would rather die than be targeted again!" he angrily said. "We just came through this nightmare and now they want to threaten us again tomorrow? All the youth are ready to die to protect their families!"

Nasir replied earnestly, "We must do what we can to ensure that nothing happens to the community Zubaan*bhai*. We should ensure that nobody loses their lives."

Zubaan replied in fatalistic rage, "Nasir*bhai*, what's the use of living like this? I am telling you, *Allah ki qasam*, these young men would rather die than live in this humiliation. You know what the Hindus start shouting about us in this parade? They call us all kinds of insults and tell us to go back to Pakistan! How can they talk to us like that? This is our home!"

His emotions were palpable. Vijay was angry too, while Nasir displayed a sullenness I had never seen before. The community had multiple questions as we met with them throughout the day. Almost everyone, except the young and middle-aged men, left for areas away from the route of the parade where they would be safe.

After talking to Zubaan about the Rath Yatra and seeing the mood of the camps, Vijay, Nasir and I went to have our evening tea. We decided to walk along with the parade.

"At least then we can warn the community in time before anything bad happens." Vijay said, barely taking a sip of his tea. "We can also try and urge them to save themselves rather than fight and die."

"You're right Vijay." I added for emphasis. "Especially if all three of us go then, just in case any trouble starts brewing, we can fan out and warn those men who are still remaining in the community."

I was scared of more violence, and was desperately hoping it wouldn't come down to that. If indeed we were in the dire situation of having to warn them, the idea of urging them to run was important. I had no desire to fight. The thought of more bloodshed filled me with dread.

"Jaram*bhai*, the three of us should probably sleep at the main office of the camp, because from here we can easily walk to the parade route." Nasir suggested. "If you go back to the new city, tomorrow morning you won't find any auto rickshaws that will bring you here. The entire city will be closed down tomorrow during the *yatra*. So the three of us should stay here."

Vijay nodded in agreement. I was loath to spending a night away from Maria and Abhay, but knew that I had no choice if I wanted to join Vijay and Nasir the next day.

"I suppose you're right." I said, nodding with resignation. "It makes sense for me to stay with you two tonight in the office. Let me just make a phone call to Maria and Abhay now letting them know that I won't be meeting them tonight."

I went to the teashop we frequented in the evenings, and called Abhay's cell phone, a newly acquired gift from his mother. He and Maria were on their way back from Vatwa. I could hear the din of the chaotic road as they made their way back in the auto rickshaw. I told them that I was planning on staying back in the camp office, so that Nasir, Vijay and I could walk along with the *yatra* and warn the community in case anything untoward happened. Maria got worried.

"Is it really necessary for you to do this Jay?" she asked with concern.

"Maybe not Maria, but I want to go with Vijay and Nasir, since we decided together to do this. It's important, I feel. In the off chance that some violence starts, we might be able to run back to our friends here in Gomtipur and warn them. We can convince them to run rather than stay and fight. Most of the community members are safe...away from the main route of the parade. Some men are staying back just in case..."

Maria retorted, the worry still evident in her voice, "Oh god...please be careful Jay...this is crazy. If something happens, just get the hell out of there or go to the nearest police station. You speak English and you're from Bangalore. The police will shield you from any violence."

My heart swelled with affection for her.

"Of course Maria, don't worry." I reassured her. "And anyway, Vijay and Nasir are with me. This is their neck of the woods. They know where to go in order to be safe from any violence."

And so saying, I said my goodbyes to both of them and hung up.

Nasir and Vijay were waiting outside the tea shop for me to finish my conversation. The three of us hung around drinking tea and smoking. We decided to have dinner at the same eatery we normally ate at, next to the tea shop. *Parathas* and mutton curry. By now my stomach lining stood up to the spicy gravy with aplomb, and I tucked in happily. I was also happy to note that Vijay and Nasir were enjoying the food as much as I was. They weren't only focused on ensuring that my plate was full. I could sense it as another small step in our strengthening friendship.

After dinner, we walked back to the main office of the camp. It was well past dusk. We set out straw mats right outside the office, the breezy openness of the dusty cement porch being overwhelmingly preferred to the sweltering claustrophobia of the office itself. We slept next to each other.

The camp was different at night. Not as crowded as it was in the day time. Quite a few people went back to their destroyed houses, all at various levels of crude reconstruction. Some stayed back to sleep in the camps. A handful of men, including Zubaan, sat around in a circle, playing cards in front of the mosque. The atmosphere was quieter, more serene, in stark contrast to the chaos during the day. It was a new experience for me.

The night was uncomfortable though. The straw mat was hardly soft enough for my middle-class bones, but I did my best to feign comfort so as to not have Vijay or Nasir try to do something to alleviate the situation for me. The weather, while better outside, was not exactly pleasant, with a mosquito or two every now and then keeping me at my self-slapping best. The discomfort was more than offset by the amazing feeling of comradeship I felt for the two men lying next to me. Under the starry skies, in the area where we bonded as activists, about to go on a self-imposed mission, I felt a rush of political camaraderie for them as I slowly drifted to a restless sleep.

We woke up the next morning a little weather-beaten.

"We can wash up and go to the latrine in Zubaan*bhai*'s house nearby, and then walk towards the parade." Nasir said, sleepily wiping his droopy eyes.

The camp didn't have any of its usual bustle. Word had spread about laying low during the *yatra*. The three of us trudged to Zubaan's house, and I found myself wishing for the toilet in the apartment I lived in; a loo on which I could sit contentedly with the newspaper. But right then I would have been happy with a hole in the ground for a good shit before we left for the *yatra*. My unerringly regular bowel movement would have ensured that I would be worrying about more than just potential fascist violence if I didn't take a dump that morning. Luckily, Zubaan seemed to have successfully reconstructed the toilet in his house, which I learnt was almost completely burnt down in the violence. There was also enough water to wash up, which I was particularly thankful for.

The streets had an eerie calm to them. We walked back to the tea shop, where we had some sweet buns with tea. I smoked my morning wake-up cigarette with my second cup.

A little refreshed, we soon made our way out of the tea shop and walked towards the path of the parade. Nasir and Vijay seemed to know exactly where to go, so I followed them.

As we walked, Vijay said, "We have to make sure that if something happens, we call Zubaan*bhai* immediately. He told me that he will wait around the tea shop all day until the *yatra* ends. After we call him, he will inform the others and we can then run back to organize things with our friends to ensure that they get to safety."

Nasir and I nodded.

"We must also make sure that we take side roads and stay away from the mobs." Nasir added. "They won't know that I am Muslim or that Vijay is Christian just by looking at us, but we should still take care to run away taking the smaller street."

I felt a surge of adrenalin as they spoke. It suppressed my fear. There was no way I would have done this alone, but being with them and their effortless courage had a transformative impact on me.

As we neared the parade, I could hear the din of drums and blaring music on loudspeakers. Another surge of adrenalin shot through my body. We soon joined the commotion, and walked along with the teeming masses of the parade.

It was a sight to behold.

A disgustingly macho, martial sight to behold.

Young bodybuilders, flexing their muscles on trucks as they passed the parade route. Well-oiled. With sunglasses on. Some of them lifted dumbbells or barbells on the trucks.

Swords. So many swords. Real ones for the adult men. Toy ones for the children. Waved around with flair or just held menacingly on display. Tridents and spears too. Some held in kill poses as they stood on the slow-moving trucks.

Large speakers along the route and on the trucks blared nationalistic songs from early Bollywood movies. I found myself taking particular offence to that. It was like they had stolen something from me and claimed it as their own.

As we walked along the route, ever so often young men would lie supine on a board of nails, one on top of the other at times, place a different board on their chest and then another young man would drive a motorcycle over them.

People cheered. How they cheered. Women and children waved from the balconies of the houses along the parade route, cheering on the masculine madness.

Local politicians and party leaders stood on top of makeshift stages set along key junctions of the parade route, and shouted slogans of encouragement, complimenting the martial valour of Hindu youth in Gujarat.

Hindu symbols and colours adorned everything. Large idols alongside the bodybuilders and weapon-wielders on the trucks. Men dressed as Hindu gods while carrying their weapon of choice.

Saffron. A lot of saffron. The colour was omnipresent.

As I walked with Vijay and Nasir, drinking in the insanity, I wondered to myself – how many of these men were among the bloodthirsty killers who mobbed the streets only a few months back? How many raped and butchered? How many burned and pillaged?

We walked along for a couple of hours with the noisy parade. I was simultaneously mesmerized and nauseated by the display. I clicked more photographs of that parade than any other single event in my life. When the body-builders and weapon-wielders saw me working the camera, they tried to get my attention by posing for me.

Nasir, upon seeing my interest, smiled and whispered in my ear as we walked, "Jayram*bhai*, you should see the young men during our *Muharram* festival. They're much stronger."

Nothing happened eventually. Every foot of the parade route had a posse of policemen or paramilitary personnel to prevent any outbreaks of violence. It was evident that the criticism levelled at the Chief Minister had some effect. The media and the central government had piled the pressure on him for holding the *yatra* with such ferocity despite all that had transpired. So the man got riot police to line the entire parade route.

As the parade ended, I wondered again – why hadn't he been able to mobilize this kind of police presence when it mattered? I knew why of course; but I allowed myself to wonder nevertheless.

The parade ended without any reason for us to warn our friends. I heaved a sigh of relief as Vijay and Nasir walked with me to the nearest auto rickshaw stand, but the deep disquiet inside me didn't leave. I had been on edge the entire duration of our walk alongside the parade. I was fearful of violence breaking out and thought I would feel happy when nothing untoward happened. But I didn't. What I saw didn't give me any reason to.

Vijay and Nasir hugged me goodbye before I got into the rickshaw, as if they were accepting me as one of their own. It was brief, but powerful. And it was the only thing that provided me a measure of solace at that moment.

~ Chapter 17 ~

Notwithstanding occasional moments of fear and foreboding, things were moving well for me. While Nasir, Vijay and I were bonding as a team and handling our work with increasing confidence, life for me on the other side of the river was getting positively blissful. Maria and I had now become a loving couple. It seemed imminent from the moment we met. There was the proverbial chemistry we shared combined with the common cause we were working towards. It was a heady mix. Without labelling or having a conversation about what we were getting into, we started revelling in each other. Shared auto rides, eating out, getting drunk, laughing freely, melting into each other in bed. I knew that I was falling in love with her, and with an intimacy I had never experienced before. Indeed my heart knew that I *loved* her, with all that the notion signified. She made me feel alive in a way nobody else had until that time. It was painful even. Maybe it was because she was there when I was in a particularly raw state of being that it felt so electrifying. But it was also because of her. She drew me in with her sexy intelligence and unabashed political rage. Abhay even joked that our names might as well have been hyphenated. It was something I had never experienced before.

At the back of my head, I knew there was something unsustainable about it. But I was in new territory, an exciting place, where emotion thrived, pleasure was sought after like it was oxygen, and the light Maria radiated was like a life-raft that kept me from drowning.

The night that we gave in to each other encapsulated what I shared with her. It was scary, yet exhilarating. I knew it would happen. She was amazed at my patience, my peace with the way things stood between us. I was not pushing for it to move any further. I knew I wanted it, but I was also scared of it. It was only a matter of time though. It was a little anxiety-ridden for me, yet so very beautiful. I think I was frightened by the intensity of her soul. I couldn't match it. It was like she would eventually find out what a callow little child I was – obviously not good enough for her. Yet, despite my nerves, she led me through a beautiful apex of intimacy and uninhibited love. My anxiety didn't matter much to her; she was even a little irritated at it – like she was talking to an immature, yet eager, idiot and trying to explain high philosophy that came easy to her. But she explained it with affection, not arrogance. It was sensational.

Simultaneously I had interesting feelings towards Abhay; feelings I had never experienced before for a man. I'd always thought I was heterosexual in the most blinkered way. But in meeting him, and feeling his affection, his amazing depth of thought, I started to rethink my own sexuality. I would always hug him when I saw him in the evening. I looked forward to that hug every day. Abhay laughed and listened to what I had to say, unlike so many other men wiser than I who often looked at me as a young man-child with big ideals that would get blown away in the winds of reality soon. There were a couple of inebriated nights when we even playfully kissed each other on the cheeks. One of those kisses lingered for that extra second. It felt wonderful.

Being with Maria however prevented me from going any further with Abhay, despite him openly talking about his bisexuality with both of us. I was also not ready to accept myself as anything other than straight in bed just yet, having just started a very mercurial journey – but also because it was so amazing to be with Maria. My internalized heterosexuality was nevertheless shattered, if in an unacknowledged manner. I was excited at the prospect of understanding my sexuality in a more unshackled way. But I didn't know whether I had the courage to proposition Abhay. It was confusing. The liberation of sexuality was something I was swimming in now. I felt that if I took a step back, I would not be as free, however scary that freedom felt.

I wondered how my open-minded, yet rather conservatively rooted family back in Bangalore would understand this. I thought about the email Appa had sent to our family and friends. Would Amma and he accept my rapidly liberating sexuality? Would they accept a new me in more ways than just what that beautiful email so obviously indicated?

It was interesting how this dual, rather scatterbrained, life on either side of the river had become the most important chapter in my life. There was an intense pain, but an unknown excitement, as a tempestuous political liberation was coupled by an equally intense personal liberation. It was difficult, at that moment, to reconcile the two – primarily because they were happening in two different worlds, with a river between them. On auto rickshaw rides either towards the camps to work with Vijay and Nasir, or back to the apartment to be with Maria and Abhay, I wondered if these two liberations would ever be fully reconciled.

Would Vijay and Nasir be comfortable with the kind of open sexuality that Abhay, Maria (and slowly, I) functioned with? Vijay, Nasir and I rarely spoke very deeply about our personal lives; it usually remained on our work, and the political aspects of our work. With Maria and Abhay, it didn't just remain there, but delved into other aspects of our existence. There was internalized condescension in the way my functioning with Vijay and Nasir panned out, even though I loved them and thought the world of them. I wasn't able to open up to them about my own liberation. I callously failed to grant them the ability to connect with me on it or at least respect it. I unknowingly erected barriers to the possibilities of friendship between me and them.

Yet, I had an awakening with Vijay and Nasir that simply could not have been possible with Maria and Abhay, no matter how committed to the work they were. Vijay and Nasir opened up a world to me that was scary, because it took me out of my sterile comfort zone. It wasn't just the difficult material conditions of their existence or the violence their communities faced. It was more than that. It placed my own existence at the helm of benefit from their oppression.

They did this for me. And they did it without malice or rancour. They probably didn't even know they were doing it, which drew me to them even more. They did it in different ways. I was drawn to Vijay's strength, his ability to command a situation. He was my comrade in the truest sense of the word, and it was a relationship I felt, deep down, would stand the test of time – not in any small part due to the fact that we had talked about building a community organization in the neighbourhood together. It was an exciting, if still ungrounded, prospect to be able to continue the connection with him into the future. Vijay had an inner heat to his soul

103

that kept him going. I never felt like it was a violent one, like a seething rage, though I knew that he had been a street thug and bootlegger for sometime before getting involved in community-work. It was more like a flame that couldn't be extinguished, an angry passion that fuelled his activism.

Nasir had a more amiable aura to him. He was no less informed or zealous about his work, but in a *nicer* way. He was well-versed about different political issues, but unlike Vijay, who derived his politics from his conceptual understanding of what was right, Nasir was more organic in his politics. He did his work because it made sense, because it was right, and not just because he understood it to be right theoretically. There were times when I felt like Nasir was almost juvenile in his ways, but only when I was looking at his outer shell, the facade that covered his true being. When I would get glimpses of that being, over tea and cigarettes, it radiated with a mature, organic goodness that I wanted to defend with my life. He was the kind of activist who came into fighting for a good cause, not because he was a political guy, but because he was a nice guy. It was always pleasant to be around him, unlike Vijay, who sometimes got crotchety. Every once in a while though, Nasir would surprise me with the amount he actually believed in and the strength of his convictions, even though Vijay was louder about it.

Both were fighting comrades, the kind you wanted in the trenches.

But the three of us only connected temporarily every day. I was always going *back* to the other side of the river. Back to Abhay's warmth and Maria's love. Back to their safe embrace and drunken jocularity. Back to bootlegged whisky and restaurant fare. Back to a toilet where I could take a shit while reading the newspaper. This made me reflect on something else. I knew it as the white elephant in my mind, which I only occasionally acknowledged. I had to ask myself if *my* world was ultimately on the side of the river with Maria and Abhay. After all, it wasn't very different than the way things were for me in Bangalore.

Yet the similarities were superficial at best. The moment I looked a little deeper, even that world was so radically different from what I had in Bangalore. I might have been more personally comfortable with Abhay and Maria in our apartment, than in the camps with Vijay and Nasir, but both worlds were still galaxies apart from what I left behind. And both worlds were still soldered together at a very important level, if only in my head. It was like I had been reborn into a dual-world existence, one world completely new, and another that resembled my past life in form alone while still crucially different at its core because of a dialectic connection to that new other world. They informed each other, in a new reality for me. One couldn't exist without the other. And the person I was becoming, suspended between these two worlds, rejected what I had left behind in Bangalore.

It was confusing.

I was treading water in the Sabarmati, desperately hoping to not be swept away by the currents that would take me away from both sides, and possibly...(shudder)...back to Bangalore.

~ Chapter 18 ~

While my dual-world existence on either side of the river with these four amazing people formed the placental core of my rebirth, they weren't the only folks I interacted with. Every few days, we would get short-term volunteers who joined *Shanthi Samudaya* for a brief while. Groups of volunteers, who were part of a movement or organization in their region, coming in solidarity with the survivors of the violence in Gujarat; or individuals who did the same thing, but on more of a whim than anything else. Some of them tested our patience. Like a group of irritating students from a prestigious law school in Bangalore. For the entire duration of their ten-day stay, they didn't do a damn thing other than whine about the fact that their talents were going to waste; how they could have easily contributed doing legal writing work for the Public Interest Litigation, but instead were being made to conduct surveys; and how they were under the impression that they would be making an actual difference in the legal campaign through their skills.

For the entire duration of their ten-day stay, I had to fight the irresistible urge to line them all up and punch them; a sentiment that I imagine was not too different than what Mani experienced with when I first landed.

But there were also people whom we worked really well with, from whom I learnt a great deal. One of them was a chain-smoking journalist from Delhi, Sunita, with intense eyes, and an even more intense countenance. When she spoke, I listened. Sunita was beautiful, and in more ways than just the stereotype of feminine beauty. She had a daunting beauty. It felt like she had been scarred, like she was carrying some deep trauma that I never found out about. It only made her presence that much more intimidating. I tried joking around with her, but she laughed only when she wanted to, on her terms. Maria was not happy that I spent so much time with her, but she was assigned to the camps that I worked in, so there wasn't much I could do about it. I didn't hide the fact that I was quite taken in by her presence though. It boosted my ego to see Maria getting a little jealous.

Sunita came with me to conduct surveys in the
Gomtipur camps. She had jet-black, long curly hair with
almond eyes set in a dusky, stunning face. She wore numerous
bangles on each hand, along with flowing *kurtas* and skirts. As
we walked everyone turned their heads to look at her. It was a
little uncomfortable, and I didn't know what to do about it.
She knew it was happening, and it looked like she was used to
it, though by no means happy about it. She knew what must
have been going through the heads of some of the guys. The
previous night, she had shown me a knife that she carried
around in her shoulder bag while travelling around in Delhi, a
city notorious for its dangerously macho sexism.

"If some guy tries to mess with me, I seriously will
gut him." she said, calmly brandishing the knife. "In Delhi, a
woman has to be tough."

I had no doubt that she was being dead serious.

We walked around the camps doing surveys. The
stares ended once we started going about our work. Sunita
was exciting to be around. We smoked together when we took
breaks from the work. She offered me some good cigarettes
from Delhi. Everyone stared at us in incredulous shock. A
woman smoking was beyond comprehension to everyone in
the camp. A conservative moral compass shrouded in
patriarchy often resisted even the most mundane challenges to
those social moors. One evening as we were done with
surveys, we sat by the side of one of the burnt houses we had
just finished surveying. Vijay and Nasir sat with us as usual.
Sunita offered me a cigarette. I took one and lit up. Vijay lit
one up as well. Some of the women we had just surveyed were
also sitting by the doorway. They had their stitching on their
laps.

One of the middle-aged women said, while threading
a needle, "You know, you should not be smoking."

I said in response, "I know. It's a bad habit. I'm going
to try and quit soon."

She replied, "No, no. It's ok for men to smoke. But
women should not smoke."

She turned towards Sunita as she spoke, and promptly
received a polite earful.

"Why do you only say that women should quit? Huh? Don't you think these are double standards on your part?"

"No double standards ma'am. Just that women should not smoke. It's not good for them to smoke."

"Oh...so it's ok for men to smoke then?"

"No...but...women particularly should not smoke."

"Why is that? What's so special about women not smoking?"

"I don't know ma'am, but they just shouldn't, that's all I know."

Taking another drag of her cigarette and pointing at me, Sunita said, "If you're telling me to quit smoking, then you should tell him too. What is this notion of 'only women should not smoke'...whatever rules we have should be there for both men and women, don't you think?"

The woman in the house didn't say anything. She snorted in disagreement and went back to her stitching. I sat, staring at them like a buffoon, not knowing what to say. We soon had to make our way back, so we took our leave. Sunita smoked on the auto ride back to the apartment, and we got stares from folks throughout the trip each time we stopped at a traffic signal. They looked disparagingly at her puffing away, and clearly for reasons other than health concerns. The moral compass at least had transcended religious divides on both sides of the river.

We soon got to talking about the incident once we reached the apartment.

I asked her, "So, is this something you constantly face?"

"Is what something I constantly face?"

"You know, people looking at you in funny ways because you smoke...and facing constant harassment on it."

She smirked, "Hmph...you really don't know much about what it means to be a woman in this world huh?"

I felt a little foolish now, and blubbered, "I know...uh...I'm sorry. I was just asking because I don't face anything like that. It must be awful."

She softened up a bit and replied, "Yes, I know. It's something I constantly face...you know, because women who smoke are considered to have low morals and nonsense like that."

"Well, it's a good thing you told her off then, right?"

"Maybe, but remember that I essentially used my class-privilege to tell her off, rather than engage with her properly on a gendered argument."

I looked at her questioningly, not understanding fully what she meant by that.

She smiled, clearly sympathetic to my density.

"It's not like she's convinced of what I said." she explained, now looking at me directly in the eye. "She just stopped talking because she saw me as someone in a position of relative power, and didn't want to challenge that. That's not really helping bring down the institutions that are propping up those kinds of thinking."

I nodded, finally getting it.

She continued, "Jay, I'm sure you realise that the woman who asked me to quit smoking probably faces far greater pressures of the patriarchal system than I do, because she also faces daunting prospects as a poor Muslim in this poisonous environment."

I nodded, trying to internalize what she was saying. Maria and Abhay were the two people in my life right then who were teaching me how to think. It was rare that I ever derived even a smidgen of that kind of knowledge from others, especially those who came in for a short duration of time. With the allocation of work, and constant deadlines with short-term volunteers, there was rarely any moment where in-depth conversations could take place. But there were always exceptions like Sunita.

After a few more days of surveys, Sunita's time with us came to an end. I walked with her to hail a rickshaw that would take her to the railway station. We found one. She thought of hugging me as she got into the rickshaw. She paused, briefly looked at me and smiled. None of the hardness. None of the intensity. Just pure affection. She didn't hug me, and instead shook my hand. But I could tell that for one brief moment, I had seen her core. In that moment, we had a visceral connection.

There were also volunteers who taught me about my political baggage in different ways; taught me how much I had to learn, and unlearn, in that regard. Vijay and Nasir had unknowingly taken on that role on a day-to-day basis, but every once in a while I would find others who did the same.

We had a group of volunteers who were affiliated with a large NGO in Northeast India. All of them lived under an Indian military presence aimed at suppressing the many nationalist groups there either fighting for greater autonomy or independence. Abhay, Maria and I were asked to be in charge of putting them to work for the two weeks of their stay with us.

I had found in the past that one of the toughest things for any organization to do was to find work for short-term volunteers. It was a problem I was familiar with when I volunteered in Bangalore with a student-group addressing gender-based violence. The key was to ensure that there was something, anything, that they could participate in without feeling useless. So, new volunteers who came in were asked to tag along for events and workshops until they got the hang of it.

This was not a problem in *Shanthi Samudaya* as long as people were willing to do whatever we asked them to do. We didn't have time for fussy volunteers. The activists who came in from the Northeast were anything but that. They were willing to roll up their sleeves and do whatever was needed, regardless of age or station in life. It was interesting to see this, because it was difficult to find this attitude of egalitarianism in some other parts of the country. Elsewhere, the older and more titular you were in society automatically presumed doing less mundane work. In general we only had this problem with urban, English-speaking brats from large cities like Delhi, Mumbai, or Bangalore.

We put them to work in procuring rations, and getting some more survey forms filled out. Rations-delivery worked well, but getting surveys done was much harder because most of them spoke only English and their respective native languages, with no Hindi. They soon started data-entry for the PIL, which they were only too happy to do. I learnt a lot from one of them.

My imbibed nationalism growing up meant that I always supported the Indian state and military presence fighting militant groups in the Northeast and Kashmir. In all of three and a half months in Gujarat, through conversations with Maria and Abhay, who were resolutely sympathetic to the aspirations of self-determination that the people in those regions had, I was radically transformed. It didn't make sense any more to support the Indian military apparatus or even a homogenous idea of India. I wasn't sure what I believed in any more politically – socialization is tough to get rid off – but I was slowly getting a framework on how to place myself in any political engagement.

It ultimately boiled down to power (who had it and who didn't), and oppression (who faced it and who didn't), with all the grey areas to be negotiated with constantly.

It was easy to engage with the activists from the Northeast. They sensed that Maria, Abhay and I were not typical Indians who bought the nationalist rhetoric. I only had to cling on to the critical thinking of Maria and Abhay, not yet having developed my own. The volunteers were staying in the BSC dorm, so the three of us joined them there a couple of times after working in the camps. The usual booze was there, which some of them declined to my surprise. I had always stereotypically pictured the Northeast as a place where the best parties happened. But I learnt that Gujarat was not the only state in India where alcohol was legally prohibited; two states among the Seven Sisters of the Northeast also had prohibition laws in place, primarily because they were Christian-majority states.

I had become pretty good friends with one of them. Bobby and I discovered a common love for Led Zeppelin, and both of us played in college bands. I was hanging out with him separately from the rest of the group one evening. Our conversation eventually stopped being about hard rock legends, and soon turned to the troubles in the region.

I asked, "So, what's it like living in the Northeast? We hear stories almost every day in the news about the problems there."

Bobby replied, "Well, for the most part, it's not very different than your life in Bangalore I think. The only difference being that we have the fucking Indian army there all the time."

I probed further, "I can't even imagine what that would be like. To live under military occupation like that. How do you cope?"

I think he appreciated my calling the presence of the Indian military an occupation – a term most Indians outside Kashmir and the Northeast would never have used. I had Maria to thank for that.

"Well, the most important thing is that we have to keep living, and keep doing what we normally do. One of the biggest issues for us young people is some viable career choices. So we have to come far from home to study in good colleges. I even have a cousin and a couple of friends in Bangalore."

"Oh yeah? That's wonderful. I had a close friend from the Northeast. He and I were in the band together. Phenomenal guitarist." I said, smiling.

"That's cool...yeah, rock music is really popular where I come from. It's like an escape I guess." he said, nodding his head.

"So, um…where do you plan on going?" I asked.

"I think I'll go to Bangalore also, and if I don't go there, then maybe Mumbai or Calcutta, possibly Chennai. My last option is Delhi...I hate Delhi."

"Why? Is it because of the aggressive behaviour?"

"Ya man. They treat us like second-class citizens there." he said with a passion. "Always calling us 'chinky' or 'chinku.' And girls from the Northeast, those fucking Delhi boys think all they're interested in is sleeping with them, so they treat our sisters like pieces of meat. It's terrible."

He paused and shook his head

"Tsk…we wouldn't have to worry about any of this if we weren't living like we do." he continued. "Otherwise we would just stay at home, and go to the colleges there itself, but where are the job opportunities in the Northeast? The conflict ruins everything. Unfortunately many of us are forced to leave to other parts of India."

I remembered that my friends and I back in Bangalore always used to call folks from the Northeast 'chinky' even to their faces. I had even used the term with my band-mate, thinking it was just light banter. I was certain that Bobby's cousin had faced it as well, but he chose to be polite and not castigate the city I was from.

I asked, "Have you faced any problems directly from the conflict there in the Northeast?"

"Of course man." he replied, surprised that I would even think he hadn't. "My friend was killed by the army. Shot dead from point-blank range after rounding him and a couple of other boys from his village. They called him a terrorist, put khaki pants on him after killing him, and then put out a press release. He wasn't even close to any militant group. He was just a student."

He shook his head again and looked down.

"His brother got so angry," he continued ruefully, "that he ended up joining one of the militant groups. They're better than the army, at least they don't terrorize us constantly. It's terrible. Our land is so beautiful there man. But the army and the conflict ruin it."

I nodded. I couldn't imagine living like that.

"I don't know what to say brother. I can't even imagine what that must be like." I said, trying to sound sympathetic.

He looked up, and said with a smile, "Don't worry my friend. It's not all bad. We still have fun and enjoy ourselves. We all manage."

I then asked, "So, what prompted you to come here to volunteer in Gujarat?"

With a wide grin, he said, "Solidarity man...we're all brothers and sisters after all."

Bobby left with his group a couple of days later. As I hugged him goodbye at the railway station, he gave me an open invitation to come to his town and spend some time with his family. I thanked him and said that I definitely would. I knew at the back of my mind that this was likely going to be our last interaction, but I didn't feel like acknowledging it right then.

He smiled, and pulled me closer to him in a tight embrace before boarding the train.

~ Chapter 19 ~

I was learning a great deal during my time in Gujarat; more than what I had bargained for. It helped me reflect on things better, and the more I reflected, the more I learnt. It wasn't fun though. As the weeks and months passed by, my work with Vijay and Nasir soon made me realize my own utility-value on the ground. I rarely took a step back to examine it, but when I did, it was a sobering realization for my bloated ego. My work was not defined by my abilities, mental or otherwise. Nor was it defined by my self-perceived zeal for social justice. My work was almost singularly defined by where I came from.

I was nothing more than a privileged go-between. A bridge between the larger NGOs in the movement and the *Shanthi Pathiks*. All that I brought to the work was my class position. Indeed, I soon realized that it was all I that was needed for, primarily because of the baseline of mistrust that NGOs staffed by English-speaking middle-class folk, however well-meaning, had for the poor. Activists like Vijay and Nasir were not trusted to handle organization monies, while activists like Maria, Abhay and I were. I handled the money and "coordinated" work with Vijay and Nasir. I didn't have the grassroots capacity or community-networks to do any real work, other than act as a cog in the class-ridden status quo.

I was the white missionary, the foreign aid worker, the relief organization representative, the person who had to be nothing more than a glorified middle-man for large organizations who wanted to do "good" work sans any disturbance to the prevailing social order. I had a multitude of fancy names like Liaison, Coordinator, Advocate, or even Director.

I was nothing more than a humanitarian pimp.

I didn't do or say much about it though. Rationalized it. Convinced myself that it wasn't the battle to be fought now. Maybe I was right to some extent. There *were* things to be done, urgent issues to be taken up, and I did have a certain utilitarian value to the work, however non-descript. Was it worth rocking the boat right now? Talking about how the movement could have been more egalitarian when there was so much to be done in the midst of a giant insanity. Would it achieve anything?

Honestly though, the rationalization was merely to justify my existence. Truth is, I liked being in that position. Made me feel like I was doing something. If I had tried to figure stuff out and muck things up, one of the things I would have needed to do was come to terms with my own redundancy. I didn't feel like doing that. I liked working with Vijay and Nasir. I liked going back to Maria and Abhay. I knew I needed the rebirth that was occurring on both sides of the river. I also knew that the feeling of *doing* something, something good and worthwhile, was crucial to making the birth process that much less agonizing. I needed it. I needed to feel good.

So I didn't bother. I let things be as they were. Let the river run through it so to speak. Crossed it every day, but never tried to figure out how to challenge the divide.

~ Chapter 20 ~

One day Vijay, Nasir and I had to go to a locality near Gomtipur called Gulbarg Society. This was one of the most featured localities in the national news after the violence broke out, because among the many victims who were brutally killed by the mobs, was a former Member of Parliament, Ehsan Jaffrey.

The three of us went to try and help with some rations-distribution problems that some of the *Shanthi Pathiks* in the area were facing. Distribution of rations had slowed down since the start of the livelihood project. People were able to slowly get their own food through the regeneration of their livelihood. However distribution was still to be phased out gradually, since it would take some time for the community to completely get back on its feet. So rations would still be distributed periodically.

In general, rations consisted of wheat flour, rice, lentils, salt, cooking oil, and sugar. Once in a while we would get vegetables, and even more rarely, meat. This time in the Gulbarg Society camp there was a shortage of wheat flour and lentils, so not everyone in the camp would have received their allotted share. We did have sufficient quantities of rice, so decided to trade in the rice that we had with a local grain depot in exchange for more wheat flour and lentils. This way, everyone at least got enough to make *daal-roti* for their meals. The depot was contracted by the state to distribute grains to different ration shops, but *Shanthi Samudaya* also got rations from other government sources through national relief programs.

Every now and then though, aid-workers on the ground had to negotiate with local depot-owners in the area to barter. Some were very kind, while others were corrupt cretins. In this case, Vijay, Nasir and I weren't sure, since we had never dealt with him before. We would need to appeal to the guy's sense of compassion and community. But I also ensured that a bunch of hefty guys we had befriended, whom I knew were the local toughs, came along so that the depot-owner would be more amenable to make the barter at cheaper exchanges than the market rates without much of a fuss.

The depot was close to the Gulbarg Society camp on a narrow messy street like the ones in Gomtipur. We were able to negotiate an exchange of rice for wheat flour and lentils. I knew that he would sell the rice on the black market to make a profit, since he now had too much. Vijay and Nasir had explained this to me weeks earlier when we conducted similar actions for the Gomtipur camps. It was a win-win for both of us. I was a little surprised at myself that I didn't flinch when they told me about this black market dealing. Despite growing up with the privilege to abide by and be moralistic about the law, I now reacted like breaking it was the most natural thing in the world.

We managed to do this and get it back to the camp late afternoon that day. The camp residents were waiting with their cloth bags and plastic buckets to collect the rations. The truck reversed to a halt with its back facing the residents waiting for distribution. It sputtered black fumes as the driver manoeuvred it and brought it to a halt.

I stood on the back of the rusty truck and told the camp residents what had transpired, that there wasn't enough wheat flour and lentils, so we had to go to the depot in order to procure enough of those items in exchange for the rice. I expected a volley of insults, accusing us of selling the rice and pocketing the money, but to my pleasant surprise they were quite happy with it. The fact that some of the younger male residents of the camp had accompanied us, and nodded in affirmation as I spoke, helped. Our sweaty, grimy demeanours were also useful in winning them over.

The distribution of rations went quite smoothly, primarily because it was only two items. The people were also tired of waiting, so once the rations came, they were happy to be done with the wait and took whatever was on offer.

After the distribution, the three of us went to meet with the camp coordinators. One of the coordinators was a woman, a rarity I was now starting to realize. There were many female *Shanthi Pathiks*, but very few of them were in coordinating roles. Her name was Uma. She had a pleasant face, and a charming smile that never seemed to leave. She was small, almost waif-like, but had a loud fire-cracker laugh.

And she was Hindu.

I was a little surprised, and first thought she was a Dalit Christian with a Hindu first name, like Vijay. Then I spotted a small charm around her neck with a goddess on it. She seemed to know Nasir and Vijay quite well. Nasir and Uma joked around in the way that I used to joke around in school with the girls I had a crush on. It was adorable. Uma was giggly, and in a permanent state of cheer. She was shorter than Nasir, who himself was quite a small guy.

"So, Nasir*bhai*, when are your parents going to fix you up?" Uma playfully chided. "You're now eligible for marriage no?"

Nasir replied in mock bravado with a grin on his face, "*Arrey*! I'm not one of those guys who gets married as soon as they can. I want my freedom...not to be imprisoned by some woman who will nag me all day!"

Uma whacked him on his shoulder with surprising strength, and teased loudly, "Fool! You talk like as if there's a long line of women waiting to get married to you, scrawny runt. Who will want to marry you? You're saying all this because no woman wants to marry you I think."

Vijay guffawed loudly at this. "Uma*behen* you are absolutely right!" he said, nodding his head vigorously. "He's too ugly...doesn't even have a proper moustache...all the women look at him as their younger brother, no one wants to marry him. They all tie *rakhis* on his hand during *Raksha Bandhan*...they only want him as a brother. Eh Nasir, what do you say?"

Nasir took this ribbing on his masculinity well.

With a wave of his hand, he said, "You fools don't know anything...huh, I'm having to fight these women off with a stick. They're all waiting for me to say 'Nasir is now ready to get married', and then they'll all swoon. You see...soon I'll have the most beautiful woman in the world as my wife."

I then piped in, "But wait...Nasir, you just said that you wanted your freedom, didn't want to get married and all. What happened to that?"

"That's true Jayram*bhai*, but when I do decide to get married, you won't believe just how many women will be lining up!" Nasir replied, cheekily.

"Shut up...scrawny runt!" Uma said, whacking his shoulder again, with some more force this time. "I pity the poor woman who is so desperate that she has to marry *you*!"

We laughed some more. The silly banter was nice to be a part of. The fact that I was organically taking part in it made me slowly feel like a member of their little community. It was always nice to bond with Vijay and Nasir like this along with other friends in the community we worked in.

The chatter stopped soon enough. Uma explained what the conditions of the camp were like, and what had transpired at Gulbarg Society during the carnage.

"What happened here was unimaginable. They killed so many people here, and then just piled up their bodies and lit them on fire." she said in horrified recollection. "What happened to the women...oh my god...too much."

As she spoke, she pointed to a spot near one of the bigger houses in the locality.

"And here was where Jaffrey*saab* was killed." she said. "He tried to protect the community in his house. He called his contacts in Delhi to try and get them to stop the violence, but nothing happened."

She paused and shook her head.

"One old woman saw everything." she continued. "The mobs came and dragged Jaffrey*saab* out. He then tried to pacify them and tell them to go away. Nothing worked. They told him to shout 'Jai Sri Ram' and when he refused, they chopped him up and burnt him. Then they killed everyone else too...did all kinds of horrible things. Too much *bhai*, too much. That old woman who survived...I don't know what she must be going through."

The mood got more sombre now between us.

Uma continued, "The camps now...I don't know how we manage. The government doesn't do anything for us. We just do what we can, and try our best. Sometimes the residents get angry, but what can we do?"

Nasir nodded and said, "I know. Even we at Gomtipur talk about how the losses in Gulbarg Society and in Naroda Patiya were the worst. So many people got killed in these two places."

The second locality that Nasir mentioned was even

119

better known. I knew of Naroda Patiya. In fact it was the first locality I learnt about before I got to Gujarat, even before hearing about Jaffrey and the Gulbarg Society massacres. Naroda Patiya was where the leader of a Hindu mob, killed a pregnant Muslim woman by driving his sword into her stomach, shouting "Jai Sri Ram!" This made the news everywhere. I remember the numbness that washed over me when I heard it, from afar, sitting in my living room in Bangalore.

I also remember a weird feeling then, that I couldn't quite get a grip on; a feeling I was now able to articulate a little better; the feeling of knowing that your life would never be the same.

The four of us talked for a little while longer, and then we took our leave of Uma. We had to check in on a little work in the camps in Gomtipur specifically for the livelihood project. After saying our byes to her, we made our way back to the Gomtipur camps, and met up with the belligerent residents. There were some more arguments regarding the distribution of materials. By now they weren't accusing us of malfeasance any more. We had proved ourselves as sincere and hardworking. We had also come through on our promises to get the materials to the neediest of the survivors, while not promising anyone the world. This brutal honesty worked in ensuring people didn't think we were crooks. We had gained their trust. But we also disappointed many when they came with their problems and didn't find us useful in any way. For folks who had gone through such a high level of trauma, it might have helped to hear even a false promise. But that was something we had resolved not to do. Vijay said that these people had been fed false promises of development from the government every day. They didn't need it from us too.

We had had a long day. I was dog tired and really looking forward to our regular evening tea and cigarette before I headed back to the apartment. We sat down by the tea stall near the main camp. The owner was by now quite friendly with us, and as soon as we approached, he would have three teas ready for us, and some space at our usual table near the entrance. We sat down. I took a sip of my tea and lit up. The day was ambling to an end as usual, and it was close to sundown. The dust was settling on the street. Folks were winding down from doing whatever they did for their daily sustenance. A couple of stray dogs loitered around the overflowing piles of garbage, while a handful of guys were standing by their auto rickshaws nearby smoking *beedis*. A few women were walking with bags of vegetables in their hands, while the *kabab* vendor was sweating it out in the heat of the open-fire stove where he was roasting deliciously spiced pieces of lamb on skewers, to be served with buttered *paav*, raw onions, and green chillies.

It was a scene out of any poor locality in any part of India, save a few changes in the details.

It never ceased to amaze me, every now and then, how *normal* everything looked. This was a locality, among a few others, that had seen probably the worst episode of bloodletting in India for decades. Yet life went on. Of course it had to, but we had just heard yet another example of the depths to which the violence had gone. It wasn't just killings that had occurred in Gujarat. It was more macabre. And yet, here I was sitting in the epicentre of the carnage that had taken place only a few months back, and there wasn't anything out of the ordinary that one could see at first sight.

When we met Uma today, the conversation was all fun and jokes, nothing too different than a conversation I might have had with my friends in Bangalore. But it didn't take much to shift to the violence, the *dhamaal*, and all the suffering. It didn't take much to shift back too with consummate ease. Life went on. It had to.

Vijay and Nasir were in a lighter mood. Vijay and I had lit up, and were enjoying our cigarettes along with the tea. It was clear that Nasir liked Uma, and Uma liked him back. The fact that he had seen her and spent so much time with her had put him and Vijay, his bosom friend, in very happy spirits.

I asked playfully to Vijay, "So boss...it looks like our friend Nasir has a girlfriend eh? What should we do about him?"

Vijay laughed loudly, "I don't know Jayram*bhai*. This fellow is a lost cause...so smitten by Uma*behen*. I think we should just have them run away together!"

I had rarely seen Vijay laugh with such abandon. It was beautiful to witness this happiness he had for his friends falling in love with each other.

Nasir replied in mock-bravado again, "What are you talking about? Run away for what? Boss I don't know what you all are babbling about. No woman can ever control the heart and life of Nasir Khan...King Khan."

He lifted his collar in faux-macho style as he said this, and straightened his thin shoulders as if he was squaring up for a fight with an imaginary opponent.

Vijay continued ribbing Nasir, "Huh...all nonsense. The moment you see Uma, your knees shake, heart goes racing. You can't even speak properly man!"

I then interjected, taking another dig at Nasir, "Sorry boss...I have to agree with Vijay. You are like a Romeo to her Juliet...a total *aashiqui* eh? We should do a Bollywood movie about your story some day."

Nasir replied, showing a toothy grin, "*Arrey*, there's no Bollywood actor who's bloody half as handsome as I am who can play me...I'll have to play myself!"

We sat around joking for some more time. The conversation was light-hearted and silly. But at the back of my mind there was a nagging thought that I wasn't fully willing to acknowledge yet. Uma was Hindu. She wasn't even Christian, like Vijay. It wasn't unheard of to see Christians and Muslims get married to each other, especially if they came from the same community and fell in love.

But a marriage between a Hindu and Muslim? That was *the* division...the one that families would be most torn apart by.

It was made particularly acute by the fact that this courtship was between a Muslim man and a Hindu woman. It was the apex of sacrilege. The fascists often screamed about how *their* women were being stolen by *those* boys. Hindu women who had married Muslim men had not been spared during the carnage.

The familiar chill slowly crept up my spine and I instinctively dug my thumbs into my kidneys.

Back home in Bangalore, I had read about the Civil

Rights movement in the United States and the fight for racial equality. I had learnt how white supremacist groups there were particularly incensed when white women married or slept with black men. *White niggers*, that's what they were called, and they weren't spared when the groups went on lynching rampages.

I tried to hold down the shudder that was threatening to unleash itself as I thought about the love shared by Nasir and Uma. I felt a gnawing sensation in the pit of my stomach when I realized how much I cared for him, and how much I wanted this to succeed between the two of them. It was the moment I realized that I would do anything in my powers for them.

The three of us laughed. We had to. Life had to go on. Surviving with even a smidgen of happiness was half the battle I realized.

~ Chapter 21 ~

I had erroneously assumed that English-speaking, middle-class
folk, like Sunita or Bobby, were the main source of outside
volunteers for *Shanthi Samudaya*. I soon realized that they just
happened to be the ones I interacted with the most. However
many of the outside volunteers, if not the majority, were
working-class or rural folk engaged in a movement or NGO
in their region. I didn't hang out with them as much. In fact,
once Abhay, Maria and I left the BSC dorm and moved into
the apartment, the interactions were even sparser. Most of the
volunteers who spoke, ate, and carried themselves like us
would stay over in the apartment. Those who didn't stayed at
the BSC dorm. This was a divide that didn't need a river. It
was unacknowledged of course. It was not something we
wanted to deal with. After a long day at the camps, all we
wanted to do was get drunk and laugh. It was a status quo we
were comfortable with.

I wish that there had been greater efforts on my part
to interact with them. I could have learnt a lot more from
them than I actually did. What I did learn stuck though.

A pair that stood out were two men, best friends –
one Hindu, one Muslim – from Rajasthan. Ramesh and
Ahmed worked as masons, and helped immensely with shelter
construction in the camps when they arrived. They were both
part of a militant labour-peasant movement in Rajasthan.
They completed each other's sentences, spoke to each other in
Rajasthani, spoke to everyone else in a thickly Rajasthani-
accented Hindi, held hands in the way that many men in India
often do when walking (that international tourists find to be
curiously homoerotic), wore similar pointy Rajasthani shoes,
and swaggered with the unique kind of macho masculinity that
one found in North India. In short, they were bosom friends,
and it showed.

They had come to volunteer together in *Shanthi
Samudaya* as a way of showing solidarity, showcasing their
friendship as a model for others to follow. And they were
open about their religious identities, which they held dear.
Ramesh had a red *tikka* on his forehead along with a locket
that had a picture of Hanuman on it, while Ahmed had the

quintessential Muslim beard sans moustache and wore his pants above his ankles. Both were not just culturally Hindu or Muslim, they were staunch followers of their respective faiths.

Ahmed was more vocal, while Ramesh was a little quieter. We only interacted while working at the camps, but we got along famously. For whatever reason, they both took a shine to me. This, despite them obviously not liking some of the other English-speaking folk, especially those who were in positions of authority, like Mani. I think it might have been because I asked them earnestly for their advice, and not out of some condescending notion of artificial egalitarianism. I genuinely needed their supervision in building the shelters and keeping them up. Mani gave out tasks in a calm way, but without much engagement or discussion. He acted like he knew what he was doing all the time.

This worked well for people like me, especially in the beginning of my stint, because I obviously didn't have a clue; while *Shanthi Pathiks* like Vijay and Nasir essentially respected Mani's age. The three of us eventually learnt to get the broad gist of what he and the coalition wanted, but ultimately did it our own way, because we knew what was happening on the ground. We also played the game effectively in ensuring that we managed to do what we thought was best for the community without ruffling too many feathers in the leadership of the movement.

But Ramesh and Ahmed were both older, and less inclined to diplomacy, than the three of us. They were also very experienced in movement-building, and came from a region of India where the pressures of masculine honour took on bizarre proportions. The manner in which Mani and the rest of the coalition leadership functioned wasn't just an insult to their experience as activists, but an affront to them as men. So they didn't take too kindly to being told what to do without taking their thoughts into consideration. They never admitted to it outright though – doing so would have been a sign of weakness. It was only natural that they would take to me quite kindly when I sincerely asked for their advice.

I was also happy about their friendship. I was at a place where I was secretly celebrating every little smidgen of hope I saw for humanity coming through the horror that had transpired in Gujarat. Their friendship was one such smidgen, a friendship so obviously transcending that dehumanizing divide. I went along shamelessly with the masculine bonding, despite assuring Maria that I would come to terms with my internalized sexism eventually. One evening we were drinking tea. I had become quite friendly with them and asked,

"So Ahmed*bhai*, Ramesh*bhai*, what is it that makes you two such good friends? What are the things you have in common?"

Ahmed replied with a manly slap on my back, "*Arrey* Jayram*bhai*, ultimately a man is a man no? So we pray to different gods. What difference does that make? I still need a nice wife, who will take care of my children. So does he. We both have to eat, both have to take care of our families, both have to work."

I was barely able to keep up with the accent of his Hindi, but understood for the most part.

"Of course, of course." I said, nodding my head. "But it can't be very easy. I mean, there are some areas, like here in the Old City, where it's probably very difficult, no?"

Ahmed said with a wave of his hand, "What's so difficult? I don't understand. Hindus and Muslims have been friends for decades...centuries even. The Brits came and tore us apart, and now the leaders of these horrible political parties are doing it to us. It's all their fault. It's not like we are born hating each other. *Arrey*, in our town, we would always invite each other's communities to Holi, Eid, Ramzan, Diwali, Dussehra...no problems...we would enjoy being with each other."

"I know...it's just sad that this horrible brutality happened here."

"Ramesh and I have always been close. Since childhood. We attended each other's weddings, children's birthdays, family gatherings, festivals...everything. We're like brothers."

There was a pause.

Ramesh then quietly joked, "Plus we both see Raveena Tandon dancing on the TV and become very happy eh?"

Ahmed burst out laughing at this. I looked at them

and smiled.

"You're right boss...when Raveena dances, all religious troubles stop, because everyone will stop killing each other, and start staring at her moves!" I said, miming an hourglass figure with my fingers.

We laughed some more. Then spontaneously Ahmed broke into a dance number singing *Tu Cheez Badi Hai Mast Mast*, while Ramesh provided beats by clapping. Vijay and Nasir, who were checking in on work at another camp, arrived just then and smiled. Without asking any questions, and following a beckoning from me, they joined in. Nasir got into the thick of things, pulling off a sensational kneeling dance move on the ground. Ramesh then danced in feminine form, hands on hips, swaying his ass in faux-sensuality. Ahmed started clapping now, and cheering his friend on with Nasir.

It must have been a sight to see, the five of us indulging in this uninhibited joy for a few seconds.

It was nice to work with Ahmed and Ramesh, but they eventually got into a major fight with Mani. Tensions boiled over, and they decided to advance their return to Rajasthan by a few days since they had already achieved what they had come to do. They were not happy with Mani and the way he talked to them, but they were warm to me as I accompanied them to the train station.

We hugged goodbye, standing beside the second-class compartment, and Ahmed said to me, tightly clasping my hand, "Whatever happened with the other leaders of the group doesn't matter my brother. We're very happy to have worked with you Jayram*bhai*. You have to come to Rajasthan and stay with us. It was a real pleasure to have worked with someone so good-hearted as you."

Ramesh nodded in agreement, "Absolutely. We really enjoyed working with you. You're a true worker for the people. Please come to Rajasthan...we will feed you authentic Rajasthani food and treat you to some wonderful music...it will be great fun!"

I gushed at this. I had done nothing but just look at them as human beings, fellow-activists with experiences and histories of their own right, and they were praising me like I had saved their children from drowning. I was sad to see them go. As I waved to them after they took their seats, I wondered how much work we could have done together had they stayed longer.

~ Chapter 21.5 ~

I was beginning to realize something as I journeyed onwards in my brief stint in Gujarat - holding a position of being easily heard automatically presumed correctness. First World to Third World, urban to rural, rich to poor, men to women – there was a hierarchy in perceived right to conduct discourse that this experience was laying bare for me. It seemed like a ridiculously simple truism once acknowledged, but it took a while for me to realize it.

It was primarily the work I did with Vijay and Nasir, and reflecting on my highly undeserved position of on-the-ground leadership that pushed me to a better truth. But other nuggets of experience, like what I shared with Ahmed and Ramesh helped too.

Possibly the most important nugget was a brief interaction I shared with a socialist activist, a gentle soul called Ayaan, from the rural hinterlands of Uttar Pradesh. When Ayaan came to volunteer for a short while in Gujarat, it turned out that Maria knew him from an earlier time. They had both attended a gender-rights workshop in Delhi together, and though Maria recognized his dusky face, she didn't recognize his name.

"For some odd reason, I don't remember your name, though I recognized your face immediately." Maria said, as she and I sat with him in the BSC dorm soon after he arrived.

He smiled pleasantly, and said, "That's because my name wasn't Ayaan at that time. It was Sriram."

My interest rose since that was very close to my own name. Both were nominal variations of the deity Ram, whose invocation was shouted out by the marauding killers during the violence.

At first I instinctively thought that he had changed his name because of the way it had been usurped by the fascists. I had briefly thought of doing the same, but decided against it because I convinced myself that such an obviously Hindu name was strategically more powerful in fighting Hindu fascists, especially when I spoke to folks from similar backgrounds. Truth be told, I was just too damn lazy.

Ayaan was made of sterner stuff though. Turned out

it was the gender-rights workshop he and Maria had attended that pushed him to change his name.

"You remember how they had talked about the patriarchy in all religions?" he asked Maria.

Maria nodded, "Yes. It was during the second day of the workshop."

Ayaan continued, "Well, that workshop changed my life in so many ways. When they spoke about how all religions, regardless of where they came from...Christianity, Hinduism, Islam...all of them had strongly patriarchal structures, it really hit me how gender-oppression is so ingrained in all of us. Everywhere we go."

I then piped in, "So how did that change your life?"

He continued, "So many ways. One of the most important things was realizing that I would have to fight against gender oppression my entire life. It's not just about thinking that women are equal...it's much more. I had to look at the different ways in which sexism played into every aspect of society."

He shook his head with a smile as he recollected his epiphany.

"I realized that even in my activism, which is politically radical, there is a lot of patriarchy, a lot of sexism." he said. "We think 'ok we're socialists...so once the revolution comes, there will be complete liberation for women as well...so let's first work for the revolution.' But the revolution is happening now, we cannot wait for the revolution to occur, and then hope that gender oppression will automatically stop. It has to stop now."

I listened intently, while Maria nodded with a knowing smile, like he was saying something she had understood her entire life.

I asked him, "So how come you changed your name then?"

"See, the main issue for me was that I couldn't reconcile with having an obviously religious name that had such patriarchal connotations." he explained. "The story of Lord Ram is a huge epic, with many different nuances, and one of those nuances is that it is also a story of patriarchy. Ultimately the way Ram treats Sita in the end is a caricature of patriarchy in our society. Sita's destiny is controlled completely by Ram, whether it's in rescuing her or rejecting her later because he believes she is impure."

What he was saying was profoundly illuminating for me. It wasn't just the content, but his way of being. He spoke in a rich, authentic Hindi and didn't personify the stereotype of a progressive intellectual that I had in my head – English-speaking, middle-class, urbane. He came from a working-class background, carried himself in the way small-town or rural folk do. He was more comfortable sitting on the floor than on a chair and eating with his hands rather than a fork or spoon. I didn't grant him the ability to think the way he did, assuming it to be the domain of people who talked and looked like me.

He continued, "I was not happy to have my name associated with such a story so I changed my name to Ayaan. I did it well before the violence here happened, so it wasn't because of the violence here...though it's just as good a reason. I have so many Hindu friends who despise these people for giving such a bad name to their religion and their god. My reason for changing my name was not that though."

It was almost like he was reading my mind as he said that. I imagined he had been asked about his name-changing in connotation with the violence that occurred in Gujarat on a couple of previous occasions.

We had to depart for the camps soon after the conversation. Ayaan was also a certified children's therapist. One of the things he was hoping to do in his short time volunteering at the camps was to conduct some therapy-cum-play sessions with the children in the camps, and ask them to draw what came to their minds. He went with Maria and Abhay to Vatwa, so we decided to regroup in the evening at the BSC dorm before the three of us went back to our apartment.

I came back to the dorm that evening after another tiring day at the camps. Maria and Abhay were chatting, and I asked them where Ayaan was. They said that he had gone to get some provisions for the night from the shop around the corner outside the BSC campus. He had said he would show us the drawings the kids made when they returned from

Vatwa, so I sat down with them, waiting for him.

Soon Ayaan came in. He looked petrified, like he had seen a ghost. Maria immediately went to him and put her arm on his shoulder.

"What happened Ayaan?" she asked him, with concern. "Is everything ok? You look really scared."

Ayaan sat down on a mattress, putting the tiny plastic bag of groceries down on the floor.

He said, "Oof...I just saw how deep-rooted this hatred of Muslims is in this place."

"Why? What happened?" I asked worriedly.

"I was walking by, past the traffic light to the store, and saw a couple of tough-looking guys sitting by a tea stall look at me very angrily as I crossed the road." he recalled, with fear in his eyes. "They didn't say anything then, but then as I was walking back from the store, they shouted 'mullah bastard!' after I walked past them."

I felt a chill go up my spine. I frequented that tea stall often to have a smoke after dinner. I think I could even picture the guys Ayaan was talking about. I found myself feeling a particularly cold-blooded fear knowing that this happened so close to our own living space.

Ayaan had a beard, and was wearing a long *kurta-pajama* that gave the outward appearance of a Muslim. It wouldn't have mattered anywhere else but here. I felt sick.

He continued, "You should have heard the tone he used. It was so dark and evil. I just glanced back and quickly walked out of sight from them. I was so scared..."

I pictured this soft-natured, beautiful young man being abused in this manner, and it made me wonder how they could have felt threatened by him.

He shook his head to get rid of the anxiety.

"Anyway...this day has been quite crazy." he said, changing the topic. "Especially after the sessions with the children. You all should see the pictures they have drawn. These children play like normal kids in the camps, but they've seen everything...the killings, the burnings, the blood...and it all comes out in the drawings."

He took out a stack of papers from his battered leather satchel and gave them to us to see. His hands quivered a little as he laid down the drawings on the floor. All of us peered at the sheets of paper. Weapons were drawn in black crayon. Many of the tridents and swords were drawn larger than the humanoid stick figures. Fire was represented through swathes of yellow, while blood was drawn using a deep red hue. There was a lot of red and yellow in the drawings, lashings of it, liberally applied onto the sheets of paper by tiny little hands.

I looked up into Ayaan's eyes. They were red with emotion as he scanned the drawings. After we had seen all of them, he picked them up, hands still quivering, and placed them back carefully in his satchel. Ayaan left Gujarat after a few more days of art therapy in Vatwa, back to his hometown and the socialist movement he was a part of. Maria and Abhay spoke about him a lot after he left, the wonderful comrade he turned out to be, and especially how the kids in Vatwa had taken such a shine to Ayaan*bhai* and his artsy games in the brief time he worked with them. We were sad to see him leave. In the midst of a noxious atmosphere he was like a breath of fresh air, something I had taken for granted until then.

~ Chapter 22 ~

Notwithstanding occasional moments of vicarious trauma, I could always rely on the work with Vijay and Nasir to ground me. It was the ballast that prevented my mind from capsizing. It was the eye of the storm where brief moments of blue-sky-like clarity emerged in the midst of swirling madness; often in ways that took me by surprise.

One day in the middle of the afternoon, we were taking a break after a few gruelling hours of filling survey forms and distributing livelihood materials. We were ready to call it a day, and headed to our regular spot for some tea and a smoke.

We sat at our usual table by the entrance of the shop, and Vijay ordered our teas. We had not yet eaten lunch, so we ordered some spicy buns as well. Normally the owner would bark at the kid who worked for him to get the tea for us – in double-quick time since we were regulars. But this time he got up and brought it. He even brought an extra tea for himself, and sat at the same table we were sitting at, removing a *beedi* to light up with us. I had, until then, never really had a proper conversation with him. He usually sat by the entrance, at a small table with a cash register. We would order our teas with a wave and smile, and he would wave back with a grinning sideways head-bob. That was the limit to our interaction.

Vijay and Nasir knew him well enough to be comfortable with him sitting next to us. I was a little piqued at this interruption to our routine. Nasir asked him about his family and the business. Vijay enquired whether things had looked up since the *dhamaal*. He was one of the luckier ones. He hadn't lost anyone close – a distant relative and a couple of acquaintances – but his immediate family had survived.

He wasn't there for small chit-chat though. Judging by the way he was looking at me, he wanted to speak specifically to me about something important. By now, a lot of the community in Gomtipur had seen Vijay, Nasir and I work hard, so we were treated well by most people, barring a few whom we had to be unavoidably harsh with because we weren't able to do anything for them. This man was always very warm towards us. We came by almost every day to his tea shop, and he would always welcome us in, even charging us lesser than he did for other customers, sometimes even declining payment.

He was particularly welcoming to me at all times. I was still seen as an outsider. Vijay and Nasir were almost expected to do good work being *Shanthi Pathiks* from the community, but I had come from outside so if I did good work, I was commended a little extra by the community. I was still seen as someone who didn't *have* to do this, so it was appreciated just that little bit more, however undeserving.

He put a bony arm around my shoulder, in a particularly open expression of warmth.

Without batting an eyelid, he asked, "So, Jayram*bhai,* being a Hindu, what made you come here to work with us?"

"Well, I'm not really a follower of any religion." I replied, still a little irritated. "I just believe in humanity. We're all human after all."

He continued, like this was nothing new to him, "I know all that, but I also heard you condemning your religion once. I want to know if that is because you're working here."

I didn't know what he was talking about.

"I don't think I understand. When did I condemn any religion?" I asked.

I was curious now to see where this conversation was going. I shifted a little to face him more, giving my full attention now.

"A few weeks back." he replied, assuredly. "I remember the three of you sitting here, along with some woman from Delhi I think. You said some horrible things about your religion, when you said that you didn't believe in god any more, that Ram or any god who makes people kill others was not worth believing in any more. You also said that you would never ever follow any religion ever again. Remember? You were very angry, and I was sitting at my table over there with the cash register, so I was able to hear everything."

I jogged my memory. Every day was crazy here, so my weeks and months had turned into a blur. But I knew what he was talking about. It was a conversation, as usual, about the violence, and I had gone on another empty rant about religious fundamentalists.

I still couldn't quite understand where he was going with this though. Did he think I would convert to Islam now? He was a good deal older than I, so maybe he thought that I could be brought into the fold by him.

I nodded softly, "Yes, I remember now. But what is it about that comment that is troubling you uncle? It's definitely not because I work here. I love the work here. I just condemn what happened in the name of religion and don't want religion in my life anymore."

He shook his head dramatically, "Ya Allah! I need to talk to you about this very thing! I wanted to tell you...I think you are a great person for coming here, so far from home, and doing so much good work with these two wonderful young men. But my son, you're very wrong to be saying things like that about Ram, and your religion."

I was a little taken aback. Vijay and Nasir chuckled a little at my surprise. I couldn't fathom why.

I replied as politely as I could, "Um...ok...but I don't understand uncle. Why would you care about what I say about my own religious traditions if it's used by some people for such evil purposes?"

He shook his head again.

Trying to reassure him, I added, "I uh...I hope you know, uncle, that I would never insult *your* religion, or any religion for that matter, and of course I would never question anyone's right to believe in whatever they would like to believe in. I just don't want any religion in *my* personal life."

He nodded as if that wasn't even the problem, "I know my son. I know you would not say anything like that. You have come here so far from home to work for people from a different community. Of course I know you will defend anyone's right to their religion."

His eyes widened as he continued, "But that day when you described how angry you were with the Hindus here, and what they did, the way you said it made it look like you're angry at the entire religion. When I heard that, when I heard what you said, I couldn't sleep my son," he said, raising his hands a little bit to the heavens, and shaking his head.

"I tossed and turned all night," he continued, still

shaking his head, "and then late in the night Allah told me to talk to you about it, and convince you of your wrongs. Allah told me to tell you that you shouldn't discard your faith as a Hindu. Allah told me that He will love you even more if you follow your religion, and you will surely come to heaven. So I really wanted to tell you this."

I listened. Dumbfounded. Even Vijay and Nasir were a little surprised.

He continued with the same warmth, like he was talking to a precocious child, "See my son. None of your gods are bad. They're all great. Lord Ram was a great god. Only some of the people who invoke his name, they are bad. See, there are bad people in all religions. You shouldn't condemn your religion because of a few bad people who think they're Hindus. They're not Hindus. They're just using such a wonderful religion for their own purposes."

I puffed on my cigarette, taking another sip of tea. What he said was touching to say the least.

I replied, "I know uncle. I never meant to condemn all Hindus, or the entire religion. I was just saying that for me the only thing that mattered was humanity, and not religion. Religion should never be placed above humanity."

I noticed Vijay nodding in full agreement with what I was saying, while Nasir seemed to be more on the side of the owner, though still acknowledging me.

The old man retorted, "Of course my son. But without a belief in god, without a belief in the almighty, how will you survive in this world? You do such wonderful work, but you need to have that belief, otherwise it will be very difficult for you to come through difficult times. The *Quran* says that we all must have that belief, and submit ourselves to the almighty, otherwise it will be impossible to surpass tragedy or loss."

I politely repeated my earlier assertion, "But uncle, I don't say that people shouldn't believe what they want to. In fact I will defend and fight for the rights of everyone to believe what they would like to as long as it doesn't hurt people. I'm just saying that *I* would rather believe in humanity than in some system of religious belief for myself. It helps me survive in this world better."

He didn't relent. "But son, listen to me, our faith *is* our humanity." he said, clasping his palms tightly for effect. "And without our faith, we cannot have as much belief in humanity. Without god what is a human being? Nothing. Just flesh. That's why Allah told me to convince you to go back to your faith, to go back to believing in the wonderful gods you have. Allah told me this, my son, and He will love you for it. You don't have to be Muslim to have Allah's love."

There was a pause in the conversation now.

I looked at his eyes, set deep under his wrinkled brow. There was a passion in them. For a moment it was just the two of us. Vijay and Nasir ceased to exist. This was the first real conversation I had ever had with this man whose tea shop I had been coming to almost every day for the past few months. I didn't say anything. It was obvious that he was arguing from a core belief, one of those perspectives that give us reason for living. I would never have been able to convince him to move a millimetre from that position.

I slowly understood the nuance with which he was talking to me though. I think my condemnation of religion as a tool to oppress people was taken by him as a full condemnation of religion itself, which was not far from the truth. He wanted me to be religious, not just because he wanted me to have the security of faith, but also because it validated his own belief system. It didn't matter whether it was Hinduism or Islam or Christianity. For him, all that mattered was whether or not one had faith.

The fallouts of religion sometimes sprang some surprises on me. There was an irrational construct of faith, of belief, present in all religions that, funnily enough, united them all. This gentle, warm man in a Muslim prayer cap and with *henna*-dyed hair said nothing too different than my uber-religious grandmother who claimed the high ground of Hindu piety, or one of my best friends in our college band who refused to play bass guitar for our cover of *Hotel California* because he considered it anti-Christian. They all said the same, irrational thing. We need faith. God. Without this rigid system of belief we won't have anything to turn to when the rational world ceases to work in our favour. They all parroted the same thing like it was oxygen to them.

And yet, there was something beautiful about what this man was telling me. True, he was trying to convince me of something that I would never be convinced of. All I had seen of religion, *all* religion, was that it was a system of control. I did like a lot of what was said in the various good books I had read. But it was the lack of discourse, lack of thinking for oneself, lack of evolution in thought that irritated me. The fact that I couldn't challenge or disagree with it, have a discussion on it that could improve it conceptually, the blind obduracy of it all, was something I couldn't stand. And I hated, *hated*, religious leaders who controlled people.

But this man was not exemplifying any of that. He genuinely cared for me in a weirdly parochial way. He didn't want me to suffer any bad times. And in his worldview, he felt that I would best be able to avoid that suffering by staying rooted in faith – *my* faith, not his, which was what particularly endeared me to his paternalistic advice.

What he said didn't change my beliefs one bit, but after a long pause, I clasped his hand and said to him, "I promise you uncle, I will take your advice fully into my heart for the rest of my life. Thank you so much for telling me this."

He smiled. Wide. So wide that I could see the *gutka* stains in a good number of his teeth. I smiled back at him with what I hoped was equal warmth. But I decided not to tell him that he was living, albeit somewhat ironic, proof that humanity was far greater than all religions combined. It didn't want to risk losing that smile.

~ Chapter 23 ~

After Uma had told Vijay, Nasir and I about the woman in the Gulbarg Society camps who had witnessed all the bloodshed, I promptly went and told Mani. Although he had assumed some leadership of the movement at large, he was primarily coordinating the health unit. He said that he would like to talk to her to start her on some trauma counselling. A lot of the trauma counselling was primarily to ensure that those who survived could at least continue a semblance of life again and also to prevent potential suicides. So whenever volunteers met survivors, especially vulnerable ones like elders or children, who had witnessed tremendous bloodshed, it was our prerogative to inform the leaders of the campaign so they could take appropriate action in trying to heal that person.

The camps all over the city were slowly starting to wind down. This was primarily because of the apathy and hostility of the Gujarat government. The Chief Minister wanted to showcase normalcy to the rest of India by portraying the state-funded – and non-existent – relief program as a success. The steady progress of the livelihood-generation and house-reconstruction projects of the campaign occurred despite government apathy. However, while very few people actually slept at the camps, we couldn't afford to close them down because many still hung around there during the day either waiting for rations, livelihood materials and housing materials, or to attend community meetings in order to talk about the most salient needs they had.

Through Nasir, I learnt from Uma that the woman we needed to meet, Naseema Bibi, was in the camp that day. So Mani and I travelled together that morning from the BSC campus in an auto rickshaw to the Gulbarg Society camp.

"So Jayram, how have things been going?" he asked me, in his thickly Tamil-accented English. "You seem to have settled down really well here. A couple of us at the coordinators meeting were talking about the wonderful work you're doing with Vijay and Nasir. Very happy to see the three of you working so hard."

I smiled with pride.

"Thanks Mani." I said, as we trundled across the

Sabarmati. "It was tough at the beginning. But it's amazing to work with Vijay and Nasir. Also Maria and Abhay help me figure out what to do at times when I'm a little stuck. It's great to be with such wonderful people. I feel really lucky."

He replied with a paternal smile, "That's good, very good. You have to take care of yourself when doing this kind of work. Ensure you support each other. If you're not strong and healthy in every way, you won't be able to fight for the rights of others. You're one of the longest-serving volunteers. I think only Abhay and Maria have been here longer than you, and that too just a couple of weeks longer. We're really glad that you all have this dedication. Most of these kids come for a short while and then leave."

I remembered the early cantankerousness that Mani had showed when I first got to Ahmedabad. I now understood why that was, but it was nice that he had shifted so much in his attitude towards me. Especially in the last couple of months, when he saw that I was eager to learn and put in the hard hours. He was friendly to me whenever I met him, which was once every few days usually to update him on work in Gomtipur or get some instructions for ongoing projects.

"Well, whatever it is, it's great to be around lovely people who care about the world. I just love it. It's not something that others wouldn't do if given a chance." I said, trying to sound gracious.

Mani smiled knowingly, like he could see straight through my facade of false-humility. And false it was indeed; it wasn't just a purer ideal of social justice that drove me to do this. One of the reasons was because of the camaraderie it brought with it, and the spirit of encouragement. It genuinely *felt* good to be with people that were engaged in this kind of work, to be able to say that I did good work. And to get their tip-of-the-hat was awesome. I revelled in it. It gave my ego a huge boost and pushed me to work harder.

Mani and I reached the Gulbarg Society camp where Vijay, Nasir and Uma were waiting for us at the entrance. I had called Uma from the BSC office phone before leaving so they knew we were coming. I caught Vijay's eye and smiled at him.

He nodded back without gesturing too much. Whenever I interacted with Vijay and Nasir in front of Mani, our usual back-slapping bonhomie receded. They would act more formal, like we were three students talking to our school principal. It was irritating, because it highlighted the power differential between Mani and the three of us. And the fact that I talked less deferentially with Mani than they did, further indicated the power differential between me and them. I wanted to erase that differential because it made me uncomfortable and forced me to be more reflective than I cared to be. Easier said than done of course. Vijay and Nasir trusted me, despite my coming from a much more privileged background, but they didn't trust Mani. They would revert back to our ways of comradeship only when he was not around.

Mani and I stepped out of the auto rickshaw. He started paying the driver, while I walked up to the three of them standing at the entrance. I shook hands with Vijay and Nasir, while touching my chest politely to greet Uma.

I asked, "So where is Naseema Bibi? Is she in the camp or do we need to go to her house?"

"She's in her house Jayram*bhai*." Nasir replied. "It would be best that you and Mani sir go there with Uma*behen*. Vijay and I will wait for you at the camp office. We have to take care of some work anyway with some people in the community."

I nodded and said, "Ok. That's probably best. I don't know what we can do though. I think Mani just wants to at least ensure that she's eating something properly, drinking water, taking care of herself. Then later he might want to start some proper care, and ensure she has some livelihood and all. I think he'll also try and get her together with some family she has in Vatwa, I think. That's what you said right Uma*behen*?"

Uma replied, "Yes Jayram*bhai*. She has some family members in Vatwa that she can be with. At least she will be with people who care for her. She won't be alone. She had already lost her husband before the *dhamaal*, and her children were grown up, had left the house to other towns for work. So she was basically alone, but now it's probably better for her to be with family."

Mani soon walked our way. The three of them immediately straightened up a little. He shook Vijay's and Nasir's hands, while respectfully nodding at Uma. All three greeted him with deference.

Mani asked, in formal Hindi, Tamil accent and all, "So, what's the situation brothers and sisters? How're things running in the camps? Are you all managing well?"

All of us nodded.

"Things are going well Mani sir." Vijay said, with the same commanding tone, now tinged with a little reverence. "Sometimes it takes time to deliver the materials for the people, either for their livelihood or housing. They then get angry and we have to also be stern, and say that we're doing our best."

Nasir nodded, and said, "That's right Mani sir. We are able to do good work but it's sometimes tough to get it all done in quick time because things on the ground are not as smooth as what the coordinators of the campaign would like them to be. And the community sometimes blame us because we're the people they see. But overall, it's good...we have a great rapport with the community mostly."

Mani, who probably hadn't really dealt directly with the travails of work on the ground, said a little patronizingly, "Of course, of course. But you should not get angry with them. They're after all suffering a great deal. Whatever they say, we have to do our work with a smile. We have to show compassion at all times."

I wondered if Mani had truly internalized that Vijay and Nasir *were* from the community, so the need for artificial sweetness was something they couldn't afford. It was easy for people like Mani or I to put on a fake smile in the face of angry folk from a community we weren't really a part of. We just left for our worlds, so it didn't matter if they didn't see us for who we truly were. Vijay, Nasir and Uma couldn't afford to take that chance. They had to have an honest engagement, even if it included bitterness and anger. When they went home, they went to the same community they worked in.

Vijay and Nasir nodded. I knew it was because of Mani's age and station in life though, rather than anything he was saying.

Once the pleasantries were over, Mani asked, "So Uma, we should see this Naseema Bibi, yes? I want to make sure she is at least eating properly, and taking care of herself. We can then later start some proper treatment for her, and make sure she has some support system in place."

Uma replied, "Ok Mani sir. Let's go to her house. She's expecting us. I told her yesterday that you would be coming along with Jayram*bhai*."

I didn't know why I had to be one of the people meeting her. I went along nevertheless, just in case there was something, anything, I could do. Vijay and Nasir told me they would be at the camp office checking in on some work. Mani, Uma and I walked across the camp, where there weren't many people around, save a few children playing cricket with an old bat and rubber ball by the graveyard. They had placed a few sturdy-looking stones one on top of the other to serve as a wicket. They were screaming in laughter as they ran around.

I secretly wished I was playing with them.

The three of us made our way past the graveyard and exited the camp. I had not seen much of Gulbarg Society, since most of my work was in Gomtipur. I was amazed at the extent of the damage. Gomtipur had more open spaces but Gulbarg Society, especially the part where the most bloodshed occurred, was walled in. It was a slightly better-off community, evidenced by the fact that a former Member of Parliament lived there. We walked past that area, and I could imagine the carnage. At least in Gomtipur, there were escape routes. In Gulbarg Society, if the mobs had come in through the main road, they would have completely cornered the community. A massacre would have been easy.

There weren't any people there. The houses were all still charred. The results of the violence were plainly evident. I saw a slightly larger two-storey house as we walked by. Uma pointed to it, and told us that it was the residence of Ehsan Jaffrey, where many people came to be shielded from the mobs to no avail. His house was probably the largest in the community.

Mani and I looked at it without saying a word. The familiar chill crept up my spine again. I had now become more adept at blocking it and preventing it from moving upwards. I

gritted my teeth. I did that a lot now and immediately dug my
thumbs into my kidneys. This helped again in preventing the
chill from affecting the rest of my body.

We walked past the locality with me digging both my
hands surreptitiously up my sides and tightening my stomach
muscles.

We finally got to the house of Naseema Bibi. The
entire house was no bigger than my living room in Bangalore.
Inside was a small room that served as a bedroom cum TV-
viewing room cum living room, and adjacent to it was a small
alcove that acted as the kitchen. There was almost no
ventilation. The bathroom was attached just outside, only a
little bigger than my wardrobe in Bangalore. The entire house
had corrugated tin sheets for roofing. The same tin sheets that
had been distributed weeks before.

These were the houses they destroyed?

Naseema Bibi came out of the alcove that was the
kitchen and asked us politely to sit down on the bed. All three
of us sat on the bed, while she sat on a floor mat. She was
sweating, and wiped her brow with her *dupatta*. She was old,
old enough to be Mani's mother probably, but looked strong.
Her cracked hands and calloused feet were lined with fading
henna, and showed a life of hard toil. We sat there smiling at
her. She had a vacant look. Uma made to say something when
we heard a hiss from the kitchen. The milk had boiled over.
Naseema Bibi immediately got up, and went to the stove. She
poured four cups of tea and brought them to us.

We took our teas and sipped them. She sat down
again. She was going through the motions of politeness to
guests, but her eyes were distant. She was not present. It
wouldn't have taken a particularly sharp person to know that
this woman had seen too much. She was on the edge.

Uma spoke first.

"Naseema *aapa*, this is Mani sir and Jayram*bhai*." she
said, sweetly. "Mani sir wanted to talk to you to make sure
you're taking care of yourself, and wanted to see if there's
anything we can do for you. You can tell him whatever you
want. Jayram*bhai* works with me in the camps, so we can try to
get you whatever support you need."

Naseema Bibi nodded mechanically. The distant look

in her eyes didn't change. She looked like she had given up.

Mani asked, "Naseema*ji* I wanted to know how you are doing. We know you've seen a lot. We want to make sure you're at least eating properly, drinking water."

Naseema Bibi looked out the window with the same vacant stare, and said, "Allah will take care of me. I've now come to the end."

Mani continued, "Are you ok? Please tell us if there's anything we can do."

She continued, shifting her empty gaze to the floor, "What is there to do for me *baba*? I am finished. What is there to live for after all this?"

Mani asked softly, "Please tell us what you're feeling now. We will help in whichever way we can. Please..."

There was a pause. She had one hand on a raised knee, half covering her mouth, as she squatted on the floor. She kept staring at the ground. Her tea cup, still full, milk starting to cream over, was on the floor beside her. In her other hand, I noticed Muslim prayer beads that she held onto in a vice-like grip.

"They came in hordes." she then said, without any warning.

Mani sat up now.

"Don't know why they hate us so much. What have we done to them?" she continued. "I ran to Jaffrey*saab*'s colony, like the others. They were already there, and had surrounded his house. So many people were in there. I hid in one of the neighbour's houses, and saw everything through the mirror."

She was still gazing at the ground.

"Women...men...children...all slaughtered...what all they did." she said, her tone getting louder, slapping her knee now in a steady rhythm. "Ya Allah...what all they did!"

She was phantom-like. Her eyes could only see what happened that day, the images forever seared in her memory. She lifted her face and looked out of the window. She couldn't bear to see us. Her vacant gaze had transformed into one of death; morbid and red-eyed.

"I saw Jaffrey*saab* come out with his arms raised, trying to pacify the mobs." she continued. "They pushed him around. Threw him to the ground. Stamped on him. They asked him to shout 'Jai Sri Ram!' and he refused, begging them to leave the people alone. They butchered him, cut each of his fingers first, before killing him. They burnt the house with everyone in it. The women whom they caught...Ya Allah...they didn't just kill them...that would have been better. They then killed everyone, cut them up with swords, and then piled up the bodies and set them on fire."

I started shivering. I pressed my thumbs deep into the sides of my abdomen. It didn't work. I could feel my stomach turn and the bile rise up in my throat.

Mani tried to interject, "Mother...you should try to ensure that there is some support for you. You shouldn't be alone after what you have seen."

She didn't hear him. Her deathly gaze didn't flinch. She banged her open palm against her forehead. It was like a thunder clap. Her bangles jingled violently. She hit her forehead again. And again, and again. She let out a monotonic wail, a sound that was beyond anguish, like it was coming from her gut, not her throat.

"ALLAH!!! Please take me away from this nightmare! Take me to your arms...please! Ya Allah...save me from this hell...save me, save me, save me...ALLAH SAVE ME!"

The words rang out in a banshee-like howl.

Mani tried again, his tone sounding more desperate now, "Mother! Please go and stay with your family in Vatwa. They will at least take care of you, and make sure you're eating properly. Please mother...we'll arrange for whatever you need."

She wasn't listening. She hadn't heard a thing. I could sense my body reacting violently inside me and found it hard to control the quivering.

Mani looked at her. He knew it was a lost cause.

"Mother...we'll ensure Uma keeps checking in on you." he still implored, the futility evident in his voice. "We'll arrange for some transportation to Vatwa, where you can stay with your family. Till then, mother, please drink at least 3-4 glasses of water every day. Eat something three times a day. Please mother. Please! We'll try to do whatever we can for you. Please just take care of yourself."

The directness in Mani's voice shook her out of her

reverie. She didn't say anything, but was in immense distress. Mani looked at Uma and me, indicating that it was probably time to leave. Before we could get up, Naseema Bibi got up hastily and came up to us, abruptly placing her hand on each of our foreheads one by one, tugging our hair a little, like a blessing she was giving to her three children. A soft, low wail emanated from her as she did this.

A tear drop rolled down my cheek. We left after politely saying our byes, with Mani repeating that Uma would come back to check in on her. She didn't say a word, just walked to the doorway with us, the empty look not leaving her countenance. The low wail emanating from her gut hauntingly followed us as we walked away.

The three of us walked back the way we came. We didn't say a word to each other. Mani and Uma weren't reacting the way I was, though I had calmed down now. I couldn't understand what happened to me. It wasn't like it was the first time hearing about the killings. I had heard much of the same with other residents. None of what she had said was new. Maybe it was because of the conditions she lived in to begin with before the mobs came. She was dirt poor, and the only thing she had was her humanity, and they wanted to take that away too. Or maybe it was because she wasn't really present the entire time. It was like she had been stuck in a traumatic time warp.

We walked past the central colony of Gulbarg Society again, past Jaffrey's house. I was barely able to look at it.

We met up with Vijay and Nasir at the camp office. I planned on staying back to continue the tasks for the day with them, while Mani would head back to the BSC office. He bid goodbye to them, thanking them for their work.

Then, turning to me, he said, "Jayram, please walk with to me to the rickshaw stand."

I wondered what he wanted to talk specifically to me about. We walked across the camp towards the auto rickshaw stand.

"Look Jayram," he told me in a disciplinary tone, as we walked, "you should know that showing your emotions in front of those who have suffered is not a very useful thing at all. We must be strong. All of us will go through what you went through, but we cannot, simply cannot, show that to the victims. That's not good."

I looked ahead as we walked, internalizing what he said. I felt foolish now for having become so emotional in front of Naseema Bibi.

He continued, "You should seek support from your friends and fellow activists. But we must not put ourselves in a position where we're too weak to be able to fight. Else it becomes about us, and it's not about us, it's about them! You're doing good work Jayram, but you still have a lot to learn."

It was a reprimand. I took it, and deserved it. He was right, especially about making it about me. But I hated the fact that I had to conceal emotion. I couldn't figure out why that was necessary. It just seemed a little cold. I nodded nevertheless.

We reached the auto rickshaw stand and beckoned for a driver. It was someone I knew well, so he knew exactly where to go. As Mani got into the rickshaw, he put a paternal palm on my shoulder and gave it a squeeze.

"Don't worry Jayram. We all have our moments of weakness. I know you'll come through this well, and continue doing good work."

I smiled. There was genuine warmth in his voice, even as he disciplined me.

"Thanks Mani."

~ Chapter 24 ~

In Bangalore I used to enjoy a drink or two with friends every couple of weeks. But I never needed alcohol to have a good time. I might have smoked a grand total of two cigarettes in the first twenty-two years of my life before I came to Ahmedabad. But it was never a stress-reliever. In fact I was vehemently anti-smoking and hated the idea of alcoholism. I was an athlete, and a decent one at that. The idea of regular smoking and boozing was an abomination to what I wanted to see myself achieve physically. As a young teenager, I had even thought of maybe taking up athletics professionally for a few years. Give it a shot, I thought, I might make it. Had dreams of becoming India's first Olympic medallist in track and field. My dreams of Olympic glory were summarily dashed through a combination of hard realization in my lack of talent and the fact that I had a much better chance of a good life via pursuits of the mind. But I still ran regularly, participated in amateur road races, and did pushups to stay strong. I never once thought I would be a smoker and compulsive alcoholic. Within a few weeks of coming to Ahmedabad, I was drinking and smoking every day.

Woke up in the morning – tea and a cigarette with Abhay and Maria.

Crossed the river – cigarette on the auto rickshaw journey over.

Finished a stressful meeting or complete surveys – cigarette with tea.

Took a break during distribution – cigarette with Vijay.

Had a late lunch or snack – cigarette while chewing paan.

Crossed the river back to Maria and Abhay – bootlegged whisky, with a few cigarettes.

Ate some dinner that I was barely interested in – cigarette before going to bed.

Woke up the next morning – repeated everything.

Vijay, who offered me my first cigarette when I came here, had begun saying that I smoked too much. Abhay, who was a

fellow smoker in the mornings and evenings with me, said
that he was worried that I was smoking way more than he
was. Maria hated kissing me after I smoked, and threw away
my pack of cigarettes in disgust on more than one occasion.
Nasir would constantly try and get me to quit out of concern
for my health.

I laughed them all off.

Food, which was one of my biggest pleasures, now
tasted awful. I didn't enjoy eating any more the way I used to.
I looked it as a chore rather than an enjoyment. Exercise,
which was something I was obsessed with in my college days,
had all but disappeared from my life. All I craved were
cigarettes and booze.

I had heard that most smokers and drinkers got
addicted in their teenage years. Not so with me. I got addicted
at the relatively ripe old age of twenty-two, and it took all of a
few days in a miserable hell hole for it to happen.

The ironic part was that the hell hole was one of the
only states in India where prohibition laws were in place. An
old colonial era law of sorts that prohibited the sale, purchase
or manufacture of alcohol. It was ridiculous of course. The
zenith of hypocrisy in the anti-bacchanalian legal system was
that Gujarat, with all its pseudo-Hindu piety, had one of the
highest per-capita alcohol consumption rates in the country.
An intricate network of legal loopholes and lax enforcement
made sure that those who wanted to drink, could. The poor
drank hooch. The rich got hard-to-obtain purchasing-licenses.
The rest of us went to bootleggers for cheap whisky.

I knew about the bootlegging operations from Vijay,
who had worked for one himself. He told me that the guy
paid him some money to go to the border of the state on his
motorcycle, strap on bottles of whisky onto his body, cover
himself with a jacket, and ride back. It was decent money, but
he became too scared of getting caught. With good reason
too. It would have meant a nasty beating at the hands of the
cops, usurpation of the booze, and a potentially dangerous
bootlegger on his tail for payback. So he stopped running
booze after a few weeks at the job. He did hook us up with a
guy to get our stuff though.

Our bootlegger was a guy going by the moniker

"KC." It must have stood for something but it didn't matter. He got us our booze. We weren't exactly spoiled for choice. We just drank whatever he had at that time, at slightly higher rates than the rest of the country. Mostly whisky. But once in a while we would get a nice bottle of rum or vodka. It provided an artificial reason to drink some more.

We had many of those – reasons to drink.

One of the volunteers found out they got a job – booze.

Another just heard that they had become an aunt – booze.

Someone's birthday – cake and booze.

The reason didn't matter really. If we weren't able to manufacture any, we drank to relieve the stress. All that mattered was having a bit of fun. Lots of laughter. Anything to forget what we had seen or heard during the day. Maria, Abhay and I especially craved it. We had been around longer than any other outside volunteer. The booze and laughter kept us going I think. I know it certainly kept me going. It wasn't healthy, but we weren't exactly in the land of salubrity.

~ Chapter 25 ~

Things were starting to slowly unravel for me, and the process was manifesting first with Maria. Our relationship had hit a bit of a bump on the road. The headiness of the initial few weeks of our courtship had long passed. But that wasn't the real core of the problem.

The place was getting to me. And I irrationally blamed the people around me, on both sides of the river.

I started acting crotchety with everyone around me and the smallest things became sources of irritation. Vijay and Nasir were spared some of it, because there was so much work to be done that I rarely had time to be irritated with them. But the passion had ebbed. I did it because I knew it had to be done. Both of them, bless their souls, did their best to ease my mood, offering to take up a larger share of the tasks at hand. But the work was also the one thing that kept me going.

Maria faced the brunt of my irascible behaviour. I kept pushing her affections away, and she had no idea why I was being so hurtful. Abhay tried his best to lighten the tension between us. It worked, if only temporarily. Soon, the only way Maria and I could laugh with each other was when he was around. Because the three of us lived together, often with other short-term volunteers, this was generally the norm. But the times when the two of us were alone was choleric.

The downward freefall of my moods did more than just cause a rift between Maria and me.

It was late afternoon one day. I returned early from the camps to the apartment. I needed to write up a small report on the livelihood generation project for the coordinators of the campaign. I found Maria in the living room, packing. She was heading to Mumbai for a few days to meet her mother, and check in on the editing for the documentary she had completed before coming to Gujarat. I was secretly happy that she was making the trip. It was a welcome break from the tension that existed between us. But I also knew that I wanted her to come back. I would have been desperately sad if she had left for good.

The tension was palpable as I put my backpack down and went to kiss her. The kiss was brief, neither of us wanting to linger, merely going through the motion of greeting each other as a couple. The ease with which we shared our love, the comfortable silences, the unencumbered intimacy, the gentle bond – all of that was gone. It was difficult. It was the kind of shroud-like stress that increased the intake of cigarettes and alcohol.

I went to the kitchen and poured myself a drink from the whisky we had procured a couple of days back. The bottle was already half empty. I took my drink, lit a cigarette, and sat in a corner of the living room. Maria continued packing. I penned through an old magazine that was lying on the floor. I was in no mood to write the report. I was in a sullen mood whenever I was around her now and just about anything ticked me off.

I asked her in a disinterested tone, not bothering to look up from the magazine I held, "So, what's this documentary that you're checking in on the editing for?"

I knew it was about caste-violence and the movement fighting it in Maharashtra but asked anyway.

She replied sharply, "You know what it's about. Or did you forget already? We talked about it a few weeks back. It's about the Dalit liberation movement, following in the footsteps of Ambedkar. At the time you said you were really inspired by it. Maybe you were drunk."

Maria had an acid tongue, but not as bad as mine.

"Yeah I must have been a little drunk." I replied, mockingly. "Anyway, sorry to make you repeat it. You obviously are too busy to have a decent conversation."

She swatted away my attempt at sarcasm without a pause from her packing.

"Don't talk crap Jay." she angrily said. "You knew what the documentary was all about. You even asked some incisive questions about it. So don't give me this shit about you not knowing. You're just trying to rile me up."

I didn't say anything. I continued to look down at the magazine without registering what was on the pages. I tried to make like I didn't care but was angry that my petulance was so sharply found out and thwarted.

Still not looking up from the magazine, I said in a condescending tone, "Well, anyway...I think I must have just been trying to make you feel better, when I said I liked it."

She didn't say anything but I could sense her getting angrier as she continued packing, which gave me more fuel.

"I don't know what Dalit liberation you're talking about." I continued in the same tone. "But in Karnataka with reservation for everything, all these lower castes get everything they need....seats in college, jobs. The upper caste folk always have to fight on merit. We don't have reserved seats for us. So maybe you should take that into account too for what you're doing with this documentary of yours."

Maria was livid. She knew I was debasing myself just to get her riled up. She stood up from packing and looked directly at me, arms akimbo. She was almost quivering with rage.

"You petulant BRAT!" she exploded. "What the fuck do you know about what Dalits go through, huh? Don't talk garbage just for the sake of trying to make people angry. Asshole!"

I didn't look up and pretended like what she said didn't matter. But I was kidding myself. What she said stung, and for all the reasons that she intended it to. She was peeved at me as her boyfriend, but she was particularly angry at me as her comrade.

I was unwilling to budge at that moment however. I continued flipping the pages of the magazine without looking up, took a sip from my drink and a drag from my cigarette.

"You can call me whatever you want Maria." I said, in the same tone. "I can't argue with you when you're like this. *You're* the one who's acting petulant. All I said was something normal and you're acting like I killed someone."

This infuriated her even more. Her eyes were red with anger. I had never seen her in such a quivering rage. Her tone got a little quieter, but angrier.

"The reason I'm so furious Jayram," she replied, in simmering rage, "is precisely *because* this sort of thinking kills people! Whether it's with Dalits or Muslims or women or whatever marginalized group...just because you don't go and physically oppress them, doesn't mean that you're not part of the social and cultural system that does! Who the hell do you think you are to be talking about them in this way anyway, when you have no idea what they go through?"

She paused to see if I would respond. She was breathing hard with rage now. I didn't say anything. She never called me by my full name unless she was furious. I was now a little scared. I could take Maria being angry with the way I was as a boyfriend, but not as a comrade. I didn't have the courage now to look her in the eye.

She hurled a book she was packing in anger at my silence. It smashed against the wall and thudded onto the floor. I flinched a little.

"The worst part, the worst fucking part," she continued unrelentingly, "is that unlike those other privileged assholes, you don't even have the excuse of ignorance on your side! If you're angry or pissed off at me for whatever bloody reason, that's one thing...but don't ever, don't you ever fucking talk about people who go through horrendous oppression and then belittle their resistance, without knowing what the fuck you're talking about! I will never talk to you again, as long as I live if you pull this bullshit again!"

I continued looking down at the magazine, still too scared to look up at her. She kicked her suitcase away in disgust and stomped off enraged to the kitchen, not waiting for me to respond. I caught a glimpse of the hot tears starting to flow from her eyes as she hurried away.

I was completely beaten down. It wasn't just the shit I said that got her angry. I had said equally stupid and offensive stuff before in earlier conversations soon after we met up. But conversations with Maria and Abhay helped change that, and aided in my growth. This time it wasn't coming from a place of ignorance. It was malicious, devoid of innocence, and she would have none of it.

I sat and continued taking small swigs from my drink, and lit up another cigarette. The intensity of her reprimand was slowly sinking in. I was still angry and feeling morose about the whole thing, but somewhere deep inside me I also knew I was wrong. I could feel the sadness well up in me. But the anger I noticed was a different anger; one directed at myself, stemming from shame. I didn't know what to do as my feelings vacillated between petulant defence and honest acceptance.

I got up to pace the room, feeling claustrophobic in my thoughts. As I got up, I could feel the effects of the whisky and swooned a little. I paced the room for a few minutes, puffing away, with the drink in my hand. The entire living room was a little smoky now.

I felt like dirt. I made my way to the kitchen, and could see Maria's back through the screen door separating the kitchen from the attached veranda. She was leaning against the metal railing, looking ahead in the distance. The clothes we had put up to dry the night before were fluttering in the wind. As I looked closer, I could see a drink in her hand. I noticed the opened whisky bottle near the stove. I got a little worried. Over the last few days, she had started drinking to forget the pain I was causing her.

I walked towards the veranda, stopping to pour in a little whisky, and opened the screen door. She turned her head at me. It was obvious that she had been crying. Angrily. Dried tears along her soft cheeks were set in contrast against the deep disappointment and aggravation in her eyes. I went and stood by her. She shifted away from me in disgust. There must have been something in my expression that expressed remorse and weakness though because, despite shifting away, her face softened a little.

She asked irritably, "What do you want Jay? Can't you just leave me alone?"

Her reverting back to my term of endearment made me feel better.

I stuttered, "Listen...Maria...uh...I'm sorry. I don't know what I was thinking. I shouldn't have talked to you like that."

It only worked in part.

"It's not just the way you talked to me Jay." she retorted, still angry but now softer. "It's what you said. I'm not that angry with you about the tensions in our relationship. It's what you said about Dalits that is pissing me off. If we're having problems as a couple, that's one thing. We can figure it out, and I might be angry at you, but not the kind of rage I felt when you said what you said. Like an ignorant buffoon, you just said the same nonsense that all these upper-caste people give."

She took a sip of her drink, and continued, "*That's* what made me angry Jay. It was immature, and worse, it was dehumanizing to so many people."

There was a pause. She was right and I had to own up to it.

"You're right. I'm sorry." I said, the sincerity in my voice coming more naturally now. "I was angry at this place, and it was starting to irritate me, it kept gnawing at me. I then forgot all that we had talked about that was so important for me to understand, and instead went back to that crap that I grew up with. I didn't believe in it, even as the words came out of my mouth. Really, please believe me."

I could feel the relief of truth flood over me. Maria looked at me. She didn't say anything, but I could see the affection once again. Tears welled up in her eyes, and she smiled.

I continued, "I need to learn how to separate things. I was getting angry at this place and I took it out on you all. But I also started getting angry at everything I associate with this place, even subconsciously. Things I didn't realize I was associating with this place."

I stopped to take a drag of my cigarette.

"It included everything that I've learnt from folks like you, Abhay, Vijay, Nasir," I continued, "because in my head, since it came from here, I started getting angry at that knowledge as well...I'm starting to hate this fucking place. That was wrong of me. I'm getting angry at the wrong things simply because it's within reach."

I paused and took a deep breath. My lips quivered as I exhaled. I think I apologized just as much because I feared losing her as I did to undo my shame. Maria held my hand over the rail. It was the first time there had been any real affection travel between us in what seemed like ages. She didn't say anything. She didn't have to. I felt a flood of painful happiness wash over me. It was like the feeling I used to get when I hadn't eaten all day, and suddenly had a bite of good food. My jowls ached with salivary excitement upon taking that first bite. It was the same feeling, the ache of bliss.

We stood on the veranda, sipping our whiskies. I lit up another cigarette, which we shared. Ahmedabad had cooled down following the monsoon, and the evening breeze was crisp. It was lovely to be with her on the veranda, our friction abating, at least for now.

Abhay soon walked into the kitchen, and waved at us. He was carrying food from a local *dhaba*. Through the kitchen window I spotted butter chicken, *palak paneer*, and *raitha* in clear plastic bags, as well as what must have been *naan* wrapped in aluminium foil. My mouth started watering. I felt my appetite return for the first time in days.

He placed the plastic bags on the counter next to the stove, poured himself a drink and joined us on the veranda, greeting us cheerfully. There were no other volunteers apart from the three of us. Abhay had valiantly laboured through the tension between Maria and me with his usual infectious smile and jokes. The place was getting to him too, but he was more concerned with our rift, and tried his best to ease the tension. He sensed the lightness in the atmosphere as he walked out onto the veranda. I immediately felt his relief.

He sat on one of the old wicker chairs and leaned against the wall, with a big smile on his face.

"Dinner's ready, comrades." he said, the happiness evident in his voice.

Maria and I smiled back at him.

He continued, "I decided to get some food for us...I know that both of you like our local *dhaba* so thought we could eat some of this and then go for a late-night show. I hear from my friends that one of the worst Hindi movies ever made has recently been released. *Jaani Dushman.* Apparently it was funded by the mafia in Mumbai, so they forced all these huge stars to act in it."

Maria and I looked at him incredulously, our smiles getting wider. He was excited, almost child-like.

He ended emphatically, "We *have* to see it. It's running in the local drive-in. The weather's nice, so we can take a few mats with us, and sit outside on the ground."

I started, "Um...wait, you want to see..."

He interrupted me with a dramatic shake of his head, "Nothing doing. No refusals. We're going to see the movie and that's that. We've been putting in maniacal hours. We deserve a break...and there's no break like a mafia-made Bollywood movie...especially when it takes itself so seriously."

Maria started giggling as he went on his description of the movie, and was laughing by now. It was lovely to hear her beautiful laugh again and see that wrinkle on her nose.

Abhay then said, without giving us a chance to respond, "*Chalo*, let's eat. I'm starving, and we should finish dinner and head to the theatre soon."

We headed in to feast on the food that Abhay had brought in. Dinner was amazing. When we first started eating together, months back, they had been amazed at my gargantuan appetite. Recently, Abhay had remarked a couple of times that I wasn't eating as much. I ate like a horse this time, as much as both of them combined. I noticed both of them becoming visibly happier.

We cleared up the dishes and soon headed over to the drive-in to see the worst movie I had ever seen in my life.

It was lovely. Pleasant. In the shortest of moments, we were back to being the comrades we were before depression hit us all.

~ Chapter 26 ~

The legislative elections were taking place in the state. There was a buzz around town. All the news channels and pollsters were predicting a close election, and there was a cautious optimism among all the volunteers in *Shanthi Samudaya*. It was a toss-up between the Hindu nationalist Bharatiya Janata Party – the same BJP that had conducted the carnage and governed the state – and the more secular, centrist Congress party. The political pundits were predicting that the violence the BJP had perpetrated was bound to backfire on them. Gujarat would not accept this sort of fascism and bigotry. When the results of the elections ultimately came in, it didn't surprise me.

I think the entire elections – the campaigning, the political speeches, the fight against fascism, the voting patterns, indeed the undeniable fact that democracy was ultimately about the will of the people exercising their inalienable right to representation of their choosing – could be encapsulated in a poster that I saw one day on an auto rickshaw ride back from the camps. It was barely a couple of seconds but the image was unforgettable.

The poster showcased what the elections were all about. A young, obviously Hindu, girl was pictured, crouched up against the wall, quivering hands on knees, eyes wide open, petrified with fear. A silhouette of a man, an obviously Muslim man, with a beard and traditional turban, was shown approaching her menacingly, his crooked hand raised with clearly malevolent intent. It was a graphic image that pushed the viewer to imagine what was about to take place, what that scary Muslim man was about to do to the trembling Hindu girl. Objectively speaking, it was brilliant cerebral manipulation. Nothing evoked fear like the unbound imagination of a brainwashed mind.

Underneath the image was pictured a saffron lotus, the party symbol of the BJP, and a single caption in Gujarati:
Apna Kaun?
Who will stand for us?

The BJP won the elections in a landslide.

~ Chapter 26.5 ~

The camps were starting to close down on orders from the Gujarat state government. The writing was on the wall ever since the elections ended and the incumbent government got voted back into power. We had been told as much the minute the results came in. You're on the clock, we were told; get the work done quickly because there's no predicting when the camps will be closed down.

The government never wanted to open the camps in the first place. It would have been an admission of guilt. Due to increasing pressure from human rights movements like *Shanthi Samudaya*, and civil liberties groups, a reluctant green signal was given for the camps to be opened; with scant help from the state though.

It was small mercy that the communities were slowly starting to rebuild their houses and get back into their regular work through the periodic, if haphazard, distribution of construction and livelihood materials.

It was nothing short of criminal, what was happening. After the carnage this was the proverbial salt on the wound. It also meant an ongoing transition for all of us towards community-organizing rather than emergency relief work. But we couldn't ever let go of relief work either. It was tough, and the balancing act often got the better of us. There were times when we had to figure out solutions on the fly.

We were having some trouble at the camps in Gomtipur with infighting among the residents. Both Maria and Abhay offered to come for a day or two with me to Gomtipur just to have another mind resolving the problems. Finally it was decided that Maria would come, since she was leaving in another day to Mumbai, and couldn't take on responsibilities for any new projects in Vatwa. I was a little nervous. I didn't know whether I was hoping she would come or not. We were doing a lot better following the night of our teary reconciliation, but there was still some way to go before we could get back to where we were. I was still feeling the shame of having said what I said. I didn't know whether it was because of what I said or because it made me look bad in front of Maria. It was probably a bit of both, but it was shame nonetheless.

She was gracious about it though, which made it easier. She didn't mention it again. She was back to her regular vivacious self; jokes, sharp politics and all. It helped deal with the rawness of my ignominy.

Maria and I hailed an auto rickshaw and made our way to the camps. Along the way we didn't talk much, but I could sense a happier energy as I sat next to her during the bumpy ride. I soon realized that I had a smile on my face which had crept up without my noticing it. She asked me how the work was going in Gomtipur. I updated her, and she was genuinely amazed at the progress that Vijay, Nasir and I had made, especially with the livelihood project. Her positive affirmation of our work did wonders for me. It was uplifting in a way I hadn't experienced in weeks.

We got to the camps and, after paying the driver, walked towards the camp office. By now, Maria had come with me enough number of times to the point that the obvious gawking had stopped, but people still cast a glance at her as we walked by them. With her smiling good-looks, clad in a jeans and *kurta*, she was difficult to avoid noticing. I had come on occasion to the camps with other female volunteers. Once in a while, Nasir or Vijay would joke around with me, calling me Romeo or *aashiqui*. It irked me a little to see Maria being objectified like that. But I knew both of them respected her a great deal, so went along with it.

We found Vijay and Nasir in the office having a loud argument with some of the camp residents. Their tone was a little harsher than I had seen before. Even the normally beatific Nasir was showing strains of anger. I could see the stress getting to both of them. Rations were dwindling, while materials for livelihood and house reconstruction were delayed again. And it didn't help that the camps were all but closed down completely except for distribution purposes. People were also asking questions on the surveys that we had been completing for the legal campaign. We were at a low point in terms of delivering materials, because our focus was shifting to community organizing, and materials were getting harder to procure. This was normal. The work often went in ups and downs. But there were still people who needed relief materials, and there just wasn't enough to go around, which made tempers fly.

Maria soon calmed things down. Seeing a new face among the volunteers acted as a temporary abatement of anger for the people. She also had an amazingly calming presence in the face of hostility. She gently asked Vijay and Nasir to step away from the crowd and towards me, and started talking to the crowd. Vijay and Nasir were only too glad to sit down near the entrance by me, with a sullen look on their faces. Maria faced the crowd, and gently directed their focus away from Vijay and Nasir. She asked them what the problem was.

One of them, a slightly older woman, said loudly but politely, "*Beti*, we are in need of rations right now while we're waiting for our livelihood materials. We've been waiting for the materials for so long. If they come, then we wouldn't need rations. But if we have to wait for our livelihood, then we don't have anything to buy food with. We are then forced to beg from our neighbours. How much can they help us?"

Another man piped in, "And we're not looking for charity. If we have something to do our work, we can get our own food, but how can we be forsaken like this, when we don't even have anything to buy food with?"

Maria said that something would be worked out, but also requested them for the same thing that Vijay and Nasir did, but in a much calmer way – their patience. She asked them to go to their houses or wait inside the vicinity of the camp.

"I promise you that we will do our level best to make sure something happens." she assured them in a calm tone. "If needed, I'll see if I can get some rations diverted from elsewhere if it's there. But please be patient. We can't do this if we have to fight with all of you as well...and we will do the best we can, I promise."

The last line especially calmed them down some more. They dispersed, and Maria walked towards the three of us.

She asked Vijay and Nasir, "Ok, so we have to find a way to get some rations...anything. They're obviously desperate. What are the options we have in front of us?"

"Maria*didi*, that's the problem." Vijay replied in frustration. "We don't have any options in front of us. We're not getting rations supply from the regular government source for another few days. Our other route also is closed down. We don't even have anything to exchange in the black market, otherwise we could have gone that route, like what we did a few times before. What else can we do?"

As Vijay ran through the lack of options to get rations, Nasir nodded with equal strain on his face. They needed a break from all this. I felt a wave of brotherly protection towards both of them as I saw the stress on their faces.

Maria said collectedly, "Ok...let's not fret. We have to think this through."

We looked back at her, hoping for an answer. We were obviously spent.

She continued, "If we stress, then we can't think clearly. Let's go through the different options in our head, and then we'll see which ones are at least possible to try. Maybe we can get a little from different places, and then at least deliver something that will tide over the people until regular rations arrive. Is there the possibility of maybe going to some other source that we haven't tried before?"

We sat around quietly and thought for a little while. My mind was blank, and I was willing to go with whatever suggestion anyone could come up with.

Vijay then straightened up from his hunched position. I could see a visible light-bulb moment on his face.

"There's one more possibility." he said.

Maria asked, "What is it?"

Vijay replied, still thinking about it, "It's only a possibility. I don't know...well...we have to see how it might come through."

I replied a little impatiently, "Whatever it is, let's try. If we don't get rations today, these people are not going to have food, and they're going to be really angry at us."

Vijay nodded.

"Ok, I'll see if my friend is still there." he said. "He can maybe help us in an emergency like this...or at least I hope so."

He left the office purposefully without telling us more. Maria, Nasir and I sat around looking at each other a little quizzically.

I asked Nasir, "Do you know where he's going?"

Nasir shrugged, "I don't know Jayram*bhai*, he has all kinds of contacts. Vijay was quite a street thug a couple of years back, a real *goonda*. His nickname on the street was Boxer...so maybe he's gone to get one of his old contacts. Who knows?"

I was a little unsure about this.

"Um...ok...but what has this got to do with getting rations?" I asked.

Vijay had mentioned to me in passing that he endured a pretty rough past as a street tough. It didn't bother me, especially as I had asked him for his bootlegging contacts on more than one occasion. I wasn't so sure about how it would pertain to us procuring rations though.

Nasir shrugged again, and said, "I don't know...you have to ask him."

We sat in silence for a couple more minutes, Maria and I exchanging looks, wondering what was going on and hoping for the best.

Vijay soon came back with one of the camp residents, a thin, toothy young man with a wispy moustache. He had a bit of a shifty grin that I couldn't quite place. Vijay introduced us and said, "He says that his boss can get us rations."

I looked at him and asked, "Really? That would be very helpful."

The young man nodded cockily, and with a wave of his hand, proudly proclaimed, "No problem *bhai*, my boss can get anything done. We'll go to him now. Come, come...let's go."

We got up and followed him out of the office. The swaggering punk led all of us down an alley across from the camp entrance, his irritating smile not leaving his face. We then turned onto the main road, and went towards what looked like a shop selling cheap Chinese-made goods.

The chap asked the man behind the counter, "Is our *saab* there? I have some folks who work at the camp with me who want to meet him."

The man behind the counter waved us through, and we made our way to the back of the shop

At the back of the shop was a large man sitting behind a lovely wooden desk with a shiny glass top. On the desk were a couple of gold-plated fountain pens, a stack of papers neatly arranged in one corner, and three phones, one black, one pink with gold sequins, and another rainbow-coloured. The wall was decorated with rich tapestry and gaudy pictures, as well as some Islamic symbols. The man was wearing a crisp white *kurta*, and had gold rings with unnecessarily large gem stones on six of his ten meaty fingers. He sported an immaculately trimmed moustache along with a well-dyed head of hair. On one side of the room sat three burly men, looking quite fierce, two of whom held menacing submachine guns resting on their laps.

The scene was straight out of a B-grade, Bollywood potboiler. If ever there was a caricature of an underworld don, this was it.

The cocky young man was now the epitome of boot-licking supplication, hands behind his back in humility, as he stood a little to the side of the desk after entering the room.

"Siddiqui*saab*, some people have come to see you. They work in the camps, and are having some problems with the rations. I said they could come see you." he said, head a little bowed.

The man behind the desk didn't deign to even acknowledge the young guy. He didn't look at any of us in the eye. Instead he looked straight ahead and stood up rather grandly, placing his hands on the desk to heave himself up. He held out his hand to shake mine, and I realized that he was standing out of politeness. I eagerly took his hand and shook it. His grip was beefy and strong. He then shook Vijay's and Nasir's hands as well. Vijay was polite, while Nasir acted almost as deferential as the brat who brought us there. The man didn't shake Maria's hand, but instead touched his chest and bowed his head in respect as he turned towards her. Maria folded her hands in a *Namaste*. He then opened a gold-plated casing on the desk and gave us each a colourful business card, which read:

Ismail Siddiqui
Social Worker
Working for People

It had the same thing written in Hindi, Urdu, and Gujarati, and gave the address, of what I presumed to be this shop, on the back of the card. As we were reading his business card, Siddiqui gave a grunt to one of his henchmen, who immediately brought chairs for all four of us. The youth stood by the side of his master in humble attention, hands behind his back, while we all took our seat. The don didn't sit until we all sat down. Till now he hadn't uttered a word to any of us, nor really looked any of us in the eye, or even changed his stern expression. He then gave a curt nod towards another one of his henchmen, who got up immediately and brought us four teas with biscuits. I remember thinking how funny it was that I didn't feel scared or particularly nervous as we sat in the work space of Gomtipur's Godfather.

Siddiqui indicated for us to drink the tea. As we sipped it, the young man then officiously beckoned me to explain the problem.

"Go on, go on...tell *saab* what the problem is." he bossily said. "Come on, come on, quickly."

I felt like punching the cheeky little bastard in the face. In any case, I turned to Siddiqui and addressed him politely. He didn't look at me, but seemed to be paying full attention. He alternated between looked ahead or down towards his table as I spoke.

"Siddiqui*saab*, see...um, the main problem is that we've exhausted all our avenues for getting rations for the people in the camps." I slowly ventured. "Many of them, especially those who haven't yet received livelihood materials are a little desperate. I don't know if there's anything you can help us with sir...but if you can..."

I trailed off with my sentence, not knowing exactly how to ask for help from a mafia don.

He nodded.

"How many people in the camps?" he asked in a deep voice, still looking past me.

I fumbled around for an answer, "Um...well...there are people in the community who need the rations also, so totally I would say...uh...Nasir, Vijay, what do you think...seven to eight thousand?"

I turned to Vijay and Nasir for confirmation, and they nodded.

Vijay replied, turning to Siddiqui, "Yes *saab*, if we can get rations for around 8000 people...even just rice or *atta* with some *daal*, then we will be ok till the next batch of rations comes through."

Siddiqui continued to stare ahead, and gave a sagely nod after we had finished our pleas. He then looked down at the desk, and flipped through a couple of papers. He lifted the receiver of the black phone, and dialled a number. Someone on the other side answered, and he spoke.

"Yes. Mmm...it's me Siddiqui. I need *atta* and *daal* for Gomtipur. Which one do I call? Hmm...hmm...say it again....ok. Ok, *khuda hafiz*."

He put down the phone, and then picked up another one; the ugly pink one.

A similar conversation took place, with him saying that delivery of the rations should be arranged for the camps in Gomtipur.

"I'll cover the payment through our regular ways." he ended.

His cell phone rang as he was putting down the receiver of phone number two. He took out a sleek-looking black cell phone from the side pocket of his *kurta* and seemed to have the exact same conversation.

"Siddiqui here...mmm...what? Ok...hmm, ok...just do it...payment will be covered through our regular ways. *Khuda hafiz*."

The four of us looked at each other. None of us had a clue as to what he was up to. He seemed to be talking in a ridiculously clichéd code language. Meanwhile, the cocky punk was standing there by Siddiqui smiling at us with pride, raising his eyebrows and bobbing his head as if to say, "Look at what my master can do...and I got you to him."

I had to admit though – it was pretty impressive from where I was sitting.

Siddiqui then put his cell phone back in his pocket, and placed his hands, a little too slowly, on the table. He looked straight ahead, again not catching our eyes.

"It's done. Please expect the rations to come today afternoon. I'll send one of my men to ensure that distribution happens properly." he said with a nod towards one of his henchmen.

I wondered why we needed a gun-toting beefy man to distribute rations, but then realized that it was probably Siddiqui's way of ensuring people knew where the rations came from. I just hoped the henchman would hide the gun before coming. Siddiqui then stood up. I sat and continued looking at him in – I must confess – a little awe. I then realized that others were standing up too. The meeting was evidently over. It was interesting to me how, during these last few months in Gujarat, stereotypes I had held were simultaneously de-centred and reified; often in really surreal ways. He was a mafia don, but he also came through when the people were desperate. I'm sure it wasn't all Robin Hood-like altruism that guided his work; he must have used the popularity he was bound to get to further solidify his network, but at the same time he didn't *have* to do it. Something in me felt like he genuinely cared.

We shook hands. I think I acted a little more humble and polite than I did when I first shook hands with him. I couldn't help but feel like I was participating in the local Gujarati version of *The Godfather*. Maria was none too impressed however.

We made our way out of the shop, and as we stepped out onto the street, the young man said proudly, "See? My *saab* will be able to handle anything. Don't you worry, the rations will come. Anything else you need, just let me know."

Vijay replied, "Ok *bhai*, thanks for doing this. We will take our leave now."

I sensed Maria's revulsion to the guy. The young man waved cheerily and set off in another direction, while the four of us made our way back to the camp office. Along the way, Vijay and Nasir told people who were waiting for rations that it would arrive in the afternoon, and to inform the rest of the community. I asked them whether they needed help with distribution, or whether Maria and I could head back since she needed to get ready for her trip.

"No problem Jayram*bhai*, we'll take care of everything. You can leave." Nasir said.

Both of them thanked Maria profusely for helping to dissipate the anger of the people. Maria and I then made our way to the auto rickshaw stand. We got into one and headed back to the apartment. Along the way, we talked and I could sense the lightness between us, primarily because Maria was poking fun at me.

"I think all you boys have some macho gene in you that makes you salivate like idiots in front of such masculine nonsense." she exclaimed incredulously with a smile. "That guy was straight out of some low-budget Hindi crime movie, and you were almost ready to kiss his ass!"

I smiled and replied defensively, "I wasn't salivating or anything. I was just impressed that he could get the rations so quickly. You have to admit, it was pretty cool. I've never seen anything like that in any case. But you're right...it was quite the stereotype."

Maria smiled back.

I then said, after a pause, "Did you notice that he used three different phones for three different calls?"

Maria burst out laughing, nodding her head, "I know...I have no idea why he used a different phone for that second call. I had to try so hard to prevent myself from laughing!"

I laughed too.

"I have to admit, I was amazed that I didn't feel at all scared or anything like that." I then said. "I mean, normally one would think we would be petrified to be in a don's presence, especially when he had guys with guns behind him. But it didn't seem scary at all."

Maria replied, "Well, ultimately this place is out of our comfort zones. You and I are coming here with our stereotypes. If we lived here, it would be much more normalized. Already, think of how much you've normalized in just a few months."

I nodded in agreement.

She continued, "At the end of the day though, these

will always be experiences you have as an outsider to this place. We're surprised when we have a new one because we're not truly a part of the conditions here. I mean, think about it, how many nights have you spent in Gomtipur ever since you came to Ahmedabad?"

Not one, I realized, barring the one night in the camp office before the Rath Yatra. But even that was an emergency.

"I haven't spent any nights in Vatwa either." she added, not wanting to seem like she was taking me to task. "Ultimately, you and I are outsiders here. I always have to remind myself to not take that for granted. It's dangerous to the people we work with if we do."

I thought about what Maria said, something I had known intuitively since I started working with Vijay and Nasir. No matter how much I wanted it, I would never be a full insider. I was surprised by how much it hurt to think about it.

~ Chapter 27 ~

One morning, foreign representatives of a couple of the international NGOs that were part of *Shanthi Samudaya* came to visit the various camps in Ahmedabad. They wanted to interview survivors and write a report on the work in the camps. Mani called me earlier that morning and begged for Vijay and me to be in charge of ferrying them around. He knew that I would not want to do it because I felt it was a waste of time. They particularly wanted to see the Shah Alam camp, which was the biggest one in Ahmedabad. He sweetened the request by informing us that the NGOs had hired a taxi for the entire day and were paying for meals in proper restaurants. I was to act as a translator since Vijay couldn't speak English. And in case any of the survivors or volunteers spoke only Gujarati, then there would be a two step translation, with Vijay translating for me from Gujarati to Hindi and then I doing the needful from Hindi to English for the *firangis*.

My post-colonial mindset felt a little irritated at the fact that I had to spend a whole day ferrying a couple of out-of-towners, especially when there was so much to be done at the camps. We had enough to do in Gomtipur. Nasir was the least happy of the three of us.

"I cannot cope alone with the two of you gone Jayram*bhai*." he whined. "There's so much to be done here in Gomtipur. Why do *you* two have to ferry these stupid *firangis* around? All those fat office people are just sitting around in the *Shanthi Samudaya* office anyway, why can't they go? Those of us who work on the ground have so much to do. This is nonsense."

I replied in like tone, "Boss...it's not my decision. There's no one else to take them around. Everyone's busy with the work in various communities. Mani literally begged me. Nobody who speaks Gujarati, Hindi and English is able to go, so Mani asked me to take one of you with me and travel with them."

He was not buying it, and was still sullen.

I added with exasperation, "Listen...they say that this is important because they will be able to get greater funding from larger international organizations, and maybe even take this issue to the U.N. or something like that. I don't know...it's only for one day. If anything comes up, just postpone it for a day until we get back."

Nasir nodded, but didn't stop pouting. I don't know whether it was because he was alone doing the work in Gomtipur or because Vijay was going with me instead of him. Vijay was needed primarily because his Gujarati was a little better. Vijay's family was a little more trans-Gujarati. Nasir, like a lot of Muslim communities in some parts of the old city, spoke mostly Urdu-laced Hindi. Also, Nasir was better integrated in the community, primarily because he was Muslim, so it made sense for him to stay behind for the day rather than Vijay.

In any case, Nasir's face lit up a little when I said that we would come back to Gomtipur in the evening after dropping the *firangis* back in their hotel. I also told him that the three of us could eat dinner together in one of the nice *dhabas* in the area. He was assuaged a little. I think he just didn't want our team to break. It was tough doing this work alone. I would have been irritated too if I was left alone, while my friends gallivanted around the city in an air-conditioned taxi.

Vijay and I made our way to the hotel in a rather nice part of Ahmedabad where the two visitors were staying. It was mid-morning by the time we made all the arrangements and contacted volunteers in the various camps informing them of our arrival with foreigners. I hadn't even met them and I was already irritated at them. It went away a little when I saw that one of them was a round, jovial African man from Botswana. I immediately felt a fraternal Third World connection. The other was a toothy white guy, from the UK, whose flaky pink skin was clearly not holding up to the heat and dust of Gujarat. Both were extremely nice and friendly so it was difficult to continue being put off by them.

The Brit was particularly enamoured by India, and when I told him I was from Bangalore, he remarked to me with a chuckle, "You lads are taking over the world with your technology."

I couldn't help but puff up in artificial pride as he said that, and then reprimanded myself for indulging in petty chauvinism, that too based on what a Brit had said. I had a complicated relationship with the British accent. It made me smile because my father, who was quite the anglophile, fed me a steady diet of British comedy television shows growing up. Simultaneously, it evoked a sense of annoyance because of the colonial legacy.

The scrawny bastard in front of me was eminently likeable though. He spoke with humility and showed a genuine interest in learning, rather than teaching, a rarity with office-bearers in large international NGOs. He was quite endearing in the kind of squirmy way that only the Brits had mastered.

The four of us made our way to the Shah Alam camp, which had survivors from Naroda Patiya, the most infamous locality of bloodletting in Ahmedabad. The area around Shah Alam itself was spared from the violence, but Naroda Patiya was where some of the most brutal violence had occurred. It was the Shah Alam camp that was featured in the English news channel program that pushed me over the edge to making my way to Gujarat. The name, Naroda Patiya, was seared in my mind well before I came to Ahmedabad. It represented in a microcosm what had happened in Gujarat in all its macabre reality. It was the place, along with Gulbarg Society, that was hit worst (if such episodes of bloodletting could actually be placed in a hierarchy of intensity). Naroda Patiya was the first to face the bloodlust of the mobs. There was no warning here. It was a massacre. Hundreds of Muslims were killed.

In the months that had transpired since I arrived in Ahmedabad, the ensuing confusion of traumatic political rebirth and back-breaking normalization weighed me down to the point where I had forgotten some of my starting points. I realized that I had never once made it to the biggest camp in the state, having focused all my energies in Gomtipur and then running back to my own little happy world on the other side of the river. When Mani requested me to baby-sit the *firangis*, it hadn't registered that I would be going to what was and always would be *the* representation of the 2002 carnage in

Gujarat in any construct of Indian consciousness.

It was only on the taxi ride there, as I got a chance to think for a few minutes after the irritable bluster of the morning, that I realized where I was heading to. I felt that familiar queasiness in my stomach, and the digging of my thumbs into my kidneys was now done almost subconsciously.

The taxi stopped at the central square near the awe-inspiring Shah Alam mosque, where the main relief camp was running. Life went on a little too normally for my liking. I was getting the same feeling I got when I first landed in Ahmedabad. Why was everything so *settled*? It had the regular hustle and bustle of any large locality; shops, vendors with their carts, auto rickshaw stands, noisy traffic, and busy streets.

The four of us got out of the taxi at the square, where one of the *Shanthi Pathiks* of the Shah Alam camp was waiting for us. Vijay and I had called him beforehand informing him about our trip. As we walked towards him, I could see people staring at our *firangi* friends.

The Brit was taking it all in. It always seemed to me like Westerners had a weird voyeurism for violent events in the Third World, even when orchestrated by their own governments, but particularly when it was locally produced. So, lo and behold, a steady stream of out-of-towners made their way to Gujarat once they heard of the bloodletting, providing revenue for the many nice hotels on the other side of the river. I don't know how many theses, dissertations, articles, or just plain old accounts of carnage-tourism were produced by them, but I'm guessing quite a few. Careers must have been launched or bolstered. Many probably went back to their universities and institutes to regale audiences with their brave adventures in hostile lands. Most of them were wastes of space. Some were genuinely helpful though, coming in with an egalitarianism that belied their entitled upbringing.

The Brit seemed to be one of the good ones, while the chap from Botswana was trustworthy in my mind simply because he was from Africa. Africans weren't foreigners as far as I was concerned. They were fellow Third Worlders.

We walked towards the *Shanthi Pathik* and shook his hand. Vijay spoke with him in Gujarati. He nodded vigorously, and beckoned for us to follow him into the Shah Alam camp. As we neared the entrance, the young man asked the shop keeper in the corner whether the main coordinator was inside, and the shop keeper nodded with a big smile

"Yes, yes...people are there...go on...go take the American and African and go meet them. I'm sure they will like to see them." he replied with a grin.

Vijay and I smiled back in a kind of insider bonding as we walked past the shop keeper. We went inside the camp, which was, like most other camps, on the grounds of a mosque and grave yard. And like the other camps around the city, it was winding down. Some children were playing cricket, while a few people mulled around. I could see the remnants of its former teeming ways. Worn out tarpaulin sheets, torn mats, a few pots and pans lying around, some rags, bits of charred fire wood. It was bigger than the camps in Gomtipur or the one in Gulbarg Society, but it also seemed to have held more people, so looked denser. We walked towards the main office, which was housed in a small room adjacent to the mosque, and met with a couple more *Shanthi Pathiks*. The young man acting as our guide asked if we could go around talking to some of the community members, and the others nodded.

We set off towards the houses on the other side of the camp. It turned out that the young man had pre-arranged for some youth to talk with the foreign guests at what looked like a playing field across from the grave yard. They were all waiting for us, and greeted us as we walked towards them. We soon got started with what we were there for.

The Brit and the African asked them a few questions. The usual set of queries.

"What was the violence like?"

"Who did you lose in the carnage?"

"Who do you think conducted the violence?"

"Were the police involved?"

"What has been the response of the state government?"

And so on...

I had heard it all before, and the answers were more or less the same.

"Hindu fascists with police support and government

support conducted the violence."

"They specifically targeted Muslims for their own political gains."

"So many innocent people died…men, women, children, families, friends."

"It was organized violence. The State Government was fully behind it."

And so on...

Either the Brit or the African asked the question in English to me, I would translate into Hindi to the youth there. I would then translate the answer given by one of the young men – and they were all men – back into English. Vijay would chime in to help me out.

It was boring.

"Were there rapes or sexual assaults conducted upon any Muslim women?" asked the African.

I promptly asked the question in Hindi, waiting for the same gory accounts I had heard before.

"No...not here in our area." replied the young men.

Wait...

What?

My earlier disinterest stopped abruptly. I knew that there was sexual violence conducted by the Hindu mobs.

I asked them in Hindi to clarify, "Are you sure there weren't any incidents of sexual violence? I read that there were incidents when the violence happened that…"

The young men adamantly shook their heads, a couple of them with angry looks on their faces.

"No, no *bhaisaab*...there was no sexual violence in our area. Maybe in other areas it happened, but not in ours. It didn't happen here. All the women escaped in our area."

This was strange, but Vijay indicated for me to not press any further, so I dropped it. The discussion continued for a little longer with some more questions. I couldn't take my mind of what the young men had said though. I was quite taken aback by their response. Until then, I had assumed that everyone knew and acknowledged the sexual violence that was perpetrated by the fascist mobs on the women, and yet these young men were denying it. Every *Shanthi Pathik,* every volunteer, every worker in the movement I knew had talked about it. The specific way in which the mobs targeted Muslim women was one of the most gruesomely infamous aspects of the violence conducted in Gujarat.

And yet, they denied it, and said that it hadn't happened.

We went around the locality a little more. The *Shanthi Pathik* who showed us around pointed to the house that he and his family used to live in. It was, like all the other houses in the colony, completely burnt down.

I was in another world though; unable to divert my thoughts from what those young men said.

Why did they reply in that manner?

We soon left the Shah Alam camp, and made our way to the camp in Vatwa where Abhay and Maria had arranged for us to meet with some of the local volunteers there. Vijay and I sat in the front seat of the taxi. During the ride I asked him in Hindi, so that our guests at the backseats wouldn't understand.

"Vijay...why did those young men say that no sexual violence happened in the area during the *dhamaal*?" I asked quietly. "I know there was sexual violence that many women faced in some of the surrounding localities...I don't understand it."

"Jayram*bhai*...there could be one of two reasons." he replied thoughtfully. "Well...one is that what they say is genuinely true. In their area, it's possible that everyone escaped. The media hypes everything up when poor people get killed."

I knew there was something else though.

He continued, "But the other reason could be...well, the other reason could be that they're ashamed that they couldn't protect their women, and don't want to accept it. Their honour is at risk of being completely destroyed with this."

I was sure that at least a couple of those young men very likely did know of sexual violence in their areas during the pogrom. Part of the agenda of the fascist mobs was not just violence, but the emasculation of the Muslim man through that violence. I had read numerous NGO reports about it. It was sick. Denial by those young men was a distinct possibility.

The Muslim woman disappeared twice.

I felt like I needed to vomit. I looked at Vijay and I could tell that he knew what I was feeling.

At that moment, the African tapped me on the shoulder.

"Jayram my friend," he said, cheerily, "we never asked your friend Vijay what he went through during the violence, whether he lost any friends or family members. Do you mind asking him?"

I was shaken out of my reverie. I nodded at the African, and then turned to Vijay nonchalantly.

"Vijay," I said, pointing back, "the African guy wants to know what you went through during the violence...whether you lost any friends or family members."

Vijay didn't reply immediately. He stared out the window of the taxi for a few seconds.

"I lost two of my closest friends in the violence Jayram*bhai*." he finally said, still looking out of the window. "They were friends of Nasir too. One was shot dead at point-blank range by the police, the other was killed by the mobs. He was butchered in the violence."

I stared back at him in shock. I realized then that I hadn't ventured to ask either him or Nasir what they went through during the carnage.

I had been working with them for months. They were now among my dearest friends. I was at a point where I desperately wanted to make sure our friendship lasted for the rest of our lives. We were even thinking of starting an NGO together in the long term. And yet, I didn't know this about them – what *they* had gone through during the violence.

I relayed the information back to the African, who nodded and noted it down. I then turned immediately to Vijay and looked at him. He was still staring out of the taxi window. His eyes were red. He didn't look at me directly, but I could feel his pain.

"Vijay...you never told me this...I don't know what to say...I, um...I'm so sorry."

While still staring out of the taxi window, he said, "Jaram*bhai*, I'm keeping a lot inside me. Sometimes I feel like if I start to talk, I will explode. There's too much inside me Jaram*bhai*, but working with you and Nasir helps. I don't know...it all stays inside me like poison."

He paused. I didn't know what to say and continued staring at him. He turned and looked at me. The intensity was deep in his eyes.

Until Maria asked me, I never thought about why I hadn't spent a single night in either of their houses. This, despite the months I had spent working with them and getting so close to them. I had subconsciously taken it for granted that I would not be living with them. That was another world. I knew so little about it, despite spending the better part of my days there. It was where I did my little act of social service and that's it. I didn't inhabit it the way Vijay or Nasir did, or even the way I inhabited the other side of the river.

"You know those young men...and what they say..." Vijay said, turning back to look outside the window, "I'm not saying that it's the right thing to do...of course it's wrong to deny what happened to the women. But I can understand why they might say it..."

I looked at him, feeling the intensity of our friendship wash over me in the midst of all this.

"...because sometimes Jaram*bhai*, denial is needed just to survive for a little while."

181

~ Chapter 28 ~

It was tough to see Maria leave, even for a short while. For all our problems, she had become a central presence in my life and I could always turn to her for support and love.

She said that she would be back after the editing for her film was done, but hadn't specified when exactly, which made me a little anxious. I dropped her off at the station. We hugged goodbye on the platform. Quickly, so that people wouldn't stare, but tightly nevertheless. I could feel the affection between us. I felt it as her fingers clasped the ridges on my back, and her warm cheek pressed against mine.

She sighed as we unclasped ourselves, looking me in the eyes and whispering, "Bye Jay...I'll see you soon."

I smiled and nodded.

She boarded the compartment and took her seat by the window. The train soon started trundling out of the platform and we waved goodbye to each other, each axle revolution making me a little sadder as the train sped off into the distance.

After seeing her off I made my way back to Gomtipur to hang out with Vijay and Nasir. It was quite late in the day. I had resolved to spend more time in the evenings with them, beyond just our regular tea and cigarette. But I didn't feel like cutting down on the fun-filled evenings with Maria and Abhay in order to do that. Now that she had left, I thought it would be a good opportunity to spend some longer evenings with Vijay and Nasir. We had gone out to eat dinner a couple of times. They asked me to stay at their houses and I declined each time, again.

The unique friendships I was developing with them had strengthened with our work in the trenches together. They were very different people, and I shared different relationships with both of them.

With Vijay it was like a bond between comrades because of his sense of strength and pride. He was the archetype of a masculine, working-class man. His patriarchy and belief in traditional gender roles was something we often argued about, but it was also something he was willing to be challenged on. For all his masculinity, he always believed that his wife would be equal to him. I didn't know whether he said this for my ears, or whether he truly believed it, but it seemed genuine enough. He and I bonded like comrades-in-arms.

Nasir was more of a brother, someone I felt deep familial care towards rather than friendship because of his more genial attitude. He was sweeter than Vijay, and a fundamentally gentler person. But, unlike Vijay, he didn't put himself fully on display. This made it a little harder to respect him as a comrade because he would agree to pretty much anything I said, primarily to ensure that I didn't feel bad. But I think I liked him more. Maybe it was because I saw more of myself in Vijay and found it a little tough to deal with. Considering what had transpired in Gujarat, Vijay's anger was understandable, but Nasir's sweetness was not. That endeared me to him, because it showed me something I wish I had.

It was also interesting to see how we interacted differently with each other about the future. Vijay wanted to work in building a cooperative among the women workers in the community, and was always thinking of ways in which community-mobilizing could happen. He and I spent many days talking about how the three of us would eventually form a small organization together. Nasir would chime in, but not in the detail-oriented way that Vijay planned things in his head. Nasir, on the other hand, was much more of a family man. He upheld, as sacrosanct, the responsibilities towards his parents and siblings, and eventually, as he would always tell me, his future wife and children. While Vijay was primarily interested in ensuring our continued friendship towards building an organization together in the future, Nasir was keener on ensuring that I would remain a friend of his family, coming to visit him during the holidays.

I thought about how we would continue our friendships after I left to travel to distant lands, while they, in all likelihood, would still be in Ahmedabad.

The friendships I shared with Vijay and Nasir were bonds I felt immeasurably lucky to have developed. But our worlds were different and, I had come to accept, always would be. I wanted a utopian world, where our differences would magically disappear. But I slowly began to realize that it was more important to understand those differences rather than wish them away. I felt it each time I crossed the river to be with them, and each time I crossed it to go back to my comfortable world. I traversed it every day, only to find my way back. Always a journey, never a destination.

~ Chapter 28.5 ~

My journey in Ahmedabad, suspended between two worlds, had one geographic invariable. The river running between those two worlds was a daily reminder that the truth always lay on the other side; no matter which side I was on. This river was more than just a physical divide.

The Sabarmati River – on the banks of which Gandhi founded his famous ashram, one of the many epicentres of the struggle that brought down the British Empire. The banks from where he launched the Salt Sathyagraha – a pinch of salt to challenge British taxation. This was no ordinary river. It had some fucking history to it.

But there was more to the river than that. Centuries before Gandhi, legend has it that Sultan Ahmed Shah sat on the banks of the river in 1411. He was inspired by the courage of a rabbit standing its ground against a snarling dog not too far away from where he was sitting. That inspiration led to the founding of the city of Ahmedabad itself.

I don't know how or why. It's a legend. But a good one.

It represented among the many paradoxes of India itself. A city founded by a Muslim Sultan, that had later been the political and religious home of Gandhi, was now the bastion of Hindu fascists. The river was integrally connected to those paradoxes. It had a history far richer than the fascists' virulent homogeneity gave space for.

Rivers are life in India. When plans were passed to construct hydroelectric dams at different points across the Narmada River, there was militant resistance to it. The *Narmada Bachao Andolan.* The movement brought the World Bank to its knees. It got the Bank to institute a quasi-independent Inspection Panel for all its projects around the globe, only to then have the Narmada project be taken over by the Indian government. The fight continued. The movement ultimately lost, but it also ultimately won. The dam did get built with the Indian state forcing the issue, but the movement also laid the groundwork for many other struggles against similar projects in India and around the world.

Rivers are everything to many people in India. Fights broke out between political groups in Tamil Nadu and Karnataka over disputes on sharing the Kaveri water that flowed through both states. I saw those passionate rallies firsthand in Bangalore. We were a Tamil family living in Bangalore, the largest city in Karnataka. We *had* to pay attention to it.

I'm sure the Sabarmati was equally important to the many fishing and agrarian communities along its banks. I have no doubt that, just like the communities along the Narmada, who saw that river as a matriarchal, life-giving force – *Maa Reva* – those along the Sabarmati had a reverence for it that signified more than what it was for people like me. I'm sure the Sabarmati was motherly to those communities. I'm sure it (she) nourished their crops, and filled their stomachs with fresh fish. I'm sure that people bathed in the water, uttering deep-throated morning prayers. I'm sure the Sabarmati was a life-giving force, like the Narmada or Kaveri, or the Amazon, Mississippi, or Zambezi. I'm sure it was life itself to so many people.

It's sad.

I only remember it for one thing.

A fresh water weapon for ghettoization.

~ Chapter 29 ~

Among the more sinister aspects to the violence in Gujarat was the connivance, if not outright participation, of the state apparatus. It was not so much conjectural accusation or conspiratorial theory, as much as it was irrefutable fact. It was so apparent that it was almost offensive to declare it like one had unearthed some major discovery. It was like affirming that the Nazis were responsible for the Holocaust or that the British were responsible for the British Raj - it's so obvious that it almost insults the victims to proclaim it.

And like states the world over, one of the principal mechanics of participation was the utilization of the state's body of armed mercenaries. I had heard a lot about police complicity in the carnage, but only had the briefest of encounters with them.

Nothing happened to me though.

That was part of the problem.

It was particularly late at night when I was returning from the camps one day after another strenuous round of surveys, community meetings, and livelihood material distribution. The work had gone on for a particularly long duration that evening. I found new energy to continue working late into the night since I didn't have Maria to go home to. I was dead tired and nearly falling asleep inside the auto rickshaw that Nasir was driving. He had borrowed it from his cousin to drop me back since it was quite late. He saw that I was tired and, as was his wont, decided that he would drop me. It would have been tough hailing a rickshaw at that late hour and they would have charged me double the fare. I was grateful for his caring ways.

As we rode towards the Sabarmati bridge, I noticed that the roads were pretty empty, barring a few vehicles. Some vendors and cycle rickshaw riders were sitting around in a corner smoking *beedis* and chatting. It was a pretty quiet night. We started to make our way across the bridge. All I could feel was the engine of the auto rickshaw, and the cool breeze against my face. Every once in a while Nasir would jabber something unintelligible in the breeze, and I acknowledged it with an affirmative sound.

As we were half-way across the bridge, a couple of cops ahead of us waved their batons, indicating for us to stop. There were a bunch of them nearby that I spotted as Nasir brought the rickshaw to a halt. I spotted the Inspector leaning against a police vehicle by the edge of the bridge. A couple of the constables came over to the side and asked both of us to get down. When I asked why, one of them roughly grabbed my arm and attempted to heft me out of the rickshaw.

He shouted something in Gujarati, which I didn't understand. Nasir replied calmly, raising his palms to defuse the tension, and got out.

The cop still tried to heave me out of the auto rickshaw. Unfortunately, I outweighed him by a good 20 kilograms I think, and all he could manage was a rather harsh pull at my arm without budging me. This pissed him off even more.

I put my hand up in peace to calm him down and got out of the rickshaw. Nasir was taken aside by 2 cops and asked to show his driver's license, while I was taken by the two constables to the Inspector. I was getting a little annoyed with the way they were handling me, which only made them even more menacing.

I was soon surrounded by around ten or twelve cops. A couple of them started prodding me with their batons and asking me questions in Gujarati that I didn't understand. One of them roughly held the back of my shirt and pushed me a little towards the centre of the huddle. I gave him a glare and told him in Hindi to stop pushing me. I then felt an angry whack on the side of my leg from a baton, although I couldn't make out who it was that hit me. I also noticed that I had been pushed far enough such that my back was almost against the railing of the bridge.

I quickly realised that I had stopped shaving and grown a thick beard over the last couple of months. I was also wearing one of Abhay's long-sleeve *kurtas*. They probably thought I was Muslim. I suddenly felt the growing sensation of my stomach turning over. But this was not the familiar one I used to have when I heard about the carnage. This was real fear. It was similar to the one I had when I met those goons many weeks back, or what I felt for a few minutes when walking through the Rath Yatra.

My head was swirling a little. I noticed that my breathing had quickened. I had read many accounts of "encounter killings" by police in Mumbai and Delhi, where they executed anyone they thought was even a marginal suspect and later faked a scene to make it look like they died in a shootout. Most of the bravery medals that Indian cops got were invariably for those kinds of killings.

I knew that the Ahmedabad police had done the same thing to many Muslim men in the city, as well as some activists. A couple of young boys had been gunned down recently and the papers reported it as a brave police-shootout against terrorists. Civil liberties groups later investigated and found out that they were college-going Muslim activists. As these thoughts were racing through my head, I decided then and there that if they were going to attack me, I would take at least one of them down.

I looked around and saw that quite a few of them were smaller than me, and many had paunches. I could knee the fidgety bastard on my right in the crotch and then break his neck, maybe push another over the river. At least one or two of them would be dead. Even if they killed me and threw me over the river, I would make them pay, I thought. What about Nasir? If I was to attack them, they might just let him go momentarily because their attention would be on me. Maybe both of us could even escape by jumping over the bridge into the river, but the blackness of the water at night didn't seem too comforting. And the fall would probably kill us.

I couldn't believe the madness I was contemplating.

It couldn't have been for more than a second that all these thoughts flashed across my head, but it felt like time stood still.

As the pushing and prodding continued, I tried my level best to be calm and not betray any emotion. It was hard. It took a monumental effort to control the mixture of fear and rage bubbling up inside me.

The Inspector made his way to confront me. As he walked towards me, I felt a couple of rifle butts digging into my sides, while another constable jammed his baton across my throat to ensure I wouldn't move. I gagged a little as the smooth wood pressed against my windpipe. The Inspector was the only one with a holstered pistol while the others had batons in their hands or antiquated Enfield rifles slung over their shoulders. Maybe I could quickly reach for the Inspector's revolver and shoot some of them, I thought.

He came up to me and barked a few words at me in Gujarati, while violently shaking his baton inches from my face. From what he jabbered, I only understood the words "old city" and "ID card" and guessed that he wanted some form of identification.

I reached into my pocket and took out my wallet which had my driver's license. As I gave it to him, I saw that my hand was shivering a little. My palms were so sweaty that I couldn't remove the license from the plastic casing in my wallet. Luckily it was encased in a see through section of the wallet, so I displayed it by holding it up to him. I could see the cops surrounding me visibly smirking at my state. They dug in their batons and rifle butts even deeper now. I gagged some more and coughed, trying to catch my breath. I noticed a couple of them giving me a threatening once over, from head to toe.

The Inspector took my license out of the wallet, and looked at it crudely by shining his flashlight on it. A constable standing next to him grabbed the wallet and started leafing through it. Luckily there wasn't much in it, save a couple of hundred rupees. Not sure whether he pocketed it or not.

"Jayram Krishnan from Karnataka? Bangalore, eh?" the Inspector asked, gruffly.

I nodded. I noticed that he became a little less threatening, but still glowered. He nodded at the constable holding the baton across my throat and indicated for him to remove it. He did so, much to my relief.

He then asked me menacingly in Hindi, "You're from Bangalore? What are you doing here in the old city?"

I was about to reply in Hindi, when I quickly realised that my English would save me.

I paused for a moment and nodded as a way of acknowledging the question and his authority, as well as catch my breath.

Then, with the thickest neutral, non-Indian accent I could muster, I replied, "I'm here conducting empirical research on the camps and the ongoing relief work that the NGOs and government are involved in. I'm primarily trying to examine delivery mechanisms, infrastructure as well post-relief community building measures. I'm also looking at the public-private engagement in this process with the idea of promoting a better best-practices paradigm for future projects."

I had no idea what the fuck I was jabbering about, but just wanted to make sure that I used enough difficult words for the Inspector. He became less menacing.

"Why you here...this late in night? Eh?" he asked in broken English.

I calmed down a little and replied, "There was an evening meeting with some NGOs that discussed a lot of what I just talked about. I felt it would be an important gathering to establish a strong network for my work, especially considering the data I would need to gather."

He asked, still holding onto my wallet, "So you're writing for newspaper...you are journalist or something?"

I regained a lot more of my composure. These fuckers were scared of outsiders coming and digging around, especially English-speaking folk.

I smiled, trying desperately to hide my fear, and replied, "No, no...I'm a freelance researcher, but my work gets published in different media outlets, journals etc."

He nodded, still looking at my driver's license. The constables were waiting in anticipation for their orders.

"Mmm...so you are also working for NGO or something?"

"The work is connected with NGOs, yes, because I use those networks to interview staff members. But I mainly write. I'm a freelance researcher and writer...but my work is definitely connected with NGOs."

He stared at it for what seemed like an eternity.

He then handed it back to me, saying, "You should also interview Hindus."

I didn't say anything and nodded with a smile, heaving an internal sigh of relief that I wasn't going to end up floating face-down along the Sabarmati. Thankfully, he didn't ask me for any institutional ID or anything. I would have had to weave another story since I didn't have any.

He gave back my wallet too and, without looking at me, imperiously indicated me to move along by waving his baton as he walked off. At this the other cops moved away from me as quickly as they had surrounded me. They all went back to their posts along either side of the road without giving me a second glance.

Nasir too was let go without a warning or ticket. As we looked at each other, I noticed that his lips were quivering slightly and his eyes were a little red. He had a lot more to fear than I did.

We got into the rickshaw silently. After I was seated I felt a dampness in my crotch and looked down and noticed that I had peed a little bit. I took a deep breath to calm the adrenaline surge inside me. I could still feel my heart pounding against my chest. As the rickshaw started moving, the air coming in felt particularly chilly against the sweat on my brow.

We rode off without saying a word to each other for the rest of the trip.

~ Chapter 29.5 ~

Nasir dropped me at the apartment that night after our run-in with the police. I clasped his hand tightly as we said goodbye and pleaded with him to stay with me in the apartment to avoid the cops while going back. He shook his head and said he would be fine. He assured me that he would take a slightly different route this time to avoid them and that it wouldn't be a problem. I told him to call the house phone if there was any trouble.

He drove off after saying bye again.

I went up to the apartment. My head was still swirling a little as I climbed the stairs.

I entered the apartment. No one was there. Maria was still away in Mumbai and Abhay had gone to visit a friend in Baroda for the weekend. I desperately wished one of them had been around.

I poured myself a large whisky and downed it in one swallow. I felt the alcohol burn my throat, and enter my system rapidly. I poured myself another and lit a cigarette, feeling an empty anger rising alongside the alcohol in my system. I paced around a little bit, smoked the entire cigarette while drinking my second whisky, and poured myself another. I started sweating. Paced around some more as I lit up a second cigarette.

Of course I was spared by those cops. I was always going to be spared.

Swallowed my third whisky and puffed away on the cigarette. Poured myself another with the lit cigarette dangling from my mouth. I filled the glass to the brim this time, and started swigging it. I was getting rapidly drunk.

I stumbled to the bathroom, my head spinning at the thought of what transpired in that infernal place. The blood rushed to my head as I wondered how I had fooled myself into thinking that somehow I wasn't responsible.

I looked at myself in the mirror. The figure resembled Jayram. Drunk. Hardened. I hated myself. I hated who I was. I hated where I came from.

Fuck you Jayram.

I removed my clothes, dropping them on the tiled

bathroom floor, and stood full bodied in front of the mirror, completely naked. I had the glass of whisky in one hand and the lit cigarette in the other. I looked myself over. My wretched self.

Those cops wouldn't have done a thing to me. I was always going to escape. There had always been an escape route out of this place for me.

Fuck you Jayram. Fuck your miserable life.

I took another swig of the whisky. Contorted my head as it entered my already inebriated system. Took another drag on my cigarette and looked at the red burning end. I exhaled onto the glowing ember and heard it crackling lightly.

Of course...

I slowly took the lit cigarette and pressed it against my thigh. My skin singed as the cigarette burned itself out with a soft crackle. I winced a little. I pulled the cigarette out and with it, some of my skin and flesh. I winced a little more. I looked down, and saw a small circle of slightly charred flesh mixed with cigarette ash.

It was beautiful.

I sipped more whisky to dull the pain. I then removed the blade from Abhay's razor. It was still quite new and sharp.

I sank it into my other thigh and made a thin slit. It didn't pain much. I took another sip of whisky and made another slit on my shin, and then another on my forearm. Thin slits.

They clotted quickly. It was nice to see my blood. I could barely feel it. The whisky was swimming in my system now. I took another swig. Lit another cigarette.

I looked at myself with the lit cigarette dangling from my mouth and put the whisky glass down beside the sink.

I puffed without removing the cigarette from my mouth. The cigarette smoke burned my eyes, and they became even redder.

I looked at myself and loathed what I was seeing. I took another puff, cigarette still dangling from my mouth.

I then punched myself in the stomach. It was a hard punch but not hard enough.

I punched myself in the stomach again. I tried to punch as hard as I could. The harder I punched, the more I felt I could take. The muscles tightened. The blows become harder.

I couldn't really feel anything. The whisky was now completely assimilated into my bloodstream.

I hammered my tightened abdomen. I was sweating profusely now. The ashes from the lit cigarette scattered all over my torso and arms as I hit myself vigorously.

I then started pounding my chest. Tarzan style. But in slow-motion, without the howling. Furiously I hit my pectorals. The harder I beat, the more I could take.

Harder and harder. I returned to my stomach. This time two punches at a time. Continuously, until I worked up a rhythm.

Harder and harder.

I went back to thrashing my chest.

Harder and harder.

I looked at myself in the mirror as I hit myself. I tried not to flinch. The expression had to be bare. No flinching. If I flinched, I punched harder, and tried not to flinch

I stopped. Took a breath. Heavy. My torso was red and had cigarette ash speckled all over it. My face was flushed.

I downed my whisky. Took a long drag of the cigarette. Stubbed it against my other thigh. Didn't wince. Looked at the mirror and spat at what I saw.

I took one step back and crashed down onto the bathroom floor, bouncing my head of the tiles. Stayed there for the rest of the night, the walls spinning around me, only vaguely aware of the slight trickle of blood running down the side of my face.

~ Chapter 30 ~

The spiral downwards occurred in double-quick time, almost taking me by surprise. I could see it happening as clear as day but was at a loss to do anything about it. The first casualty was my relationship with Maria. No breakup is ever pleasant, but this one was particularly awful because of the painful intensity of our love for each other.

It was my fault. Not in an amorphous I-drove-her-away, or I-became-so-distant-and-scared kind of thing. No, I was an asshole to her. I had an affair with someone else. Another volunteer who had come for a short while. Someone I knew from before, a friend from the past. She had come for a short while to volunteer in the camps, but mainly to hang out with me for a bit. We had a short affair that was beautiful and friendly.

It's unimportant who she was or what the affair was like. Maybe hiding the details hides the shame more. The consequences were, however, very significant. It broke things up between Maria and me. It happened when she was in Mumbai. Of course it did. I was a coward too. When she returned, she knew that something was up and eventually found out.

We fought about it. And like most of what we shared, the fight was passionate too. She tried to get me to own up to it as a mistake. She wasn't as angry with the affair as she was with my cowardliness. My callousness came through too, and I attempted to justify what I had done.

"Maria, you have to admit," I said, trying to sound suitably reasonable, "we never established ourselves as an exclusive relationship. We never said that we would be monogamous with each other did we? If we had, there's no way I would have broken that pact."

It was pathetic.

She didn't buy it. She merely smirked. It was the kind of smirk that a loved one who's hurting gives to cover up their hurt, to showcase just what a gulf in communication there is with a significant other, a significant other who has lost a part of their humanity. I felt very low. I thought I had hit rock bottom even before my affair. Now, with Maria's reaction, rock bottom looked like a nice place to aim for. I realized that I really loved her and had probably destroyed our relationship. The intensity of being with her – someone so much more emotionally deep and politically conscious than I – was scary. I sabotaged the relationship.

She walked away from me, shaking her head like I was a lost cause, pitying me even. But she loved me. I knew it. I could see it in her hurt. She was concerned with what I was going through. She wanted me to own up to the way I hurt her primarily to try and support me, rather than reprimand me. It made it even worse. If she was just angry at me, it would have been easier to brush off. But she wasn't. She was truly caring. She couldn't support someone who wasn't fully there though, someone who wasn't truly honest with himself or the world. I had to come clean for her to be able to engage with me again. Otherwise it was indeed a lost cause.

For the first time since coming to Ahmedabad, I felt really scared. Not scared of dying or what I had seen and how it might affect me – but about being a lesser person, someone who hurts without caring, someone who self-destructs and brings others down with him. I had never been shaken like this ever before.

We had to leave for the camps. I went to Gomtipur, while Abhay and Maria made their way to Vatwa. Abhay was feeling the stress too, I could tell. He and Maria were close, so I knew she would have talked about her pain in detail. I was scared that I would be ostracized by the two of them. I wouldn't have known where to go.

I went through the motions with Vijay and Nasir. It was a welcome relief to be with them, but I felt like shit. Both of them asked me what was going on. I didn't tell them anything in detail. Said that I was feeling a little tired. I didn't want to talk to them about my relationship with Maria. More so I didn't have the courage to admit that I had fucked up so badly and hurt her.

I made my way back to the apartment that evening a little anxiously, not really wanting to face what was in store. I found Abhay sitting on the floor with a couple of volunteers in the living room of the apartment, smoking and drinking. He seemed his usual merry self, and his gesture towards me to join them showcased his care, sans judgment. But I knew he was feeling the stress. It felt like Maria had been more gracious to me than I deserved when they talked about what we were going through. I sat down beside him, and poured myself a small drink. I shared a cigarette with Abhay and joined in for a short while, but my eyes kept scanning the apartment for Maria. Abhay noticed that I was looking for her.

Soon, as the conversation got louder and more joyful, I quietly whispered to Abhay, "Where is she?"

He tilted his head towards the kitchen veranda, and indicated to me with his large eyes that I should go there. I nodded and got up. I walked through the kitchen and onto the veranda where I found her sitting on the floor, leaning against the wall. An opened bottle of vodka was in her left hand, her eyes vacantly gazing at the sky.

She was drunk. Not out of joy, but to dull the pain. She had been drinking alone and hard. I could see it in her eyes. She didn't turn her head towards me or acknowledge my presence as I stepped onto the veranda. She took another swig of the bottle. She winced a little, half-squinting her eyes, as she felt the burn of the alcohol go down her throat.

I started getting worried now. I had never seen her like this.

I gingerly walked towards her and sat next to her. She moved a couple of inches away in disgust. It hurt sharply to see her do this. I could feel her pain and anger. It was palpable the way we felt each other's emotions without saying anything.

I started the conversation in the worst possible way.

"Maria, you shouldn't be drinking like this alone. It's not good for you."

Idiot, I thought to myself as the words came out.

She snorted with derision, continuing to stare ahead.

"Hmph...you're someone to talk Jayram. You fucking get sloshed every day."

It wasn't said with any hint of humour, just plain revulsion at my presence. Her voice was a little hoarse from the booze, her words slurring ever so slightly.

There was a pause. She then said in the same tone,

finally turning her eyes towards me in a slow drunken twist of
her head.

"Why the fuck are you here anyway? Huh? Go have
fun with the others inside...leave me alone."

I didn't say anything. She snorted again sardonically,
and looked away, taking another swig from the bottle.

I stuttered, "Listen...Maria...I, uh..."

"What do you want Jayram?" she interrupted irritably.

I made to say something, but stopped.

"For once in your life, speak up properly." she said,
with the same cynical tone.

I took a deep breath and realized, for the second time
in a few weeks, that I had to own up.

"I'm sorry Maria." I said, looking away, too ashamed
to look into her eyes. "I don't know what I was thinking. I
didn't know what I was doing. I got scared with this place, this
fucking shit-hole...and I did something stupid. I didn't mean
to hurt you, I swear. I didn't know what I was doing."

I spoke from my heart, but just as much because I
didn't want to lose her.

She softened a little, but didn't let go.

"Well...you fucking did hurt me," she said angrily,
"and worse, you tried to justify it. At least bloody own up
when you've hurt someone you say you care for!"

It felt a little better. At least she was engaging with
me.

She continued, "And don't give this bollocks about
'not knowing what you're doing' or 'being scared' and all such
rot! All of us are scared...that doesn't mean you can just hurt
people as you please!"

I was still vacillating between honest acceptance and
defensiveness, once again.

"But Maria...please also understand where I'm coming
from..."

She put her hand up to stop me from saying anything
else. I think she didn't want to be disappointed again.

"I do know where you're coming from...and I expect
the same from you." she said, now looking directly at me.
"You know how I feel about you, and you said the same
things to me. How could you hide behind this nonsense of

199

you not knowing whether we were exclusive or not? If you had just talked to me about it, I might have been fine with it or I might not have...but that's not the bloody point! The fact is you went behind my back...and I could forgive you for that too if you at least accepted right away that you hurt me."

She stopped to take a swig of her vodka, and said vehemently, "I'm not a fool Jayram. Huh...I don't need you to be anything you're not. But I do expect you to be honest and respect the love we share."

I didn't say a word. My throat tightened. I loved her. I could feel a tear drop well up in my eye and trickle down my cheek. She saw it too. It softened her up a little more, though she didn't make any move to comfort me. She was still far too hurt for that.

The tension between us was palpable, but so was the love. Things would never be the same again, but perhaps there was something still salvageable.

~ Chapter 31 ~

When I first decided to come to Gujarat, I had envisioned a certain degree of tumult in what I was likely to experience, while simultaneously knowing that it was unlikely to be very perilous. My escape from those cops on the bridge the other night had proved that, ultimately, I didn't face much risk of being killed or even injured. I had a sense before arriving in Gujarat that the experiences I was hoping to have were going to make me stronger - you know, in the what-doesn't-kill-you-makes-you-stronger kind of way - while simultaneously having enough socialized protection to not be in too much danger. I knew I was likely to feel a moderately safe amount of fear, pain and anguish, while still experiencing enough to afford me bragging rights. At the back of my head, I think I knew all of this when I landed in Gujarat.

The one thing I didn't bargain for, however, was a rapidly growing cancer of heartlessness. It was scarier than anything I had ever experienced.

One night, a couple of days after Maria and I had gone through that difficult moment, Abhay made an announcement to the two of us.

"Ok," he said with panache, "so we have to find a way to distribute a large batch of *chakla-belans* to the women in Vatwa. They have been asking for them so that they can at least roll *rotis* easily, and it's high time we did this. I've tried to get the movement to come through with it, but it's not on the priority list for them."

Maria and I looked back at him. We knew what was coming. Abhay was probably going to take things into his own hands. He was really handy in getting things done without organizational bureaucracy.

He continued, "So, I managed to raise the money from some friends of mine, and added some of my own. I also got in touch with a manufacturer who gave me a great price. We can procure the items and distribute them tomorrow. But I need both of you to help me. And Jay…if Nasir or Vijay can come, that would be of great help too. I know that maybe one of them should stay back in Gomtipur."

I remember thinking that I ought to have felt proud of him.

I nodded and said, "I'll ask Nasir to join us. He loves helping out with these things."

I managed to get in touch with Nasir by calling the teashop we frequented. I conveyed a message for him to come directly to the BSC office the next day. All of us congregated there, and then proceeded to go about the rest of the day. The process of getting a truck and then procuring the items was like all the other distributions we had done before – hectic and time consuming. I was a little grateful for the activity, as it took my mind off Maria and my own internal demons. But I was doing it mechanically, without any zeal.

We finally made our way to Vatwa by late morning. Abhay had arranged with a couple of the local volunteers there to get people ready to receive their *chakla-belans*. The women were lined up, many of them with their children in tow, in a fairly orderly fashion. Since Vatwa was on the outskirts of the city, it was a much more spacious locality than places like Gomtipur or Gulbarg Society. This also resulted in many lives being saved because of the relative ease of dispersal. The camp too was not cloistered into the confines of a grave yard or mosque ground, but had more of a village feel to it. It was also not as dusty and filthy as urban areas could get.

The distribution went quite smoothly. There was a slight scuffle and argument between a couple of residents, which was resolved without much hassle. We had a good assembly-line-style operation for the distribution. Nasir and I handed the items to the women, while Abhay and Maria set it neatly along the side of the table that we were all sitting at. The other volunteers talked to community members, answered questions, brought in those who hadn't heard of the distribution, and ensured that there was a steady stream of *chakla-belans* from the truck. In a little over two hours, we had finished the entire distribution. We still had a few extra items that Abhay gave to the local volunteers, telling them to leave it in the office, just in case anyone missed out on the distribution.

It was mid-afternoon by the time we were done.

The four of us went out to eat a late lunch at a shop that sold *kababs* and *roti*, not too far from the camp entrance. This seemed to be a regular haunt of Abhay and Maria. The shopkeeper treated them with the same warm familiarity that the teashop owner in Gomtipur treated Vijay, Nasir and I. The *kababs* were a little oily and quite spicy, but delicious. I had it with large bites of chopped onion. The pungency countered the lipids and spices perfectly. We ate well. We were hungry after all the physical work in the morning and afternoon.

We finished our meal, and ordered teas for everyone. Abhay and I lit up a cigarette each. I relaxed a little bit. The conversation was light and the mood was pleasant. Abhay and Maria joked around about the insanity of the work. As we sat there, drinking our teas and smoking, we saw one of the young *Shanthi Pathiks* from the camp walk over towards us with a slightly older man. He came up to Maria.

"Maria*didi*, this was the man I was talking about earlier." he said with a hand around the older man's shoulder. "The man who saw what happened to the crippled boy. He wanted to meet with you and Abhay*bhai* to tell the story."

Maria nodded. "Oh yes, you had mentioned it," then turning to the older man, warmly said, "*Kaka*, please sit down."

Abhay turned to Nasir and I.

"This man has been wanting to tell us a really tragic story about a young disabled boy who was killed in the riots. He saw everything firsthand." he explained to both of us in a whisper.

Both of us nodded. Nasir was visibly interested. I found myself getting a little frustrated at the thought of *another* story about the violence. I was enjoying my tea and cigarette, and had no interest in processing any more gore. I didn't want to betray that emotion either, so refrained from saying anything.

The older man sat down on a stool adjacent to us. Nasir got two more teas for them. The young volunteer who had brought him, sat next to him.

"*Kaka*, go ahead and tell them whatever you feel like." the youth said softly. "Don't worry *kaka*, they will listen and try to help you with what you're going through."

The man's straight backed body indicated that he was probably fifty-odd years old, but robust. His face though, weather-beaten by the stress of the last few months, looked older. He didn't betray much emotion. He laboured through his motions slowly but strongly. He looked at Abhay and Maria.

"I primarily want to tell you what happened because I don't know if this story ever reached you." he ventured. "I don't know if at least some compensation can be received by the family who lost this boy. Even if that doesn't happen, outsiders should know what happened."

Maria and Abhay nodded.

"Of course *kaka*, please continue." Abhay said, giving him his full attention.

The man started, "The day of the violence was I think in late February. We had heard that something horrible had happened in Naroda Patiya and Gulbarg Society the previous night. We heard that they even killed Jaffrey*saab*, so many of us were very worried that they might come to target our colony as well. Nearby localities were targeted."

I lit up another cigarette as he spoke.

"Luckily, most of us in our locality escaped because we had some warning." he continued. "But even then, the mobs came earlier than what we had thought. We had a community meeting with the elders that morning, and the mobs came soon after that. We didn't think they would come so soon. So we weren't able to gather any of our valuables or anything. We just had to run away. Our locality is on the other side of this camp near a small hill, so we ran past there for safety."

He paused to take a sip of his tea.

Nasir asked, "*Kaka*, did your family get out alive?"

"Yes, my family thankfully survived *Inshallah*." the man replied, looking up. "We lost all our belongings. But we survived…and I cannot be ungrateful for that. But as we ran away, I spotted something very horrible from the hill top down towards the centre of the locality."

He took another sip of his tea and continued.

"See, there was this one family with a crippled boy in

a wheelchair. It was very difficult for him to move fast enough to escape the mobs." he said, miming a wheeling motion. "If his family had tried to carry him, they would have been too slow and the mobs would have killed them. So I learnt that he told his parents and siblings to run away, while he would stay back to defend them from the mobs."

I could see Abhay's eyes getting red, while Maria put her head down in sadness. Nasir furrowed his brow in anger.

"I saw what happened from the hill top. I could see him from a distance." he continued, raising his hands in the direction of the hill. "He had two kitchen knives, one in each hand, and he wheeled his way to face the mobs. As they came, waving their weapons, he then tried to attack them with the knives. He didn't do anything to them. How could he? He was a cripple in a wheelchair. But it infuriated them, and they surrounded him calling him all kinds of horrible things."

The man finished his tea, and removed a *beedi* from his shirt pocket. He lit it and took a long drag to calm himself down.

"Some of them were even laughing. They dragged him out of his wheelchair, and one of them told the others to teach him a real lesson, and blast him. They dragged him to the yard, and doused him in kerosene. He wasn't able to move because he was a cripple, so he was just wriggling around as they poured kerosene."

He took another drag of his *beedi*. I took another drag of my cigarette.

"They stepped away from him, kicking him and slashing him with their swords." he continued, shaking his head in anger. "They then stuffed a kerosene-soaked rag into his mouth and lit it on fire. His entire body was burning in a matter of seconds. They kept kicking him as he wriggled around burning and screaming. They shook their swords triumphantly as they danced around him, shouting 'Jai Sri Ram' and all such slogans."

There was silence all around as he finished. It was a short story. He didn't want to prolong the pain.

"I don't know what to think or say. Every day and night I see this boy. I just needed to tell you all." he ended, and took another long drag of his *beedi*.

Everyone was visibly shaken up.

I heard the story, picturing it in vivid detail, and looked at the man telling it. He was telling it with a focused passion that a story of that magnitude deserved. It was a gut-wrenching story of blind heroism and cruel inhumanity. It needed to be told to an apathetic world that only highlighted the heroism and tragedy of the privileged, even when they paled in comparison.

Maria and Abhay, who were experienced activists, were deeply moved by the story. Abhay was close to tears and Maria was almost shaking. It was no surprise. A resident of the community they had been working in had been martyred in unimaginable desperation. Nasir, who had seen violence firsthand, was the embodiment of grief and anger. He should have been. One of his own had died the most heroic of deaths fighting to protect his loved ones from a bloodthirsty mob.

I felt nothing.

My stomach didn't turn. No chill crept up my spine.

Didn't need to dig my thumbs into my kidneys or tighten my abdomen.

I didn't have any reaction. No anger or sadness. Nothing.

I thought of what happened to the boy. I knew I ought to feel something. I knew that I ought to be reacting in the ways my comrades were, but I went numb.

Even a few days back I would have felt something on hearing that story. Now nothing. I was blocking everything out without trying to. I found myself unable to care. I literally didn't give a shit about that crippled boy who fought and died to defend his family with such bravery.

All I could think of was that I wanted another tea and cigarette. The slight irritation I felt at the interruption of my post-lunch relaxation was still present. I was thankful that the old man was done with his story. He was nothing more than an irritant I had to temporarily put up with against my will, and I was glad it was over. If that young boy had been killed in front of me at that very moment, all I would have wanted was for it to be over so I could get back to my tea and cigarette.

I had become a monster.

~ Chapter 32 ~

I needed to spend some more time with Vijay and Nasir, away from my world, on the other side of the river. I wanted to hang out with them outside of our work in the community. I had never really interacted with their families. Staying with them also served as a way to spend a few nights away from the apartment, away from the tension with Maria. It gave me some space where things were a little different. A place where I could maybe even break out of my unfeeling, unemotional prison. All of us were going through slow mental breakdowns. We could see it happening in front of our eyes, and didn't know what to do. We all could see the mental state we were heading towards. I wanted to escape it all, and thought I could do so by hanging out with Vijay and Nasir for a couple of nights.

They were thrilled. Both of them had been trying to convince me to stay with them almost from the moment I met them. We decided that I would split the time among their two houses, first at Vijay's and then Nasir's.

We walked to Vijay's house. Nasir was joining us for dinner before heading to his place. Vijay lived in a Dalit colony that was adjacent to the Muslim colony Nasir lived in. They often spent time in each other's houses I learnt. Vijay stopped at a small shop to buy some yogurt for dinner. We went down an alley towards a poor working-class residential locality.

"Jayram*bhai*, you see the corner of that locality there?" Vijay asked, pointing to the other side of the street as we walked.

I nodded.

"During the *dhamaal*, you should have seen how the Muslim youth defended their community." he continued.

Nasir nodded with pride.

"About 20-25 of them stood guarding the entrance to the community." Vijay continued. "All of them had swords in their hands. When they heard about the violence, they managed to get the women and children to safety and then stood on guard there."

I felt a surge of adrenalin as he narrated what

happened.

"The thing is Jayram*bhai*," Nasir then added, "they had no fear of dying. As far as they were concerned they were already dead. They decided to die. Nobody dared to attack the colony when they saw that. The mobs might have ultimately killed them, but they would have died fighting very hard."

I looked at the nondescript corner where this description of mad bravery took place. It looked like any other street corner in a poor working-class community.

Vijay said, shaking his head at the intensity of the story, "If someone has decided that they're dead and are ready to fight, they're the most dangerous. Oof...no one will dare to fight that person, because the very idea of fear has been thrown out of their mind. That's what those boys were like."

It sent a slight chill up my spine to hear Vijay speak like this.

We continued walking to the residential locality that Vijay's house was located in. He pointed to different markers in his life. The shop that he used to buy cigarettes from. The muddy field where he used to play football and volleyball with his friends. The small government clinic where his father worked as a security guard.

The most animated showing was a street corner where he had a fight with a couple of guys.

"We started hitting each other with soda bottles." he said, miming the action. "I was bleeding from my eye by the end. But I managed to beat them. One of my friends joined in too."

I grinned and said, "You were quite a thug in earlier days eh boss? Street fights and everything."

Nasir then chimed in, chuckling a little bit, "Just like I told you Jayram*bhai*, he used to be a big street tough. His nickname was Boxer!"

Vijay smiled. He seemed to be quite proud of his macho past, especially now that he had come out of it unscathed.

We walked on towards his house, which was situated in a small street lined with houses leading up to a dead end. Children played cricket on the street since it was too narrow for large vehicles to move into. A few auto rickshaws and two-wheelers were parked in front of the houses. Outside most of the houses were cots made out of wood and twine that older people sat on. Vijay led us into his house, and introduced me to his parents who were sitting on one such cot. They nodded politely and I greeted them with folded palms. We walked into the house. It was a typical toiling house. One big room acted as a living room cum bedroom for the entire family. A kitchen-like alcove was at the end of the room; with a door to what I guessed was the bathroom and washing area behind the house. This house had two storeys though. Vijay beckoned for us to come up the stairs.

"My brother's family sleeps here Jayram*bhai*, while my wife and I sleep upstairs." he said, pointing up.

We made our way up the narrow stairwell into an area that was similar to what I had just seen, except smaller. We walked in and I saw a small woman, sitting on her haunches, cutting vegetables on the floor. I recognized her immediately. I had seen her around the camps on occasion. She stood up as we walked in and Vijay introduced her to me

"Jayram*bhai*, this is my wife Ameena. You might have seen her in Gomtipur. She helps me a lot with my work sometimes."

I again brought my palms together respectfully, and asked, "Are you a *Shanthi Pathik* too?"

Ameena replied with a smile, "No, no, Jayram*bhai*. I work in a tailoring shop. I just help Vijay whenever I can with the work. Some members of my family used to live for a short while in the camps, so that's how I got involved."

I nodded and smiled. My curiosity was raised when I heard her name. Ameena was definitely a Muslim name, and her *salwar-kameez* had distinct Islamic patterns. Vijay was a Dalit Christian, so wondered how they managed to work it out.

They asked Nasir and me to sit on the bed inside the room, while they sat on the floor cutting vegetables for dinner. Vijay, Nasir and Ameena chatted away about friends and family, while I listened in.

I noticed the way Vijay and Ameena cut the vegetables. They peeled and removed the core of the onions carefully so as to only remove that part that absolutely couldn't be eaten. Similarly, they worked on the other vegetables, only removing the bare minimum. I reflected on how I cut vegetables back in Bangalore the few times I cooked. Carelessly, without giving a thought to how much I was wasting when I removed the roughage from potatoes or onions.

I saw that they had procured meat; minced lamb. It must have been expensive for them. A luxury, and the luxury was me. I was touched.

After the vegetables were cut, Ameena proceeded to make lamb curry with it, while Vijay joined Nasir and I, seated on the bed. The smell of the curry was divine. Ameena also made some *daal* and *roti*. Dinner was ready soon, and Vijay laid out a mat on the floor along with four plates. They then called us to join them on the floor. Vijay told me that I could wash my hands in the small bathroom situated on the balcony. I washed up and sat in front of one of the plates. They served me first – huge portions that I knew they would not be serving themselves. Throughout dinner, Ameena and Vijay kept one eye on my plate to make sure that I always had food on it.

As we came to the end of dinner, I was stuffed. Yet both Vijay and Ameena exclaimed warmly that I had not eaten a thing and ought to eat more. Before I could reply, they put more food on my plate and, despite my protests, pleaded with me to eat more. I ate it and was positively bloated. I had to remove my plate in order to prevent them from putting more food on it.

Ameena took the dishes away, while Vijay beckoned for Nasir and me to join him on the balcony to smoke. Ameena soon joined us with some *nimbu paani*, and I enjoyed a lingering smoke while sipping the sweet, lime drink.

Nasir soon left. Before leaving, he invited all of us to dinner at his house the next day.

"And Jayram*bhai*," he said, turning to me, "you stay in my place tomorrow since today you're staying in Vijay's house, ok?"

I smiled and nodded my affirmation. We said our goodbyes to Nasir, and after he left, the rest of us got ready to sleep. Vijay, Ameena and I were still on the balcony.

"Jayram*bhai*, you should sleep inside under the fan."
Vijay said to me. "Ameena and I will sleep on the balcony. It
will be much more comfortable for you."

I tried to protest.

"It's no problem Vijay. I can sleep on the balcony,
and you two sleep in your regular places."

To no avail of course.

"No, no Jayram*bhai*." Ameena replied immediately.
"We'll sleep here on the balcony. You are our guest, you will
feel much more comfortable inside."

I smiled and nodded. There was no fighting their
hospitality. I then decided to be bold and ask them about how
they met.

"Ok I'll sleep inside. But tell me…how did the two of
you meet? I ask because I'm guessing both of you are from
different religions right?"

Vijay nodded, grinning widely.

I continued, "So it must have been a love
marriage…right?"

Ameena blushed a little bit. Vijay replied, "Jayram*bhai*,
we met when we both were at a workshop in Mumbai. It was
a workshop on communal harmony. We became friends there
and soon after we decided to get married to each other."

Ameena then said, "Initially our families were a little
hesitant, but soon they accepted our marriage. It's no problem
now."

I smiled again.

"That's wonderful." I said.

~ Chapter 33 ~

Ameena woke up at 5.30 the next morning to cook breakfast for the entire family.

I heard Vijay's father come halfway upstairs and ask gruffly, "Ameena! Wake up. Is breakfast ready?"

"Yes *papa*, I'm preparing it right now." she replied while sweating over the stove.

I had already seen an inkling of it last night. Ameena woke up earlier then everyone else, went to bed later than everyone else, and worked twice as hard as Vijay in keeping the house running. All this was in addition to her day job. I felt a sleepy twinge of anger that she had to work so hard, while simultaneously feeling guilty that I was adding to her burden.

Vijay woke up a little later, and started collecting the buckets in the house. I asked him, rubbing my eyes groggily, why he had to wake up so early to do that.

"Jayram*bhai*, we get water supply to the house only for two hours in the morning and two hours in the evening every day." he replied, walking with the buckets towards the stairs. "If we don't fill up the water, then we won't have enough water for the day before we get it again in the evening. Don't worry about it…you just sleep for some more time."

I remember thinking what a royal pain in the ass that must have been. I woke up and joined Vijay downstairs so that I could brush my teeth and wash up. I couldn't sleep with all the early morning din, but I had an easy morning that day. Ameena made breakfast for all of us, while Vijay filled up the buckets with water, left half of them downstairs, and hauled the rest upstairs.

When we came back up, Ameena had made omelettes and *parathas* for us. I noticed that Vijay's parents were up there, joining us for breakfast. I again folded my palms and greeted them with a smile.

Vijay smiled and said to me, "My parents eat breakfast with us in the morning, and they eat dinner with my brother's family downstairs."

All five of us sat down for breakfast. The food was delicious, and I was surprised at how hungry I was considering my dinner the previous night. Back home in Bangalore I had never eaten breakfast without first finishing my morning workout. As was to be expected, Ameena and Vijay kept pestering me to have more until I was stuffed.

After breakfast, I asked Vijay if I could go to the loo. He said that the toilet was downstairs.

"Let me first make sure no one is there," he said, "so you can go to the toilet in peace."

He went downstairs and soon came back up, telling me that I could go. He accompanied me downstairs, past the cooking area, and pointed out to the small backyard which had the attached toilet built from corrugated steel sheets. It was barely the size of a closet, and was surrounded by a crumbling concrete wall.

"Jayram*bhai*, the toilet door doesn't bolt properly," he warned me, "so you have to use a rope hooked onto the nail by the doorframe. You should also close the backdoor of the house behind you so no one else can come there."

I nodded and thanked him. The loo was small, barely large enough for me to stand upright, and had no hook for my pants. I hung my pants on the door handle, and finished my business in the Indian style toilet with a little difficulty. Not being used to getting on my haunches to take a shit, I was grateful for it nevertheless.

I went back up to the room that Vijay and Ameena lived in. By then the dishes had been cleared up by her. Vijay's parents were back downstairs.

Vijay said to me, "Jayram*bhai*, we'll go to work now. And then in the evening, we'll go for dinner to Nasir's house. You'll be staying there tonight."

The time at the camps, or rather at the localities, went by pretty quickly with community meetings, more surveys, and some questions people had about their livelihood materials. There was something a little different with the way Nasir and Vijay interacted with me though. It was like a new step of familiarity had been taken since yesterday. It was comfortable.

In the evening as we sat at our tea shop drinking tea and smoking, Nasir told me with a smile, "Jayram*bhai*, I hope you like chicken. Because you will be getting a nice chicken curry tonight in my house!"

I smiled. I knew that he was getting it as a special occasion for me.

"I love chicken." I replied happily. "I'm sure it will be just as good as the lamb curry that Ameena*behen* made for us last night, eh Vijay?"

Vijay replied with a smile, "Nasir's mother is probably a better cook than Ameena even, Jayram*bhai*."

I found myself getting a little irritated at the fact that it was only the women who seemed to be doing the cooking – mothers, wives, sisters. But I refrained from saying anything. Now was not the time to fight that battle, I told myself. I needed to fight it in my own home first. I hadn't been able to get my own dad to help out more in the kitchen and I wasn't exactly my mom's happy helper either. I had little right to be moralistic about Vijay's and Nasir's families.

We walked over to Nasir's house. It was not too far off from where we worked. The lanes grew narrower the closer we got to his house.

"Look there Jayram*bhai*." Nasir said, pointing at his house. "My house is right in the centre of the colony. That's why it has never faced any problems of violence or anything like that."

I nodded, and looked around the locality. It was tight. Even tighter than Vijay's locality. Two or three-storey buildings scrunched up next to each other on either side of a narrow road, with small lanes snaking out on either side. The houses couldn't have been more than a room or two to a family. If ever violence were to happen here, it wouldn't take long for it to engulf the entire community.

"Even if any *dhamaal* happens, nothing happens to my house." Nasir continued, smiling. "It's completely safe."

It sounded like he was convincing himself just as much as he was convincing me.

As we neared the entrance of his house, a young boy and girl ran out from inside shouting with big smiles on their faces.

"*Chacha! Chacha!*"

Nasir laughed, and joyfully took each in one arm, hoisted the girl on his back where she clung on for a piggy-back ride, while carrying the boy in front.

"My brother's children!" he gleefully exclaimed. "They're real brats...very naughty devils!"

I looked at Nasir's nephew and niece giggling.

Of course he had to convince himself that nothing would happen to his house.

As we entered the house, Nasir introduced me to his parents. They looked a little older than what I had expected. I folded my hands again in a *namaste*.

"Come, let's go up to the terrace while we wait for dinner." he suggested with a smile, after the exchange of pleasantries with his parents. "The breeze is very nice there. Uma will also join us..."

I smiled a little, but didn't want to give too much away. I didn't know how much his parents knew. I could see the happy twinkle in Nasir's eyes though. The three of us went upstairs to the roof. Nasir was right; the breeze was lovely. We sat down on the floor of the rooftop for a few minutes talking lazily. Nasir had brought tea with him, so I enjoyed another nice, lingering smoke with the tea.

Uma soon arrived. I noticed the change in Nasir's bearing as she joined us on the roof. He straightened up a little, not wanting to present himself at his most indolent. I could see that this dinner doubled up as an excuse for Nasir and Uma to spend some time with each other without ruffling societal feathers too much. She gave a charming smile as she sat next to him.

"So Nasir*bhai*, how are you?" she asked, launching straight into her playful tone. "Still trying to find some girl stupid enough to marry you?"

Vijay and I burst out laughing immediately. Nasir soaked it in. I could tell he loved it. It was an indirect way for Uma to proffer loving attention on him. Nevertheless he reacted in his cute faux-macho style.

"Shut up...how many times do I have to tell you? The great Nasir will not be tied down by any marriage to some mindless girl who will nag me all day long."

The ribbing continued for some more time.

Soon we settled into more serious conversation. We talked about our aspirations, our beliefs, and life in general.

"Whatever we do with our life," Uma said assuredly, "we must always make sure we give something back to society."

Nasir nodded enthusiastically. They would look into each other's eyes every now and then for the briefest of moments. I sometimes stole glimpses of those moments. I could see how smitten they were with each other.

We sat in the cool evening breeze, and talked for some more time. I smoked another cigarette with Vijay. Soon, Nasir's mother called us down for dinner. We all trooped down to eat. It was a lovely evening. Good people. Good food. Warm hospitality. It was rejuvenating for me.

The next day, when I returned back to the apartment, I thought about the quality time I had briefly spent with Vijay and Nasir outside of our work. It acted like a tonic, and gave me the little spark I needed to break free from my demons. I could have continued staying at their houses. It wasn't like the opportunity to spend more nights their hadn't come up before or after that time. In fact, since I had spent a couple of nights in their houses, the invitations intensified. As I left, both of them said that I should stay with their families for the entire duration of my time in Ahmedabad.

It probably made sense to do so. The work *was* on that side of the river after all. While I worked with them in the camps during the day, I still went to back at night to leading the same middle-class life I was accustomed to. I had fun, didn't really have to worry about anything. So even when I did experience devastation, I didn't. It was so far removed from me socially that I needed to spend a couple of nights in Vijay's and Nasir's houses to merely understand how far removed it truly was. Truly if I wanted to engage with that side of my journey in a more in-depth manner, it made sense to spend more nights in their houses.

Ultimately though, I had to acknowledge the real reason for my not spending more non-work time with them. Yeah, I spent a couple of nights in their houses and I had a lovely time. But the truth is, deep down, I didn't want to.

It wasn't as comfortable for me. Physically or socially. I could do it for short periods of time, but ultimately, I was more comfortable with my guitar and being able to take a shit in a seated position; I was more comfortable with English-speaking volunteers and the social moors they came with; I was more comfortable with hugging Abhay and kissing Maria whenever I felt like it. Indeed, the spark I got by staying with Vijay and Nasir for a couple of nights was probably the realization that I had it pretty good with Abhay and Maria. Ultimately, I was more comfortable on the side of the river with them, in that apartment, with boot-legged whisky and inebriated merrymaking.

Whenever I was feeling low or depressed, all I had to do was get back to it in the evening and I could have all the fun I wanted. I could feel comforted by friends who talked, ate, drank and joked around the way I did, who lived the way I did. Abhay's humour would cheer me up, and I could sleep soundly in Maria's lovely embrace. I didn't ever seek support from Nasir or Vijay, always condescendingly assuming that they couldn't give it to me.

Truth is, I didn't want to give up my ways. It was easier being the middle-class guy who could do his humanitarian bit and go back to his comfortable ways without really having to sacrifice much. So I did just that.

~ Chapter 34 ~

While things were still a little tense with Maria, I could always rely on the work with Vijay and Nasir as a distraction to ride out any personal angst until things got better. This might have been because the work itself was never dull or short of interesting characters.

One night we were told by one of the NGOs of *Shanthi Samudaya* that a team of doctors from West Bengal were coming the next day to volunteer for two days with survivors of the violence.

Vijay, Nasir and I were given the responsibility of handling them and figuring out how best we could use them. Rather than waste time travelling to various localities across the city, we decided it would be best to run two day-long medical camps in two different localities where the health situation was quite dire. We decided to hold the first medical camp in Gomtipur and the second one in the Shah Alam refugee camp.

We had to ensure that a modicum of arrangements were in place for the camps. We crudely planned the entire process the night before through phone calls and messages to our friends in both localities, ensuring the message got to the residents that a medical camp was going to be held, and to keep any medical information they had ready. The Bengali medical team also assured us that they would prioritize the sickest among them, following which others would receive treatment. We realized that we needed to leave early next day in order to get everything set up.

Thankfully the NGO that gave us the message about them said that we could hire a taxi for the two days. This made it much easier than having to lug around a medical team, equipment and all, on buses and rickshaws. I had also developed a bad cough and was slowly falling ill, so didn't fancy trying to catch buses or auto rickshaws for the next couple of days.

Vijay, Nasir and I went to the BSC office where the medical team was waiting for us. The few times I had interacted with middle-class Bengali folk, I found them to be rather snobbish about their perceived intellectual and cultural advancement, not unlike my own Tamil Brahmin family. It often meant that, despite not wanting to, I bonded well with them in a rather tempestuous way. My first two girlfriends were Bengali, and both relationships were passionately loving and maddeningly frustrating in equal measure.

This medical team was no different. They behaved like their two days of service was the definitive act of revolutionary solidarity. Turned out that they were all members of one of the Communist Parties that was part of the ruling alliance in West Bengal. And, staying true to my mercurial connection with Bengalis, I ended up bonding with the pompous leader of the delegation.

"You see...ultimately the only way any fascism is going to be defeated," said the head doctor sagely, after I had expressed an interest in their political affiliations, "is through class struggle that is led by the working class, the proletariat."

He said this while doing health checks, and doling out prescriptions for residents queuing up to get treatment at the medical camp. His team ensured that there were enough medicines, and adequately sterilized equipment to do the checkups. Vijay, Nasir and I helped where we could and whenever we were asked for something.

"What does that mean?" I asked, while helping the doctor out with some medicines. "Is class struggle the *only* way fascism can be defeated? What about other interests, like that of Muslims or Dalits or women?"

"Ultimately, all those identities are secondary to our identity as workers in a class struggle with the bourgeoisie." he said without batting an eyelid. "This fascism that you see in Gujarat is primarily because of capitalism. All these corporations are doing business with the fascists, and the fascists are able to attract more investment capital, and also divide the working-class. If we want to defeat the fascists, then we first have to defeat capitalism."

I replied, "I agree that capitalism is a huge problem...but it's not like upper caste Hindus are facing this fascist violence. It's mainly Muslims, and in other parts of India, Dalits face it."

He shook his head like he was talking to a child.
"That might all be true," he said, smiling condescendingly,
"but we have to see the bigger picture. Ultimately these other
identities will only hinder class struggle. Initially, yes, there are
struggles around those identities. But ultimately the main
struggle is class struggle."

"Why can't class struggle also integrate these other
identities? Why can't a worker also be seen as a Dalit worker
or a female worker?" I asked, shamelessly borrowing points
from an earlier discussion between Abhay and Maria.

The doctor gave the same smile, and replied, "They
can be – as long as it doesn't take away from the class
struggle."

There was a slight pause as he handed out another
bottle of medicine to a resident.

"See, even your friends." he said pointing to Vijay and
Nasir while they were talking to some residents in the queue,
knowing full well that they wouldn't understand us talking in
English.

"They hold on to their Muslim or Dalit identity in a
political manner. But without class consciousness, ultimately
they cannot be a full part of the revolution that will bring
down capitalism, and therefore fascism," he concluded
commandingly.

I noticed that others in his team would once in a
while hear what he was saying and nod respectfully. He was
intelligent and well-read, no doubt. I was learning a lot from
the conversation. But he was also a condescending blowhard.
And I found myself bristling a little in defence of Vijay and
Nasir. I didn't say anything though. Didn't feel intelligent
enough. I almost felt like telling him to meet me after a few
years when I would have read more on this kind of stuff, and
could offer a more engaged argument.

At the end of the camp in Shah Alam, one of the
main community leaders got mutton biryani for all of us. We
all sat and ate out of a large plate. We noticed that the *Shanthi
Pathiks* and the head of the camp did not join us. They said
that, as guests, we should eat first. A few of us insisted but
they still said no. I knew they were not eating with us because
they wanted us to have our fill and get the best meat pieces.

The doctor then joked in thickly Bengali-accented Hindi, "*Accha*, now I understand. You don't want to eat with us because we're Hindus."

He seemed really pleased with himself.

At this, all of them reluctantly came and sat around the plate. They started eating with us, but barely nibbled at the food. I noticed that they were still keener on ensuring that we had large servings of biryani and the biggest pieces of meat.

The good doctor didn't notice any of this however, and tucked in with satisfaction.

"See…we can all eat together after all. In the end, we're all humans." he promptly lectured to us, spooning in mouthfuls of biryani.

~ Chapter 34.5 ~

Notwithstanding ostentatious Bengali commies, the medical camps were quite a success. After dropping the medical team off at the train station the next day, I made my way back to the apartment. The cough was getting worse, and I felt like I was burning up with fever, so flopped onto bed as soon as I entered. No one was there.

Maria was away again in the Western coast near Mumbai for a few days. She was chaperoning some kids from the camps in Vatwa to a residential orphanage-cum-school, and was due to arrive a couple of days later. She had left while I was spending nights in Vijay's and Nasir's houses.

I found myself missing her.

Abhay returned that night and I talked with him a little bit, before falling back to sleep. He ensured I ate a little something, and gave me a couple of aspirin to control the fever.

I woke up the next day, still feverish, and tried to continue the work that needed to be done with Vijay and Nasir. But it only made me sicker. I returned back to the apartment within a couple of hours and collapsed onto bed again. This time I didn't bother eating dinner. Abhay tried to wake me up to feed me, but I couldn't manage a bite. So he made me drink some ginger-lemon tea, gave me some more aspirin, and told me to sleep it off.

I could barely move in the morning, my entire body was quivering with a high fever. Abhay had to leave early that day for a round of surveying in Vatwa. He had a few volunteers that had just come in from Delhi, so he had to first get over to BSC, pick them up and then head over to the camp.

"I'm a little worried Jay...you've never fallen this sick before. Should I stay back? I can get someone else to pick those brats up and take them to Vatwa." he said with concern.

"I'll be fine man." I replied. "Don't worry. I plan on sleeping for most of the day anyway."

"Ok..." he said, not fully convinced. "I'll be back home earlier than usual, just in case."

He made me some tea with dry toast, and ensured that I had enough aspirin. Cut up some fruits and placed them in the fridge for me to eat later.

"There's some *daal* and rice, along with some vegetable curry in the fridge too," he said, "so make sure you have a proper lunch and take the aspirin. Just get a lot of rest today Jay. And don't worry about the work…if Vijay or Nasir need me for anything, they have my cell phone number and can call me. I've already left a message letting them know this."

I smiled weakly and thanked him. It felt good to be so cared for. I promptly flopped back, almost unconscious with fever, grateful for the bed and the apartment. I was even more grateful for Abhay's care, and was happy that I was going to see Maria soon. I was hopeful that the break from her would have eased the tension between us. But what really lifted my spirits was when Abhay told me how concerned she sounded when they spoke over the phone the night before, after I went to sleep. Abhay had told her about my sickness.

"She was very worried man." Abhay said, with that lovely twinkle in his eye. "Said that she would come over soon to be with you and help you feel better."

I could feel my heart lift as I lay in bed.

And with good reason too.

The moment she walked in the door, she showed the kind of affection that only came from comrades who were also in love with each other. She brought *pottu*, *channa*, and Kerala bananas that she knew I loved. We ate a late lunch together.

She stayed with me all day making countless cups of tea and chatting with me. She spoke at length about her trip, and the insane endeavour of transporting a bunch of kids to a school so far away.

"It was crazy Jay." she said, with a smile and shake of her head. "Luckily the orphanage seems like a wonderful place for these kids to grow up in, so the trip was worth it."

She saw a book next to the mattress, and enquired about it.

"What's that book you're reading?"

"It's about Bhagat Singh." I replied, showing it to her.

"I bought it a couple of days back, while you were away. He's one of my biggest inspirations."

"He was an amazing guy." she exclaimed knowingly, taking the book in her hands. "His writings are beautiful. What a sacrifice he made when he was fighting the Brits. One has to admire that kind of blind revolutionary courage…no matter how tragic."

I could feel the hair on the back of my neck stand up as I listened to her.

"It's interesting, how he has remained such an enigmatic icon in this country because of his martyrdom." she continued. "Everyone knows about Bhagat Singh…and yet, I don't think most people understand him. He was a socialist, but Hindu fascist groups like the BJP try to lay claim to his legacy."

"I know, it's crazy." I said. "It's ridiculous when one of his most famous essays was called *Why I'm an Atheist*"

Maria nodded. She was looking into my eyes now.

I slowly added, "Well…there are actually a couple of paras in it that mean a lot to me, especially now…um…shall I read them to you?'

She knew the essay well, and smiled in affirmation. I could sense her eyes welling up. Mine were too as I read his angry words.

I ask why your omnipotent God does not stop every man when he is committing any sin or offence? He can do it quite easily. Why did he not kill war lords or kill the fury of war in them and thus avoid the catastrophe hurled down on the head of humanity by the Great War? Why does he not just produce a certain sentiment in the mind of the British people to liberate India? Why does he not infuse the altruistic enthusiasm in the hearts of all capitalists to forgo their rights of personal possessions of means of production and thus redeem the whole labouring community, nay the whole human society, from the bondage of Capitalism? You want to reason out the practicability of socialist theory, I leave it for your almighty to enforce it.

People recognize the merits of socialism in as much as the general welfare is concerned. They oppose it under the pretext of its being impracticable. Let the Almighty step in and arrange everything in an orderly fashion. Now don't try to advance round about arguments, they are out of order. Let me tell you, British rule is here not because God wills it but because they possess power and we do not dare to oppose them. Not that it is with the help of God that they are keeping us under their subjection but it is with the help of guns and rifles, bomb and bullets, police and militia and our apathy that they are successfully committing the most deplorable sin against society- the outrageous exploitation of one nation by another. Where is God? What is he doing? Is he enjoying all these woes of human race? A Nero; A Changez; Down with him.

By the time I finished reading, I could see tears glistening in Maria's eyes. It wasn't just the politics in that excerpt, powerful as it was. His anger towards a metaphysical god was merely a vehicle of expression for what was the true target of his ire – cold-blooded oppression. That medium could have taken on a number of different forms. I think it was powerful more so because it laid bare the painful intensity of the events that led us to each other in the first place.

We continued chatting until I felt tired again. I went to sleep. She lay beside me for a little while, holding me. It was lovely.

By the end of the day the bond between us was back at its beautiful best. No hesitancy, no feelings of angst despite the shoddy way I spurned her love after gleefully accepting it. When I fell sick, all the tension between us just melted away, and she took care of me as if we were an intimate couple. It was a far sharper impalement, one I thoroughly deserved, than any amount of cold silences, fiery tempers, or acid tongues.

The day ended with me feeling love once more. I fell in love with Maria all over again, and felt the sweet pain of that love flooding over me.

~ Chapter 35 ~

Since we spent so much time working in the camps, we rarely saw as much of the fascist core of the city, on the side of the river where we lived. Not surprising, considering that our evenings for the most part were occupied with laughing our stresses away.

The belly of the beast was filled with nice restaurants and shops. It had malls to explore and roads that didn't crumble following the monsoons. It had opportunities for fun and amusement in abundance. We rarely smelt the bile. But when we did, it was revealing in many ways.

Mani had asked Abhay, Maria and I to help conduct a workshop on secularism and communal harmony for some students at the university campus near the BSC. They were first and second year students at the University of Ahmedabad. We were excited at the prospect. It was different from the work we were doing in Gomtipur and Vatwa. It was work that required us to be educators of sorts. He also asked us to get the help of a well known Muslim activist in the city who had done a lot of work on the issue.

"Salim Jaffrey has worked with many groups in the city on peace and harmony issues," Mani instructed us, "so it would be very wise to have him lead the workshop along with you three helping him. He runs an NGO here, which works primarily on education issues, but started working in partnership with *Shanthi Samudaya* once the violence started."

Abhay phoned Jaffrey over a speaker phone and asked if he would lead the workshop with the three of us. He was more than happy to do so.

"Why don't you three come over for lunch to my office tomorrow? We can then also discuss the format of the workshop in a little more detail." he added warmly.

We went to his office in the old city the next day, and finalized the format of the workshop. He seemed to have it down pat. There wasn't much for us to do, save whatever he suggested. Jaffrey was a soft-spoken, lean, elegant man, impeccably dressed in a well-pressed shirt and pair of pleated trousers, with an immaculately trimmed, salt-and-pepper moustache. He likely came from a well-off background as he spoke perfect English.

"I think it would be good for all of you to talk a little bit about your journeys to this point." he suggested. "It helps to personalize it as much as possible. There will be some very right-wing students, who have heard nothing but the poison that their parents have been teaching them, so we should be prepared."

"And you will lead the discussion and Q&A session after all of us have spoken?" Maria asked.

"Well," Jaffrey said with a smile, "we all will be leading the workshop. It's important that they see us all as one unit as opposed to me being some Muslim man who has brainwashed the three of you. It would help to also showcase our three different religions in a subtle manner with the fact that we're working together. It always helps to put forward a united, secular face."

We all nodded. I took some brief notes as well.

He continued, "In fact, normally whenever I do workshops like this, a very dear colleague of mine joins me. She's Hindu, so we're always a united Hindu-Muslim team. We don't make it a big deal...but rather that being together is a very normal thing. It's understated, but can be very powerful."

Jaffrey was articulate, and had a keen mind. We found out, over lunch, that he had survived an assassination attempt only a few months back when the climate of hatred in the state was at its peak.

"I was giving a small talk to a group of NGOs a few months back just after the violence had begun, early March I think." he said, as he served us large helpings of *biryani* and *daal*. "Then, midway through my talk, there was this major commotion. We all turned to see some goons from the local BJP unit barge in through the doors of the hall. They were all brandishing swords and large sticks."

He paused to eat a spoonful of *biryani* before continuing, laughing sarcastically.

"Huh...dear lord...they were so bloodthirsty. 'Where's the Muslim bastard who thinks he can tell Hindus

227

what to do? We'll bloody kill him now!' they shouted. I knew they were talking about me...I had already received quite a few death threats in those days when madness was the norm. I immediately ducked under the tables, and crawled to the back exit."

We all listened, me open-mouthed, as we ate our lunch. I tried picturing this man, who looked more like a corporate honcho rather than an activist, crawling on all fours under a table.

"My friends in the other NGOs, somehow managed to prevent them from reaching me," he concluded, with a rueful smile, "and I escaped through the back door, into my car and drove off. I tell you, it was terrifying."

No doubt.

After lunch, we said our goodbyes and made our way back to the BSC office to prep for the workshop.

The next day, the four of us went to the university. The class room was full, seating nearly a hundred and twenty people. Jaffrey led the workshop with a presentation on the roots of religious secularism and communal harmony in India; the various ways in which Islam and Muslims were integral to the very fabric of the country, just like Hindus, Sikhs, Christians, Jains, Parsis and others; that without religious diversity, the very idea of India was lost. He also spoke about the theological and philosophical similarities in different bodies of thought, as well as the richness that came with the engagement of differences. Jaffrey then listed some famous Muslims, including the then President of India, Abdul Kalam, whose nomination was supported by the BJP themselves.

The students seemed to be listening. I was surprised to see many nodding along. I had expected a slightly more hostile atmosphere.

Abhay, Maria and I then talked for a little while each about our experiences, and what happened on the other side of the river. This came as more of a shock to the students. Most of them didn't seem to know the extent of the violence that had transpired only a few months back. I could sense some ruffled feathers now. Though, for the most part, even those seemed more out of ignorance than outright bigotry.

Finally it was time for the discussion. This was one of the most important parts of the workshop, Jaffrey had told us. It was where stereotypes could be thwarted and conversations could be had in a civil manner. He told us to not raise our voices on any account and, regardless of the bigotry that might be shown, to always maintain a calm front. I decided to cede ground to Abhay and Maria if ever it came down to dealing with hostile students. I didn't trust myself to remain calm in the face of something like that.

The discussion went fairly uneventfully at first. Most of the students asked questions out of a voyeuristic curiosity, mostly directed at the three of us.

"What are the conditions like at the camps?"

"Did you face any problems?"

"How many people died?"

"Who are the volunteers in the different organizations?"

Then, all of a sudden, one of the students, whom I had marked out as one of the more attentive ones, stood up and looked at Jaffrey.

"Jaffrey sir." he asked respectfully. "Why are uneducated Muslims so violent? Educated Muslims like yourself lead respectable lives. Then why can't these uneducated ones also try and better themselves?"

Jaffrey smiled. He had been waiting for something like this. He didn't dignify the question when he responded, but was the epitome of dignity himself.

"What makes you think that they are violent?" he asked, with the same warm tone.

The boy raised his voice a little bit.

"Because they are! All the riots we see in this country are instigated by them. And they act like they're in Pakistan!"

To this, one of the girls, who was Muslim, took particular umbrage.

"You don't know what you're talking about! Without knowing anything, don't just spout garbage!" she indignantly castigated.

Without acknowledging her, the boy continued.

"You should see their neighbourhood." he said, pointing at the girl crudely. "They always fly the green

Pakistani flag! And they never support the Indian cricket team!"

I saw some heads nodding in agreement at this. I felt a little unsure as to what needed to be done. The girl responded, this time to us, but somewhat defensively.

"He doesn't even know that the flags we fly in our neighbourhood are flags with religious symbols. Just because it's green, doesn't mean that they are Pakistani flags. We all are proud Indians. People like him are too ignorant to know it!"

Jaffrey then interjected before it got out of hand.

"See, my son, ultimately you should realize that this is a free country right?" he asked rhetorically.

He continued, "People have the right to practice what they believe in and support any team they wish. What I would urge you to do is think about how we, as a people, can support each other...rather than the way in which we can harm each other. As a starting point, I ask that you try and find the areas of common ground, rather than areas of conflict"

Before the boy could respond, Maria posed a question to the larger class, but in response to what the boy said.

"Tell me this, all of you...now, I'm sure many of you want to go abroad to study. Is that also wrong? Do you think that means you are abandoning your people? If you feel like it's ok to go abroad to study, then why isn't it ok to support whichever cricket team we want to when we have the right to do so?"

Jaffrey smiled. There were some murmurs in the class and a few nods. Nobody had a ready answer.

The boy then responded.

"All that is fine. But if you're in this country, then you have to support the cricket team, otherwise these Muslims can leave India." he said imperiously before staying silent for the rest of the discussion.

The workshop ended soon after that exchange. Jaffrey seemed really pleased with the way things went.

"The good thing is that we planted a seed in all those students' minds. It's a long struggle, but it's a start." he said as he parted with us, and got into his car.

I was less optimistic. But I could afford to be.

After the workshop, I decided to go for a walk to the tea shop on the BSC campus. I ordered a tea and lit up a cigarette. As I sat on the chair outside the shop, reflecting on the workshop, I went back in time, a few years back, to what one of my high school friends in Bangalore had said, during an India-Pakistan cricket match.

"These Muslims man…why can't they support the Indian cricket team?" he commented indignantly as we watched the exciting match in my house. "They live in India, so they should support the Indian team. Otherwise they should go back to Pakistan!"

I smiled ruefully back at him.

"I agree man…if they can't support India, then they have no right to be here." I said, nodding in agreement, before getting back to watching the match.

~ Chapter 36 ~

"Jayram*bhai*, I need your help. It's really urgent." Nasir told me earnestly, while sitting in the barber's chair getting his hair cut.

"Not tomorrow. But today. Please…it's really important." he implored.

"Ok." I said, a little tentatively. "What's the problem Nasir?"

"First, promise me that you will help me, and then I'll tell you." he continued with the same earnestness, as the barber styled his hair with gel. "You're like a brother to me Jayram*bhai*, and I didn't know who else I could turn to."

Vijay nodded in agreement.

Earlier in the day, he had come to pick me up in his brother's motorbike.

"Nasir has something very urgent to talk to you about, Jayram*bhai*, so I've come to pick you up." he had said, explaining his sudden arrival at the apartment.

I nodded, got dressed hurriedly and hopped onto the motorbike.

"I'll do whatever is in my powers to help you Nasir." I said, as Nasir stepped down from the barber's chair. "Tell me what's going on…wait…"

I paused and smiled.

"Is it about Uma?" I asked.

Nasir nodded and smiled too.

"We're ready to get married Jayram*bhai*. I proposed to her yesterday morning. She agreed to marry me and went to tell her parents immediately after I proposed."

He paused to put his shirt on. I figured something must have gone wrong.

"They got very angry." he said, while buttoning his shirt. "They said that they didn't want to see her ever again, and could never accept me as a son-in-law."

I nodded. It wasn't very surprising.

Nasir continued, "My family have accepted her completely. But they've requested that she convert to Islam. I said that it wasn't necessary, but Uma said that if it's what my parents want, then she's willing to convert. Jayram*bhai*, she's willing to convert to Islam to get married to me, and she's even quit her work as a *Shanthi Pathik*."

I was touched by their love for each other, but also a little annoyed that she had to quit.

"All that is good, but why did she have to quit her work?" I asked, folding my hands in irritation. "Didn't you say something?"

"I tried to Jayram*bhai*, but she insisted, since it was my parents' wishes."

I didn't believe him fully. Felt like if he put his foot down, it wouldn't have mattered what his parents wanted, but didn't prod further.

"Ok, so what do you need? Is Uma in trouble?"

"No, no. She's fine. She's in my house with my parents, and they're treating her like a daughter. Her family have completely abandoned her, and she came back to my house in tears. But her family are not causing any problems, thankfully. They've just abandoned her."

I had heard numerous stories of Hindu girls and Muslim boys falling in love with each other, and both facing the wrath of her family. The girl's family normally hired goons from one of the fascist groups to track down the couple, beat them up, maybe even kill the boy, and return the girl to the family. I got worried.

"I hope that Uma's family won't try to go to one of those thuggish groups to make trouble." I said, a little fearfully.

Nasir replied confidently, "No, no, Jayram*bhai*. Her family is opposed to our marriage, but they're also not associated with any of these groups. Really. Uma and I had already talked about this before going to them. If they were like that, then we would have run away to Bombay or something like that. But they're not like that."

He paused again to pay the barber.

"In any case," he continued, "Uma's brother is on our side completely. He even fought with his parents, and left the house in anger. He told us that if they try anything, he would inform us immediately, so that we could run away. I have a friend in Bombay who will help us get a place, and give us jobs and everything in an emergency. So there's nothing to worry about. If there's any emergency we'll run away to Bombay."

My mind eased up a little more.

"So what is it that you need Nasir?" I asked. "I'll do my best to help, I promise."

"Jayram*bhai*, we've decided to get married on our own, without being a financial burden on my parents or anything. So…in order to do that, we need a little money. I have some money left over from my stipend, and Uma does too, but we're still a little short…" Nasir trailed off.

I nodded my head, and said, "Of course. I understand. I'll do my best, and even ask Maria and Abhay to pitch in. How much is still needed?"

He replied awkwardly, "1500 rupees Jayram*bhai*…" before quickly adding, "…and I'm looking at other avenues also. I and Vijay will ask all our friends, and they will all help, but even then we are not likely to come up with the entire amount. See, I was hoping to buy a nice dress for Uma to wear on the wedding day…"

I smiled widely.

"Of course man! I'll do everything I can to help."

And then I hugged him tightly and said, "Congratulations my brother!"

I could feel the relief in his body as he hugged me back.

I asked, releasing him from my embrace, "By when do you need it?"

"Tonight…or latest, by tomorrow morning."

I didn't realize it needed to be that soon.

"Shit…that's not a lot of time boss…"

I then added quickly upon seeing his face go down, "But don't worry…we'll figure something out. I'll go to Maria and Abhay right away and ask them for some money too."

I knew I had about a thousand rupees left in my bank account, and was pretty confident of raising the rest through Abhay and Maria. I shook hands with Nasir and Vijay, and walked out of the barber's shop, hailing the first auto rickshaw I could spot.

I barged into the apartment, a little breathless. Luckily, both Maria and Abhay had not yet left for Vatwa. They were sitting in the living room eating breakfast.

Maria asked teasingly, "What the hell's the matter with you? You look really excited."

"I *am* excited...Nasir and Uma are getting married!" I said, barely able to contain my joy. "I knew about the two of them...I'm so glad that they're finally tying the knot."

I was a little surprised at myself. My own reaction to their impending marriage caught me unawares. I thought marriages were superfluous, relic-like institutions of the past. I hated attending them too. They were boring. Yet this one elicited quite some cheer in me.

Maria smiled, but then asked worriedly, "I hope they won't face any problems from Uma's family."

I shook my head confidently.

"No...there's no problem. Nasir told me that they are opposed to the marriage, and have disowned Uma, but are not going to cause problems. Plus, Uma's brother is completely on their side, so if there are any problems, he'll be able to warn them, and they can run away to Bombay."

"You say that like it's a walk in the park." Abhay said with a snicker. "It's great that they're getting married, but I hope they've taken precautions to ensure that nothing untoward happens to them because of Uma's family."

"It's no problem...really, it's not even worth worrying about." I said, a tad nonchalantly.

"But," I then ventured, "there is one thing they need from us, and that's money. They want to get married immediately. Uma is in Nasir's house right now, and they've managed to raise some money of their own, but are still about 1500 rupees short...and they asked if we could help. I have about a thousand left in my bank account, so I was wondering if you two could help with the rest..."

Both of them nodded as if it wasn't even a matter to be discussed.

"Of course, of course...that's fine." Maria said with a wave of her hand. "And you don't have to give more...we can just split it three ways and each give 500 bucks"

I smiled.

"But tell me." Abhay interjected. "How are they able to get married so soon? To do the non-religious marriages, you know the common-law marriages, in India takes a little time to register with the state and everything..."

"Well...Uma is converting into a Muslim I believe...so they're probably getting married under Muslim law." I said, the last bit a little unsurely. "And..."

Maria asked, "And what?"

"Well...Uma is also quitting her job as a *Shanthi Pathik* because that's the wishes of Nasir's parents."

The look on Maria's face immediately changed to one of consternation, while Abhay shook his head with a sigh.

Before she could say anything, I quickly added, "Listen...I tried my best to tell Nasir that it wasn't a good idea for her to quit, but he told me that it was her decision..."

"What bullshit." Maria said, indignantly. "If she converts to Islam, that's fine. It doesn't matter. But why does she have to quit her job?"

I looked at her a little sheepishly and shrugged my shoulders.

Then she pointed at me, "You should have been more firm in the way you talked to him...this is such nonsense...why does she have to quit her job in order to get married!"

I replied, a little exasperated, "Maria...I tried my best...and Nasir *did* say that it was her decision..."

"And you believe him?" Maria asked incredulously.

"Well...not fully...but I also don't think Nasir is that kind of guy. I don't know...maybe I can talk to him later...right now there's a bit of an emergency at hand."

Maria got back to her breakfast with a huff, an indication that the conversation was over.

"Anyway," Abhay said with a knowing smile, trying to play the peacemaker, "Maria and I will withdraw 500 rupees each, and give it to you in the evening. We'll worry about other things later."

I nodded my head, and went to the balcony for a smoke, feeling like I had come up short with her, again.

~ Chapter 36.5 ~

That evening I called my dad. I thought it would be a good surprise for Nasir to get 2000 rupees instead of 1500. So I cleared my bank account, and then went to my usual revenue source for more money.

"Appa…I need a little more money…because I gave whatever I had to a friend of mine."

Appa wasn't too surprised, and asked, "Ok, no problem. But what was the reason for you to do that?"

"Nasir's getting married, so he needed some extra money right away. In any case, Maria and Abhay also contributed." I said, hoping their involvement would help convince Appa that I was doing the right thing.

"Ok…that's fine. Like I said, no problem." he replied. "I'll transfer some more money to your account. I'm glad you called actually, because we need to talk about something."

"What is it?" I asked.

"Well, *kanna*…I know that you've been doing really good work in Ahmedabad, but we recently received some replies from universities in the US that you had applied to."

Oh yes. My plan. I had forgotten all about it.

Appa continued, "Anyway, the good news is that you've received admission into a couple of good ones with decent scholarships…"

Shit – that's right.

"…and I think it's time that you returned to Bangalore, so we can plan to get your student visa soon, and you can prepare for the journey."

Fuck.

~ Chapter 37 ~

"So you're really leaving huh?" Maria asked, her voice tinged with emotion, making me feel even worse than I already did.

I nodded, looking down at the ground. It had been a couple of days since Appa had told me to start making plans to get back to Bangalore. I had told Maria and Abhay the next day. Abhay decided to join me for a short while in Bangalore to visit his mother.

"I have to..." I replied, a little sullenly, while packing my bags. "My plans were to stay here for a few months and then head back to make preparations for my studies in America..."

The words seemed hollow now.

"I know, I know...you said that already..." was all Maria could say. I saw her eyes well up.

I couldn't bring myself to think about what would happen to us, to our bond, after I left. My rational mind knew, but I couldn't bring myself to acknowledge it.

She turned to Abhay, her eyes still glistening.

"And why are *you* going too? Can't you wait until later for your trip to Bangalore?"

Abhay said, matter-of-factly, "I'm only going for a few days Maria. I need to see my mother, and thought it would be a good idea to make the long train journey with Jay for company. Otherwise it's a pain to travel for so long on your own."

"I know," she accepted, "but what will I do here alone without both you guys. It will get so lonely..."

"I'll be back." Abhay said, comforting her with an arm around her shoulder. "It's not like I'll be gone for long....it's just a week."

"And it's not like I'm running away forever either." I offered, lamely. "Gujarat will always be in my heart. I'll be back too. Come, what, may, I'll be back here. Vijay, Nasir, and I have been talking about starting a small community organization in Gomtipur. I don't want to let go of that dream."

Maria didn't respond to what I said. I think she believed it, but she was responding in silence to what neither of us were verbalizing. She and I both knew that my departure meant the end of our relationship as we knew it.

I was sad. I didn't know if I was sad that our relationship was never going to be fully realized or whether it already had been – as if this fleeting flash of love and pain was what it was always meant to be.

Regardless, it was gut-wrenching.

Maria was in Gujarat for the long haul. She had already laid the foundation for starting a women's tailoring cooperative with survivors of the violence. I wish I had her courage. I wish I could have just let it all go and stayed behind to help her with the cooperative, make Gujarat my home, *our* home.

But I didn't have that kind of fortitude.

"I should go and meet Vijay and Nasir." I said, veering the subject marginally away. "I'd like to tell them personally that I'm leaving."

Maria nodded, while Abhay got back to stuffing his small backpack with clothes and books. The mood was sombre. Even Abhay didn't try to lighten the mood. They were both sad that I was leaving for good. I hated wallowing in that kind of atmosphere, unsure of what to say or do, feeling like shit, not knowing when I would see these people whom I loved so dearly. So I was a little happy for the temporary escape, as I rode in the auto rickshaw, across the river, again.

"It's good Jayram*bhai*, that you're taking care of your future and getting a good education." Vijay said with poise, as we sat drinking tea and smoking in the tea shop one last time.

"You will need to be strong in order for you to help others." he continued, putting an arm around my shoulder.

I knew Vijay didn't see my departure as a final goodbye, which was a relief. Nasir was a little more doubtful, and wanted to satisfy himself that we would continue being in constant touch for our friendship and the organization the three of us wanted to start.

"You should make sure that you call us regularly Jayram*bhai*." he said, almost like a child. "That way, we can chalk out a good plan for starting this organization."

I nodded.

"I hope you won't forget us…" Nasir added, almost under his breath.

I looked at both of them after he said that. I then dropped my guard for a moment and barrelled them in my arms.

"I could never forget you guys…and this is not a final goodbye." I said, clasping them tightly, "Remember, we have a lot of work to do together."

Vijay gave a manly smile, while Nasir wiped a tear drop from his eye.

Uma was sitting next to us, smiling. Her eyes welled up as well, as she saw her husband crying softly. She and Nasir seemed really happy together. There weren't too many happily-ever-after endings in real life, but this was one of them. I could feel it in my bones.

As I rode back in the auto rickshaw, across the river, I wondered when I would be back. I looked at the river beneath me, as the rickshaw crossed the bridge. And just like that, as suddenly as I arrived, I was heading back, away from the river that ran through me.

~ Chapter 37.5 ~

The train journey was pleasant. Uneventful, but pleasant. I fell
progressively sicker somewhere along the Western Ghats.
Abhay and I talked a little, but mostly gazed out at the scenery
as the train wound its way along the western coast of India,
slowly veering towards the central plateau, and then trundling
southwards towards Bangalore.

The journey was partly melancholic, partly sleep-
inducing, and always reflective. It was good to have Abhay for
company. His presence alone made the journey less painful.

I kept going back to thoughts of Maria.

She had come to see us off at the Ahmedabad railway station,
and had bought fruits, bread, cheese, and nuts to give to both
of us for the journey. She linked up with both our arms as we
walked on the station platform. People stared at us. We didn't
care. It was lovely. The sombreness of the days before had
been replaced by joy and happiness, mostly I think at the
thought that we shared this love for each other. Regardless of
what the future held, no one could take that experience away
from us and we were all the better for it.

We placed our bags on our seats, and Abhay went to
buy a couple of bottles of water. Maria and I sat holding
hands on a platform bench by the train compartment. We
didn't say anything to each other. Maria couldn't stop smiling,
and neither could I.

We alternated between looking at each other, and
watching the hustle and bustle of the station.

I finally broke the silence.

"Maria…um…you know that you'll always be…" was
all I could manage before some guy interrupted me and asked
if I wanted my ear cleaned.

"Very good job I will do *saab*", he said, clutching
weird instruments, apparently meant for aural cleaning.

Maria burst out laughing. I did too, before shooing
him away. I shook my head, and smiled. She looked into my
eyes, giving that mesmerizing smile of hers.

Good enough.

Enough to last a lifetime.

Abhay came back clutching two bottles of water. The train conductor soon blew his whistle. We did our tight hugs. No words were spoken. All three of us looked at each other, as we said farewell with our eyes.

As the train chugged off, I caught one final glimpse of her eyes looking straight into me. My heart tightened as the train gained speed.

~ Chapter 38 ~

Appa said that he would come to pick up Abhay and me at the train station.

"I'll be waiting at the Higginbothams shop at the station." he said over the phone. "When the train arrives, you and Abhay just come over there."

The train slowly steamed into Bangalore City station. It felt nice to be back. Or at least I thought it did. Abhay and I lugged our bags and walked over to the book stand that Appa was waiting at. I saw Appa from a few meters away, and waved at him. He looked at me, but didn't catch my waving and looked straight through me.

I went up closer to him, standing almost directly in front of him.

"Appa, it's me." I said to him, while smiling.

He looked at me. It took a second to register that he was indeed looking at his son.

He exclaimed, "My god *kanna*...look at how much hair is on your face now! I barely recognized you. You look so different!"

I nodded and smiled. Didn't say much. I did the introductions and we soon made our way past the teeming station to the car park. I asked Abhay to sit in the front seat, so that I wouldn't have to engage in too much conversation. Appa asked a bunch of questions, while Abhay politely replied. The two of them did most of the talking. I didn't feel like saying much. Spent the entire journey looking out of the car window as we drove through Bangalore.

Could it happen here? I wondered.

Could that kind of bloodletting happen here in Bangalore?

More importantly, would I ever see her again?

I shook my head. Couldn't think about it any more. I just wanted to be.

The two of them chatted away. I was able to discern faintly that the conversation had now moved to Abhay's studies. Appa was asking enthusiastic questions about Abhay's Rhodes scholarship, to which Abhay gave embarrassed, humility-laced answers.

We dropped Abhay on the way. His house was not too far from where we lived. I hugged him goodbye and wasn't able to let go of him immediately. He complied. Allowed me to clasp him in a tight, lingering embrace, and returned it with equal warmth.

When I got back home, I was barely able to hold a conversation with anyone. I hugged Amma, kissed her on the cheek and went to my room, saying that I wanted to sleep for some time. I fell violently ill within a few hours, and was bed-ridden for days. Friends came to visit me, and I used the illness as an excuse to not interact with them or my family. I sat in front of the television in a daze or read some vapid novel. Sometimes I wrote in my journal, but the words seemed meaningless and sterile.

Did a lot of thinking, I did.

I realised that, until I came and volunteered in the relief camps, I had never really visited a Muslim's house, couldn't really speak of even one Muslim friend, and generally talked about Muslims in the third person.

I did have a few Muslim classmates in high school, but they were never really my friends.

In college, Qasim was a dear friend in my first year, but we soon drifted away from each other after he moved to the computer science batch from the second year onwards and I shifted to mechanical engineering. He had visited my house a couple of times when we were close, but I had never gone to his. It was too far from where I lived. Ahmed was a fellow volunteer in the AIDS awareness and gender rights activism we did as part of a student-group in college. He too had visited my house a few times, but I had never gone to his. I didn't even know where he lived. We started becoming friends, but then he had to concentrate on his final year studies and stopped volunteering. We never kept in touch after that. I remember really liking both of them, and temporarily becoming close buddies, but I just hadn't kept in touch with them in the same way I had with some other friends. I didn't think it was because they were Muslim per se; there were a lot of Hindu friends that didn't really last the distance either. But then again, it was weird that I didn't have a single Muslim friend, and the only friends who *did* last the distance were Hindus. Upper-caste ones. I couldn't avoid the fact that to some degree or the other, it *was* because they were Muslim.

In a tragicomic exercise, I examined it statistically in my head – Muslims were 12-14% of the population in India, and sometimes even higher in cities like Bangalore. Yet, I didn't have a single Muslim friend. All my dearest friends were upper-caste Hindu (who, for statistics sake, consisted of approximately the same percentage as Muslims). I certainly didn't have any Dalits as friends either, at least ones who were open about their caste. And I didn't think of myself as a bigoted person.

I didn't exactly spend what could be considered a long amount of time in Gujarat by most stretches of imagination. It was around six months. A blip for most.

But it was a lifetime for me.

I truly had been reborn. Everything in my life now was going to be dictated to some degree of the other by that experience. It was like opening my eyes for the first time at the age of twenty-two.

I kept going back allegorically to this scene in *The Matrix*.

Neo, played by Keanu Reeves, is just about to learn the truth about the Matrix from Morpheus, played by Laurence Fishburne. Morpheus gives him two pills, one blue, one red, and tells him that the red pill offers him the truth about the Matrix, while the blue pill will have him go back to his dream world, where he can continue to live his life in blissful ignorance, without remembering anything.

Neo reaches for the red pill, and Morpheus cautions him.

"Remember...all I'm offering is the truth. Nothing more."

Neo pauses – and still takes the red pill.

Everything that I had learnt thus far had to be undone. The heroes I idolized had to be looked over again. The thoughts that emerged from reading had to be re-examined. The framework of thinking itself had to be rebuilt, and through that, the very person I was. I felt like if I had met myself as a teenager, I would have wanted to punch that kid in the face and ask him to wake up. My life was now pre-Gujarat and post-Gujarat. Two different Jayrams. Post-Gujarat Jayram would have wanted to beat the crap out of pre-Gujarat Jayram. Spit on his face. Slap him around and ask him to open his fucking eyes.

I was not able to snap out of this unshakeable daze even after my illness subsided. My family and friends had no idea what to do. Soon most of my friends whittled away, not bothering to call or ask me out any more. I really couldn't blame them. I didn't return any of their calls, and didn't really want to be around them any way. When I was with them, I felt an overwhelming sense of anger towards them for being so sickeningly happy. Most of them avoided talking to me about politics or anything serious because they knew I would launch into a diatribe.

The only time I became alive again was when Vijay and Nasir called me from a pay phone in Gomtipur. I nearly cried when I heard their voices. I repeatedly asked them how they were doing, and reaffirmed, just as much to myself as to them, that we would see each other again. We again talked about the organization we wanted to start. I said that I would be a part of it, no matter what.

I didn't show that kind of excited fondness and affection for my family and friends.

And they saw it.

It wasn't like I stopped caring for them, I still loved them dearly – or at least I thought I did. Maybe I just needed time to internalise everything. After all, not all of my family and friends behaved like this one distant aunt I had who reacted sharply upon hearing about my stint in Gujarat.

"You know Jayram, you are very sweet and all to help these Muslims." she said condescendingly. "It's always like this. Something happens to Muslims, and Hindus always go to help them, but Muslims never come to help when something happens to us."

~ Chapter 38.5 ~

Clearly, my world had changed. I didn't belong here anymore. I wasn't even the same person. So the person they loved and cared for was gone. It was an illusion. It was like a huge chasm had been dug up between me and my loved ones. My experience almost acted like a sieve to determine who among my family and friends were really there for life. Most fell by the wayside. My closest friends still tried valiantly to get me to have fun again. My parents tried talking to me, and even admonished me for being cantankerous towards my friends.

"You've just come off a high…a very intense experience." my father said.

You don't know the half of it, I thought, as I sat at my desk thumbing through some leftist journal I barely understood, not bothering to look up at him.

"But you should realise that your friends and family here have always been there for you." he continued. "You can't lead that kind of life forever. At some point in time you will have to get back to earth and get on with your regular life. This experience should just be treated as something you can hold on to and remember at later times."

I knew that was how it was supposed to be. Yet the words didn't register. I had no idea what to do. I knew I needed to continue with my studies and make some money, but I couldn't shake off this feeling I had inside me. Like I had swallowed Morpheus' stupid red pill, and it now burned my stomach lining. I knew I had seen a truth I never knew before, but I didn't have a framework to understand it

I had found some answers. But I didn't know the questions.

~ Epilogue ~

March 2008

The airport was different now. A little swankier. The state had
seen a lot of economic development. The BJP was still in
power. They had lost it at the centre though. I remember
sitting in front of my computer in Baltimore, watching the
results of the 2004 national elections. The Congress Party, a
party comprising dynastic elitists, craven sycophants, upper-
class intellectuals and corrupt layabouts, had emerged as the
largest party, heading the largest coalition. I cried in absolute
joy. The shrill-mouthed Left Parties offered crucial support
from the outside to enable the coalition to stake a claim to
form the government. I was glad my fellow lefties were
looking at things a little more pragmatically, rather than stick
to some worn out boiler-plate philosophy. The BJP was
beaten severely, and many of their coalition partners started
deserting them.

But they still managed to hang on in Gujarat. They
changed their tune now though. Even roped in a couple of
Muslims into their party. Made me realize that fascism in India
was more opportunistic than ideological.

Didn't know if that made me feel better or not. It just
was.

Vijay and Nasir told me that they would pick me up
at the airport when I spoke to them that morning. Nasir said
that he would bring his daughter along. Vijay's son was in
school, so he said that I would see him only in the evening.

I was excited. The organization the three of us had
been talking about was finally registered.

"How would we recognize you Jayram*bhai*?" Vijay
asked over the phone, laughing a little bit. "It's been nearly six
years, so I'm sure you must have changed."

"Don't worry," I replied, with a big smile that must
have shown in my voice, "you'll recognize me. And if you
don't, I know I'll definitely recognize you."

I saw them as I stepped out of the airport. They
recognized me immediately, and waved enthusiastically. They
looked a little fuller, though still trim. I had packed on the

pounds, had been doing some heavy weight-lifting while I was away. It was a way of blowing off steam in the sterile imperialism that was America.

I waved back and quickly walked towards them, lugging my duffle bag with me.

We hugged and started talking immediately. They marvelled at my new muscles. I marvelled at their new lives.

Vijay took my bag as we walked towards the rickshaw. It was parked near the taxi stand. All of us got in. Vijay started the rickshaw and we were off.

"So," I asked them, as we rode along the smooth roads, "did you have any trouble recognizing me?"

"Of course not Jayram*bhai.*" Nasir replied, with a big grin on his face, holding his daughter in his arms. "How could we forget?"

"Where shall we go first Jayram*bhai?*" Vijay asked, as he drove the rickshaw through increasing amounts of traffic. "Do you want some tea?"

"Of course." I replied. "Let's go to our usual place..."

Vijay nodded with a grin.

"Do you still smoke Jayram*bhai?*" Nasir asked.

I looked out the rickshaw as we crossed the bridge towards the other side of the Sabarmati.

"Only in Gujarat."

About the Author

Sriram Ananth leads a somewhat scatterbrained but politically-enriching transnational life between Canada, the US and India. This is his first book.

Upcoming titles by the author:

Diary of a Privileged, Pinko Immigrant

The Messiness of Solidarity

Across the Sabarmati

www.ingramcontent.com/pod-product-compliance
Lightning Source LLC
Chambersburg PA
CBHW022155170626
46807CB00005B/2225